Rafe motioned for the driver to speed up. The quick lurch of the horses bounced Kacey toward the middle of the seat, and when she landed she suddenly found herself in the arms of Rafael Assante. She struggled inwardly against the strength and warmth of his embrace. Something inside her wanted to stay in the fold of his arms, but another force inside her resisted the man's masculine appeal. She wanted no part of an attachment now and she did not yield to her traitorous body.

She fought against the material of his suit and his rock-hard strength and knew even before she felt his searing lips that he was going to kiss her. Once again, just for an instant, her body grew weak and melted into his arms before realization dawned on her. His lips crushed against hers, and an unfamiliar feeling formed in the pit of her stomach where remnants of emotion seemed to gather and arrange the muscles of her abdomen into a huge knot. She was swimming through a haze of feelings and desires previously unknown to her, but reason won over, and Kacey pushed Rafe away.

He was the first to speak. "*Au, cherie*, so the cool Mademoiselle O'Reilly does have feelings after all, *n'est-ce pas?*"

No Greater Treasure

Ellen Kelley

JOVE BOOKS, NEW YORK

NO GREATER TREASURE

A Jove Book / published by arrangement with
the author

PRINTING HISTORY
Jove edition / December 1998

The Penguin Putnam Inc. World Wide Web site address is
http://www.penguinputnam.com

ISBN: 0-515-12408-7

A JOVE BOOK®
Jove Books are published by The Berkley Publishing Group,
a member of Penguin Putnam Inc.,
375 Hudson Street, New York, New York 10014.
JOVE and the "J" design
are trademarks belonging to Jove Publications, Inc.

PRINTED IN THE UNITED STATES OF AMERICA

10 9 8 7 6 5 4 3 2 1

DEDICATION

To my daughter, Lana, who has been my best supporter and my toughest editor, and who wanted to know the rest of the story.

To my son, Brad, without whose computer expertise I would be lost. And thanks for the copy of *Netscape and the World Wide Web for Dummies*!

To Margaret Ellen Womble Piper. I remembered, Grandma. Can't never did do anything.

To my husband, Ken, my rock on shifting sand.

And to the memory of Richard Wetherill, who first saw Cliff Palace on December 18, 1888. His determination as an amateur archaeologist and his willingness to learn the science had a profound effect on the study of the Anasazi.

ACKNOWLEDGMENTS

A special thank you . . .

To my sister, Nancy Gill Cocke, for her help in research and for her unwavering faith.

To Linda Swift Reeder, for her invaluable friendship and advice.

To Jim Finn, whose guidance has meant much to me.

To Horace and Ruby Gill . . . just because.

No Greater
Treasure

One

New York, New York
October 28, 1886

Kacey felt the excitement in the air. Even the gray misty fog that hung low over the water could not dampen the spirit of the day. New York Harbor was literally filled with boats and paddle steamers such as the one she and her father were on. The *Jubilee* was a grand steamer with its decorative gingerbread trim, and Kacey delighted in the gala atmosphere penetrating the fog. Children laughed and played around their mother's skirts while adults seemed to be suspended in time as they awaited the dedication of the great Statue of Liberty. The copper lady had been too long in storage. She was ready to breathe the salty air of the Atlantic, ready to welcome the weary voyager from the sea, ready to stand as the icon of freedom.

"Father, I'm so glad that we can be a part of this day. This is a perfect spot, if only the fog would clear for more than a few minutes at a time. I caught a glimpse of her just a moment ago, and she's magnificent." Kacey marveled at the colossal height of the statue. She changed positions on the wooden seat that flanked the steamer's railing to ease closer to her father.

Colin O'Reilly looked at his daughter and felt pride in the knowledge that he sat next to her. At twenty-two she was as lovely as her mother had been, but especially so today in her royal-blue suit. The deep color accentuated the violet in her eyes as they sparkled with exhilaration, while the coppery highlights of her upswept hair shone beneath the stylish hat.

Colin made to remove something from his eye with his free hand as he cleared his throat to speak. "Yes, yes, dear. I wouldn't have missed it for anything. I only wish ... well, that your mother could have seen it, too. You know how she loved pomp and circumstance. ..." Colin's voice trailed away as if he were transported momentarily to another time.

Kacey, whose full name was Katherine Colleen, was devoted to her father, and she did not miss the sadness in his voice now. If only her mother had not died ... but she had, and Kacey was determined not to leave her father. She would always take care of him; her hand tightened on his arm as she reaffirmed her goal.

Rafael Assante, a young Frenchman also awaiting the dedication ceremony, leaned on the railing of the *Jubilee*. For diversion he lazily turned to face the multitude of strangers, and his attention was immediately taken by a young woman sitting with her arm wound around an older man's elbow. His lips curled at the picture the attractive young woman and the older man made. So the old fellow had a mistress, he thought. Well, well, and what a lovely creature at that. Rafe continued to stare until suddenly violet eyes gazed back. His eyes seemed to lock with hers, each unable to look away. Struck by the disdain he saw in the depths of the young woman's eyes, his appraisal of her took a swift turn. *Bas bleu.* He knew the type well and he usually avoided them like the plague. *Bluestocking* was the

old English term, literary and stuffy. He much preferred
the sweet, willing type, and this one appeared neither sweet
nor willing. As a matter of fact, from the look she gave
him he could almost feel the tar and feathers.

Through the misting drizzle Kacey had gazed idly around
the steamer's deck filled with people. Then her eyes came
to rest on a young man who seemed to be earnestly returning her attention. Normally she paid little interest to
bold men who seemed to stare at her, but this man, who
wore a brown tweed suit and bowler hat, seemed to be
darkly amused. As soon as she realized how she was staring at the arrogant stranger, however, she quickly turned
her head and removed her hand from her father's arm. She
seldom fidgeted, but for some reason the scrutiny of the
man left her annoyed. She absentmindedly removed her
gloves and placed them in her lap, once more casting a
casual glance toward the stranger. She was appalled to see
him coming toward her. Quickly she turned her gaze to
the harbor. Overhead, a seagull's piercing cry rang out like
that of a hawk that had spotted its prey.

Rafe looked again at the older man beside the young
woman. Of course. He'd thought he recognized him. That
was Professor O'Reilly, his former archaeology instructor.
A glimmer of wickedness filled his eyes as the muscle in
his jaw twitched. Not forgetting the contempt the girl
seemed to hold for him, Rafe walked toward the couple
and came within inches of the lady but addressed the man
beside her. "*Bonjour*, Professor O'Reilly. This is a great
occasion for both our countries, *n'est-ce pas*?"

    Colin looked at Rafe and nodded. "Why, hello, Rafe. I
thought you had returned to France when classes ended."

    "Not yet, monsieur. I wanted to see more of this country
before I returned to France, and I could not miss this spec-
tacular event." Rafe momentarily moved his gaze to the
flesh-and-blood woman seated beside the professor.

"Yes, yes. I know what you mean. That lady will stand in this harbor for centuries to come as a beacon to free men everywhere." Rafe's reaction to Kacey did not escape Colin, and a smile crossed his lips. He remembered the young chap's reputation with the fairer sex around campus. Quite a string of young ladies' hearts were broken. He deserved to be introduced to his daughter. Kacey was a dear to him and treated him with great care, but where young admirers were concerned, her tongue was as sharp as a scalpel. Colin's eyes sparkled as he decided to have some fun. He mischievously eyed his daughter as he spoke. "Rafe, this is my daughter, Katherine, but I'm sure she won't mind you calling her Kacey. All her friends do."

Rafe offered his hand to Kacey. "*Bonjour*, Mademoiselle Kacey." The challenge in his mahogany eyes waved to her like a red flag.

Kacey reluctantly lifted her hand to reciprocate, but she was surprised when the young Frenchman firmly clasped her palm and quickly brought his lips to touch the back of her gloveless hand. His kiss on her skin was startling. The unwelcome caress left her with a warmth that rushed unwanted to her face, and the unfamiliar heat annoyed her. For her father's sake, Kacey controlled her temper. She would try to be civil to the arrogant rogue. After all, it was only for a little while. She swiftly returned the branded hand to her lap.

Kacey's anger was not lost on her father, who seemed to enjoy the display. For further entertainment Colin continued, "Rafe, won't you join us for dinner tonight? That is, if you are available."

Kacey interrupted, "But Father, I'm sure Monsieur . . ." She paused while Rafe filled the blank for her.

"Assante, mademoiselle, but please call me Rafe."

The young man's voice held an annoying quality for Kacey. He seemed so smooth, so suave. Too much so. She continued to speak as she looked into his eyes and lifted her chin even higher. "I'm sure Monsieur Assante has plans for this evening, Father."

But Colin remained undaunted. "Well, Rafe, do you have plans for dinner?"

"*Au contraire*, monsieur, I would like very much to dine with you and mademoiselle." Rafe felt honored by the invitation from Professor O'Reilly. He truly admired the professor and had learned much from him in his studies at Harvard. He'd had no idea the professor had a daughter, however. The situation intrigued him.

"Good, then you'll join us at the Albemarle Hotel at six. Do you know the address?" Colin felt pleased with himself. He rather liked the young fellow and looked forward to a stimulating evening.

"*Oui*, monsieur. What a coincidence—that is where I am staying." As he spoke, Rafe's eyes once again drifted toward Kacey and slowly surveyed the soft curves of her breasts, which were enhanced by the fitted bodice. His gaze then trailed to the patrician lines of her creamy neck before returning to the professor.

Kacey did not miss the insolent perusal by the rakish man. Her blood simmered at the outright rudeness of him, and in retaliation she lifted her chin even higher, if that were possible, and refused to look at the Frenchman. She declined to let him ruin her joy of the day, however, and tried to bring the conversation back to the ceremony.

"Oh, Father, look through the opening in the fog. They are removing the veiling from her eyes."

Colin followed his daughter's gaze and looked at the colossal statue that was about to be officially unveiled. He thought of his Irish parents, who had come to America, and all the others who had fought hardship and oppression to start a new life. He felt a deep gratitude to the people of France for the gift and did not miss the opportunity to thank the young Frenchman still standing beside him.

"You know, Rafe, your people have presented us a remarkable gift. Such generosity touches me, and I hope our countries will always be friends.''

Rafe beamed with intense pleasure. "*Merci beaucoup*, Professor O'Reilly. You have nothing to worry about. I think we shall be friends for a long time to come."

Kacey reveled in the luxurious warm bath. The rose-perfumed water trailed down her back and chest as she squeezed it from the washcloth. She had secured her lengthy titian tresses into a coil on top of her head so that she could slide lower into the tub without getting her hair wet. And she did just that, trying to shut out the face of an arrogant young Frenchman who had upset her day. But now she had to face him over dinner. She had to admit the man was handsome. But what seemed to annoy Kacey more than anything was his arrogant stance and the way his head tilted when he looked at her with those laughing dark eyes. Why couldn't she get him off her mind? After tonight that should be no trouble. She would make a point never to see him again. The thought seemed to calm Kacey, and she reached for the thick white towel that lay on the table beside the tub. She stood and wrapped herself in the cotton folds as she stepped onto the plush red carpet.

The bath had revived Kacey, and she felt she was ready to face anything the arrogant Frenchman could dispense from his expression or his tongue. She laid the towel on the side of the enameled tub and slipped her arms into a dressing gown of white lawn before she moved into her bedchamber to dress. She had brought two ensembles in addition to the blue suit. One was a pale yellow velvet with a high-necked blouse of cream voile, and the other was a cinnamon woolen suit that almost matched the color of her hair. She decided on the yellow velvet and walked to the dressing table to brush and arrange her long tresses. After once more piling the curls into an attractive style, Kacey dusted her body with a delicately scented powder and donned the yellow frock. She then took a last-minute look at her reflection before leaving to join her father in the sitting room. Her cheeks seemed paler than usual, and she did not want Monsieur Assante to think that she was pale and near the swooning point on his account. With more vigor than was needed, she pinched each cheek, then nodded her head as if to assure the looking-glass girl that she had done well.

The hotel suite that Kacey and her father occupied for the evening was opulent, and she delighted in its grandeur. Elegant Norman lace covered the massive windows that framed Central Park in the distance, where horse-drawn carriages could be seen sporting New York's elite. For the past fifteen years Kacey's father had taught archaeology at Harvard University in Cambridge, Massachusetts. Their home was adequate and comfortable, but it lacked the opulence of the suite they now occupied. And even though Kacey enjoyed the elegance from time to time, she preferred the cozy home that she and her father shared. As a professor he was not a rich man, but in the summers she accompanied him on many invitations to dig sites. What their lifestyle lacked in elegance was made up for in excitement.

Kacey still missed her mother, even though she had died twelve years earlier during a flu epidemic that swept the East Coast. As she did many times, Kacey recalled her smiling face. She could almost feel the warm hugs her mother had given her when she was a little girl. This evening, especially, she felt she needed her mother's warm embrace. Her pulse raced at the thought of facing the arrogant Frenchman over dinner.

She took a deep breath and gained strength from knowing that her mother would be very proud of her recent graduation from the women's affiliate of Harvard, the Society for the Collegiate Instruction of Women. But, darkly amused, she couldn't recall a course that had taught her how to deal with arrogant strangers who made one's veins prickle from a mere glance. She was on her own.

•   •   •

Kacey's long skirt rustled as she glided into the room where her father lightly dozed as he waited for her to ready herself for their dinner engagement. She nudged him gently.

"Father, I'm ready. Are you sure you feel like going?"

Colin smiled to himself at how Kacey fussed and fumed over him, as if he were a small puppy. He appreciated that she was so devoted to him, but he also wanted her to go out more with people her own age. That was one reason he was looking forward to dining with Rafe. He was the sort of chap who could turn a lady's head, and damn it all, Kacey's head needed to be turned. He valued Kacey's happiness above all else, but he was looking forward to grandchildren, too. Kacey was a good archaeologist, but he wanted her to share with the right man what he had shared with her mother. And if she stayed on the course that she now traveled, she would remain a spinster; there would be no grandchildren for him to enjoy in his old age. The idea did not appeal to him. He smiled at his daughter.

"You look lovely, dear. And of course I feel like going. Can't a man take a leisurely nap before dinner without everyone thinking him about to kick the bucket?"

"Yes, Father. Of course you can," Kacey said with mock contrition as she picked up her gloves from the entry table. "It's just that I know how hard you push yourself sometimes and I worry about you."

"Well, don't, darling. Save your worrying for the man you'll marry someday." Colin stood from the stuffed velvet chair to join his daughter.

"Now, Father, don't start. You know I'm never going to marry. You are the only man in my life. Besides, you couldn't get along without me," Kacey said with a loving smugness in her voice as she pulled on her gloves, before turning to assist her father with his dinner jacket.

"You are probably right, dear. Don't pay any attention to this old relic." Colin patronizingly put his arm around his daughter's shoulder and led her out the door toward the hotel's dining room.

Kacey felt a strange exhilaration when she and her father entered the hotel lobby. She straightened herself to her full five foot five, and with regal grace stood beside him as she saw Rafe coming toward them. This time she had on her gloves and she smiled to herself as she mused, *Let's see what he will do about that.*

Colin addressed the young man while offering his hand in friendship. "Good evening, Rafe."

"*Bonsoir*, Professor." Rafe shook hands with the older man before turning to Kacey with a look of lazy amusement in his smile. "*Bonsoir*, mademoiselle." He once more reached for her hand and brought his lips to the unfeeling material of her glove.

Kacey was very much aware of his masculine charm that put her feminine defenses on alert. His hair was too black and his eyes too dark. For an instant she felt as though he were the hunter and she the hunted. Ridiculously she pictured herself wrapped in his arms, his lips pressed against hers. To her dismay the vision was not as repugnant as she tried to convince herself. Mentally she shook herself and quickly regained her composure. "Good evening, Monsieur Assante. I trust you have had an enjoyable day?"

"Ah, *oui*, mademoiselle, a most enjoyable day. I have been in the company of two most exquisite ladies. Certainly a memory that I can take back to France with me."

His voice, deep and sensual, sent a ripple of awareness through her. "And when will that be, monsieur?" Kacey felt it could not be soon enough.

Colin broke into the conversation before Rafe could reply. "I believe our table is ready, and I don't know about you two, but I am famished." He touched his daughter's elbow and escorted her into the dining room, which was partially filled with people.

Rafe followed and pulled out a chair for Kacey when they reached their table.

"Thank you," she acknowledged as she gathered the long folds of her skirt to one side and seated herself.

The two men also sat down, and shortly a waiter arrived to take their orders. When he disappeared into the kitchen, Colin began the conversation.

"So, Rafe, when do you have to return to France?"

"Monsieur, I am sorry to say that my father is ill and I am leaving by steamer tomorrow morning to return home." His voice seemed husky with regret.

"That's too bad. I'm sorry about your father and I'm sorry you are leaving so soon," Colin said. "I would have liked to spend more time discussing your future as an archaeologist. You know, there's nothing else like it. The thrill of making a great discovery is something that we all dream of, but only a few live to see it. And with the digs going on right now in South America and Egypt, the possibilities are absolutely endless. I hope your father is much better by the time you get back to France."

Rafe nodded his head at the kindness in the professor's voice and replied, "*Merci*, I'm sure he will be."

The waiter brought the food and poured French wine into elegant stemmed crystal. Kacey sat across from her father, and Rafe was seated next to her. She could not deny that she was very much aware of his nearness, and although she was truly sorry about his father, she was glad that he was returning to France. She absentmindedly reached for the glass of wine and sipped its soothing nectar.

Colin noticed that his standoffish daughter was drinking more wine than usual, and he could not help the smile that formed on his lips. Eating his meal with enthusiasm, he said, "You know, Rafe, I would like to keep in touch with you and learn of your father's health. Post a letter when you get to France and let us know how things are going. And I can keep you updated on what's happening here in archaeology. Kacey has always accompanied me on digs. She is quite an accomplished archaeologist herself.''

Rafe spoke in a tone filled with awe. ''I am impressed that such a femme fatale is so . . . talented in matters of the mind. How very intriguing.'' His dark eyes bore into Kacey's own.

She did not miss the patronizing tone of the man's voice, and shot him a withering gaze. ''Why, Monsieur Assante, are you saying that intelligent women should not be beautiful as well? Or are you amazed that any woman has any intelligence?''

Rafe took in the quick flutter of silky dark lashes and the sparks that flew from her violet eyes, now a shade darker than before. His eyes grew openly amused before he burst out laughing. Colin joined him with a chuckle.

Once more Kacey felt the man's conceit to be too much. She forced a laugh to cover her own growing irritation as she reached again for her wine goblet to finish off its contents. The waiter was quickly there to pour more of the red liquid into her glass. Kacey knew she had already had enough of the wine, but she took another sip and pressed Rafe for a reply. ''So, monsieur, are you afraid to answer my question?''

Rafe's lighthearted laughter had weakened to a grin. He raised his goblet in a toast to Kacey. ''As we say in France, mademoiselle, touché.''

She felt deep satisfaction at having outwitted the witty Monsieur Assante. Her eyebrows rose in amazement that he had conceded the verbal banter, and her lips widened into a smile as she reached for her fork and took a bite of the roast duck. She felt much better, but that was short-lived as she heard the Frenchman speak.

''Professor, I have hired a carriage to ride through Central Park. Will you and Mademoiselle Kacey join me later, as this is my last night in New York?''

''Why, certainly. That sounds like a rather enjoyable

evening. We didn't have anything planned, did we, dear?''
Colin asked, knowing full well they didn't.

"Well, no, Father, not tonight. But we do have theater
tickets for tomorrow evening.''

"Yes, yes, my dear, I haven't forgotten. Sarah Bernhardt will be appearing. Have you seen the lovely Miss
Bernhardt, Rafe?'' Not waiting for Rafe to reply, Colin
answered his own question. "But of course you have. She
is an exquisitely delicate creature and captivates her audience.'' Then, as if to get himself back on track, Colin
added as he retrieved his pocket watch from its niche inside his coat, "What time should we expect the carriage,
Rafe? It's nearly seven-thirty now.''

"Eight o'clock, monsieur.''

"That just about gives us time to go back to the suite.
I seem to have forgotten my pipe. Kacey, do you need
anything?'' Colin asked.

Kacey fumbled for something to say. "Why, uh, yes, I
need to pick up a wrap. The night air will be chilly,'' she
said, rising from the chair.

The two men also stood, then Rafe flashed a smile and
bowed his head in acknowledgment. "I will wait in the
lobby for you.''

Kacey thought the Frenchman looked rather like the cat
who was about to swallow the mouse. She had reservations
about going for a ride with him, but what could it hurt?
Her father would be along. She had no desire to be alone
with the man, and besides, after tonight she would never
see him again. With these thoughts she made her way beside her father to their suite. When she had retrieved her
cloak, and her father his pipe, they left to meet Rafe in the
lobby.

He was waiting for them as he had said, and the three
went out the door to find the victoria parked at the curb
awaiting their arrival. Rafe assisted Kacey into the carriage
and turned to do the same for the professor. Colin's expression, however, held a disturbed quality as he said,

"Gads, I just remembered I have some important papers to go over tonight. I'm sorry, Rafe, but I will have to decline your offer."

At his words Kacey stood again, but Colin shook his head and motioned for his daughter to be seated as he said, "Now, dear, you go ahead and enjoy the ride. I don't know how those papers could have slipped my mind, but there's no reason for you not to go."

Kacey felt appalled and trapped at the same time. She sputtered, "But, Father, I don't have to go if you're not going. Perhaps Monsieur Assante would rather ask someone else. I'm sure he was looking forward to your company," she said as a last resort.

Rafe employed a mock look of hurt on his face while his eyes held a challenge. "Mademoiselle, I am wounded. You do not want to ride with me?"

He was laughing at her, and Kacey knew it. Her blood raced, not from his dark good looks, but because she could never bypass an outright dare, especially from conceited males. Kacey threw caution to the wind.

"Why, monsieur, of course I'd love to go. I merely thought that perhaps you would prefer to ask, er . . . someone else."

Rafe's smile was as intimate as a kiss. "*Au contraire*, mademoiselle, I would be honored to be in the company of one so lovely as you." Then he turned to Colin and extended his hand. "I understand, Professor. And if I don't see you before I leave, I'll be in touch with you when I get back to France. I'll bring your daughter back safely, monsieur. *Au revoir*."

Colin shook Rafe's proffered hand. "I know you will, Rafe, and I'll keep you posted. Good-bye, lad." Colin looked at Kacey. "Enjoy the ride, dear." He knew her well, and by now she was seething with fury. He also knew she would get over it. He turned and walked toward the entrance to the hotel.

Rafe seated himself beside Kacey in the Victoria and

motioned for the driver to go ahead. He did not attempt to move closer to Kacey but instead began conversation. "I trust you are comfortable, mademoiselle . . . may I call you Kacey?"

"If you feel you must, monsieur." Kacey knew the words sounded tart as soon as they fell from her lips. She tried to relax as she sat stiffly in the corner of the carriage. She knew she was being ridiculous. She was not some schoolgirl who swooned at every handsome male who crossed her path.

"Yes, I must. And I would like for you to call me Rafe. Would it be so difficult for you?"

"Monsieur, I see no reason to call you by your first name since you will be returning to France tomorrow and I probably will never see you again. So if we can just get on with the ride, I would be most happy." Kacey was appalled at her own words. She was not normally this short with anyone. Rafael Assante definitely brought out the worst in her, she thought.

Kacey's words fired Rafe, but he fought to keep his emotions under control. *The shrew has a tongue like a blade. She needs to be taught a lesson.*

"*Oui*, mademoiselle, we will get on with the ride, as you put it." He motioned for the driver to speed up. The quick lurch of the horses bounced Kacey toward the middle of the seat, and when she landed she suddenly found herself in the arms of Rafael Assante. She struggled inwardly against the strength and warmth of his embrace. Something inside her wanted to stay in the fold of his arms, but another force inside her resisted the man's masculine appeal. She wanted no part of an attachment now and she did not yield to her traitorous body.

She fought against the material of his suit and his rock-hard strength and knew even before she felt searing lips that he was going to kiss her. Once again, just for an instant, her body grew weak and melted into his arms before realization dawned on her. His lips crushed against hers and an unfamiliar feeling formed in the pit of her stomach, where remnants of emotion seemed to gather and arrange the muscles of her abdomen into a hugh knot. She was swimming through a haze of feelings and desires previously unknown to her, but reason won over, and Kacey pushed Rafe away.

He was the first to speak. "Ah, *chérie*, so the cool Mademoiselle O'Reilly does have feelings after all, *n'est-ce pas*?"

Kacey was glad of the semidarkness that hid the flush in her cheeks. Yet the humility she was feeling was overcome by a much stronger emotion that filled her being. She tried to mask her confusion by lashing out at Rafe. "Why, you, you . . . scoundrel, how dare you? Wait until my father hears of your outrageous behavior."

Rafe pretended innocence. "Why, mademoiselle, you practically threw yourself at me. You see, I am on my side of the carriage." His tone changed to a low, husky pitch as he leaned close to her ear and added, "You won't tell your father about this, *chérie*. You enjoyed it as much as I did."

"You're very sure of yourself, aren't you, monsieur? What would you say if I told you that I think you are despicable?"

"I'd say you are treading on dangerous territory, *chérie*. I think your lips said otherwise a moment ago."

The threat in his voice made Kacey's heart race even faster.

"Monsieur, you are no gentleman. Take me back to the hotel this instant."

"You are right, *chérie*, I am no gentleman, and I don't usually let spoiled females dictate what I should do. But I will do as you say. I've never been one to force my attentions on a lady. Shall we say I've never had to." Rafe leaned forward and gave instructions to the driver to turn the carriage around, then settled back against the leather seat.

The arrogance of the man irritated Kacey beyond reason and she seemed to have no control of her tongue. "Oh, I have no doubt as to your prowess with women, monsieur. It's just that you got hold of the wrong person this time. You should learn to better pick your . . . ladies in the future."

Rafe's voice hardened ruthlessly as he looked at Kacey. "I assure you, mademoiselle, I won't make the same mistake again."

The edge to his voice caused Kacey to glance his way as the victoria passed under a streetlight. She was stopped short by the threat she saw in his hooded eyes. Neither did she miss the passion that burned there. She sat back in her seat and silently continued the remainder of the drive back to her hotel with the arrogant Rafael Assante, whom she hoped never to see again.

Two

"Putnam, I think you are making a big mistake. This John Dunning may be on to something big. I think the Peabody Museum should investigate these dwellings," Colin said as he paced the rich walnut-paneled room. The man behind the intricately carved mahogany desk listened as he smoked a thick Havana cigar. Swirls of smoke drifted about his head, giving him the appearance of a genie just escaped from a magic lamp.

When he spoke, his voice grated like metal. "Damn it, O'Reilly, you may be right, but the board has reviewed his letter, and we think it would be a waste of time with all the important finds going on right now in Egypt. We're putting our money and our diggers elsewhere right now." The director of the museum wheeled his leather swivel chair a quarter turn and stood before moving to look out the open window of his office.

Taking the cue that the meeting had ended, Colin said to the man's back, "Very well, Professor. I hope you know what you're doing." With those words Colin turned and left the office, determined to contact the rancher and see the find for himself.

Colin strode the length of the long vaulted corridor and headed for the exit that would take him home. Classes had ended for the day, and Kacey and Mrs. Bingham would soon be waiting dinner for him. It was a short walk from campus to the modest two-story home he shared with his daughter and their housekeeper. This time of year crabapple, redbud, and dogwood bloomed profusely along the streets, but the lovely display did little to divert his thoughts from the idea that was forming in his head. He speeded his steps as he neared a gate that was set in a white picket fence. Ignoring the show of red and white tulips that flanked the red brick walk, he hastened toward the wide gingerbread-trimmed veranda that wrapped around the front of the house.

Kacey heard the front door open and stopped her task of setting the table for dinner to meet her father in the entry hall. Its walls were decorated in a delicate beige paper that was sparsely sprayed with tiny rosebuds. The rich oak of the woodwork and stair railing contrasted beautifully with the muted shades. Smiling, she moved down the hall to where he stood, and stretching on tiptoes she reached to plant a hello kiss on his cheek.

"Good evening, Father. Dinner is almost ready. Sarah is finishing dessert now. She's made your favorite—apple pie."

"Sounds good, dear. It'll go with the news I have for you. How would you like to go with me to Colorado this summer?" When she started to speak, Colin added, "Of course, I have to make some arrangements first, but I'm sure everything will work out."

"Well, yes, of course, but what will we do out there?" Kacey asked.

"There's a young rancher, John Dunning, who has found an ancient village he's named Pueblo Mesita. Putnam's not sending anyone out there, but if what the man says is true, I want to see this for myself.''

Kacey noted the high color in her father's cheeks and realized they had not been on a dig for some time now. ''Will this be a working site with outfitters and everything?''

''If I can work out the details. I want to see what's out there and what Dunning's already collected. We'll talk more about it over dinner.'' Colin patted her hand and walked toward the stairs. His mind was whirling with letters to write and what to say. After dinner he had two letters to pen: one addressed to John Dunning, Durango, Colorado; the other to Rafael Assante, Nancy, France.

Colin had not mentioned Rafe to Kacey for some time now, even though he kept in contact with the young man. He had heard from Rafe that everything seemed to be going well for him. His father was much improved, and Rafe had gone to Egypt to participate in a dig. By all his accounts it had proved to be very rewarding to Oxford University, who had financed the venture. He could prove valuable on this trip.

Colin knew that Kacey and Rafe had not gotten along well in New York, judging from the way she fumed when he mentioned Rafe's name. But they would have to put their differences aside. He wanted Rafe on this trip. Colin had resigned himself to the fact that Kacey was, after all, Kacey! He shook his head as he thought of the grandchildren he might never have and walked to his room to ready himself for dinner.

Kacey had returned to the kitchen and was helping Sarah with the evening meal. Sarah Bingham had been a member of the household ever since Professor O'Reilly had come to Harvard to teach. Kacey felt a deep affection for the older woman. From time to time she traveled to Philadelphia to visit her son and daughter-in-law, but she never stayed long, and Kacey was always pleased to have her back. Kacey suspected that she didn't get along well

with her daughter-in-law, but Sarah had never spoken of
it. After the death of Kacey's mother, Sarah had become
the mother figure in her life, and they shared mutual feelings of love and respect. Now the matronly woman's round
face was enhanced by the beaming smile she wore for
Kacey as she wiped her hands on her apron and spoke in
her faint Irish brogue.

"Kacey, darlin', when are you going to ask that nice
young man, Mr. Beecher, over for dinner again?"

Kacey had grown used to Sarah's subtle remarks concerning young men, and she smiled to herself before she
answered the question. "Sarah, Mr. Beecher is a pompous
ass, and I won't be seeing him again."

"Now, darlin', you say that about all the young men.
Surely you've seen one lad that you had feelings for."

Kacey could not stop the image that formed in her mind
of an arrogant dark Frenchman she spent much time trying
not to think about. Even after these many months, the more
she tried to forget his lips pressed against hers, the more
he penetrated her thoughts—and the angrier she got. With
more assurance than was needed, she tried to convince
Sarah.

"No, Sarah, I have not. I am starved, so let's serve
dinner."

Kacey saw that Sarah remained unconvinced, to avoid
further confrontation, she began to busy herself with putting food on the dining table. When the table was finally
set, Kacey went to her father's study to call him to dinner.
The large window behind his desk was open, and the
heavy English lace curtains floated in the spring breeze
that filled the room. Dusk had nearly settled in, and the
dimness of the study caused Kacey to pause until her eyes
adjusted to the low light. Then she saw the back of her
father's head wreathed in a swirl of smoke. He sat in his
favorite chair, enjoying his pipe. Smiling to herself and
feeling the chill in the room, Kacey walked to the window
and lowered it.

"Dinner is ready, Father."

Colin looked at his daughter and stood. "Yes, dear, I'm coming." He tamped his pipe, placed it in a nearby ashtray, and followed her to the dining room, where Sarah was waiting.

"Good evening, Sarah. I see you've outdone yourself as usual. I don't know how Kacey and I would get along without you." The sincerity in Colin's voice was genuine. He was as fond of Sarah as he would have been of a sister if he had one. Since Margaret's death, Sarah had made life easier for him and his motherless daughter, and he was truly grateful to her.

Sarah's face lit up at Colin's words. "You're too kind, Professor. Why, it means a lot to me to be appreciated and to be able to be independent from . . . some folks I know."

"Just the same, Sarah, I still don't know how we'd get along without you. I am making plans for Kacey and myself to be away this summer, and it's good to know you'll take care of the house while we are away."

"Aye, you can be sure of it, Professor. Is it a dig you're going on, sir?" Sarah asked as she passed the homemade rolls.

"Yes, Sarah, we're going to take a look at some ancient dwellings in Colorado. Then later maybe I can convince Professor Putnam to take a team out there to look at them, too. Putnam's a good man, but hardheaded." Colin began to eat as Kacey joined in the conversation.

"Isn't there still some unrest from the Indians out there, Father?"

Colin put down his fork. "No, there's nothing to worry about, dear. With the capture of Geronimo last year, I'm afraid these United States have become too civilized. Why, I could use a little adventure. In my younger days I couldn't get enough of it. Besides, danger has never bothered you before," Colin teased Kacey as he pictured her much younger, scrambling around dig sites on foreign soil. "You remember the time we were exploring King Seti's tomb and you stumbled through a secret passage? I turned around, and you were gone. I called to all the workers, and we searched for you, but you were nowhere to be found.'' Colin turned his gaze to the housekeeper. ''I can tell you, Sarah, that took ten years off my life. But Kacey found her way out and even wanted to do it again.''

With long slim fingers Kacey reached to clasp her glass of iced tea and sipped the cool drink before she said, ''Well, Father, that was a long time ago. I'm much more ... domesticated now.''

''No, dear, I think the word is *complacent*. I think we both need this trip to get our blood pumping again.'' Colin paused to curl his fingers into a fist and rapped it lightly on the table, adding, ''And, by Jove, I'm looking forward to it. This could be the biggest find in North America, and Putnam's letting it slip away.'' The excitement in Colin's eyes transferred itself to Kacey's own as he continued. ''I'm going to post a letter tonight to Dunning and ...'' He caught himself in time to stop the slip of tongue, but Kacey picked up on it.

''And what, Father?''

''Oh, nothing dear, just that I hope to hear from him right away.''

May 21, 1887

Rafe stood near the railing of the *Cunard Pride* and watched the gray waves as they pitched white against the blue horizon. As the sun floated high in the sky, a school of dolphins played in the distance, and once again the ocean did not fail to fascinate him in its magnitude. The *Cunard Pride* was a modern ship and boasted of a speed of twenty knots, making a voyage across the Atlantic in seven days. But it still wasn't fast enough.

Rafe had been eager to begin the trip from the time he

had received Professor O'Reilly's letter in late April, telling him of the planned trip to Colorado. There had not been much time to prepare, but he was ready once again to visit the United States and to work with the professor. And Kacey. The vision of the redheaded beauty filled his mind, but he was not fooled by the innocent smile. He knew how disturbing that vision could be. How would she react to him now? Recalling her actions the last time he saw her, he decided that this time he would play a different game. He would assume the role of an uninterested player. The professor never mentioned her in his letters, and Rafe never asked. Maybe she was married by now, he thought, but then dismissed the idea. He doubted that the shrew was wed to anyone.

"Monseiur Assante, are you enjoying the view? You seem to be in such deep thought." Rafe started and quickly turned at the words that seemed to drip with honey as they flowed from the reddened lips of the widow Carlisle. According to the conversations that he had had early in the week with Mary Carlisle, she had taken this voyage to try to recover from her husband's sudden death. It was difficult for a woman to travel alone, she had decided. Rafe had thought that she seemed to be making it very well, considering the attentions she received from every available male in the lounge, and the fact that she had invited herself to sit at his table during dinner every evening.

Tipping his hat and taking in the fashionable green traveling suit she wore, Rafe raised his brows and answered the young widow as a half-smile formed on his full lips. "*Bonjour*, madame. I trust you are having a lovely stroll?" Mary Carlisle was an expert at batting eyelashes, Rafe mused, as she overdid the exercise before she spoke.

"If you would join me I would be ever so grateful, monsieur. A poor girl doesn't have a chance with all the libertines on this ship."

Rafe thought she hardly fit the description of a "poor

girl," but said instead, "*Oui*, Madame Carlisle, I would be glad to escort you on your stroll."

"I just love the way you Frenchmen talk, monsieur. Why, when I was on the stage—"

"You were on the stage, madame? Why, that's marvelous."

"You think so? I'm thinking of going back into the theater since my dear Nathan has passed away. He didn't want me to flaunt myself around—you know how husbands are." The woman's shrill giggle did nothing to endear her to Rafe, and he answered a bit too harshly.

"*Non*, Madame Carlisle, I'm afraid I don't. But if the stage is what you want, then I would say for you to do just that."

"You really think so, monsieur? Of course, if the right man came along to take care of me, I wouldn't dream of going back on the stage." Once again she batted long lashes and gazed demurely at him.

Rafe felt he had endured the woman's prattle for as long as possible, and he steered their steps back to where they had started. "I beg your forgiveness, madame, but I just remembered I have an appointment in the barbershop." He did not wait for her reply, but tipped his hat and started off in the direction of the ship's barbershop, then ducked into another tiny shop to avoid detection by the forward woman. The boutique was a narrow nook, and its shelves were crowded together, holding a vast array of items from razors to silk scarves. The clerk standing behind a small counter was a middle-aged man who was fast losing his tawny locks. His hairline had receded to the middle of his scalp, with thin wisps standing on ends.

Rafe nodded to the man and pretended to shop for a few minutes before his eye was caught by a tiny box exquisitely fashioned from fine silver and inlaid with mother-of-pearl. He handled its fragile exterior and decided to buy the case as a gift for Kacey. He failed to understand his own intentions, and almost as soon as he had paid the clerk he had second thoughts about the gift. He had meant it to be a peace offering when he saw Kacey, but he was unsure how she would react, and she had a way of getting under his skin and setting him off. Rafe watched the clerk wrap the box carefully in tissue paper and then again with brown paper before handing the parcel to him. He thanked the clerk and, looking down both lengths of the deck, he left the shop and strode toward his cabin, hoping to avoid the widow Carlisle.

From now on, he decided, he would see her before she saw him. Rafe was not usually one to shirk confrontation, but he thought it would be better to avoid the woman than to be outright rude to her. There were plenty of other men on the ship perfectly willing to cater to Madame Carlisle, and Rafe did not want to deprive them of the pleasure of her company. He was willing to bow out.

At last Rafe stood in front of his cabin door, and a niggling guilt mixed with irritation washed over him. Damned if he'd ever let a woman send him scuttling to cover before, he thought. This was one voyage he was anxious to leave behind him.

Rafe entered his room and removed his hat, tossing it to a peg beside the door before carefully placing his purchase on a table in the center of the room. Afternoon light filtered through the porthole and bathed the spacious compartment in a soft glow that revealed a red velvet sitting chair, an ornate Queen Anne desk, and a poster bed covered with a gold damask spread beside a matching dresser. All in all it was an attractive stateroom, but not one in which Rafe wanted to spend the remainder of the voyage.

S'il plait à Dieu, God willing, if fair weather continued, the liner should dock in Boston Harbor tomorrow. Not a bit too soon for him, Rafe thought as he undid his tie and pitched it onto the bed. But before doffing his suit coat and tossing it aside, he reached inside for a flask of whiskey. Rafe seldom touched the container that he carried in the inside pocket, but long hours in the field as an archaeologist at times required a drink. He moved to the velvet chair and stretched his long sturdy legs in front of him as he seated himself and sipped from the flask.

Hours later when Rafe awoke, he was still in the chair, and his muscular arms hung over the sides. Only the ship's lighting came through the porthole now, and Rafe's eyes adjusted to the dimness of the room as he moved to raise his body from the chair. As he stood he ran his fingers through black hair before rubbing a face that revealed a need for shaving, while his stomach growled its need to be fed.

Cursing silently at his stupor, Rafe walked to the lamp near the door, and, turning it on, he looked at the clock beside the bed. He still had time to make it to the dining salon for the evening meal—and maybe the loquacious Madame Carlisle had already eaten. *Mon Dieu*, he didn't care one way or the other. The woman was a nuisance, but surely he could stand one more evening of her company.

With these thoughts Rafe walked to his water closet and commenced with the ablutions that would make him appear civilized. He shaved the dark stubble from his face and returned to the main room to dress for dinner. Taking a clean shirt and tie from the dresser drawer, Rafe donned the clothes, then completed his attire with a fresh dinner jacket before leaving his room and heading toward the evening spot.

In the dining area, his cautious eyes scanned the room while he waited to be seated. To his surprise, the widow was nowhere to be seen. He breathed a sigh of relief and followed a white-coated maitre d' to a table near the rear of the room. Suddenly he looked forward to his meal, which he soon ordered.

By the time the prime rib was served, Rafe was famished, and he ate heartily of the succulent fare before once more moving to the deck of the ship to enjoy the stars that twinkled in the night. As was the case so often, he could not keep thoughts of Kacey from his mind. The witch seemed to have a spell on him. He had been preoccupied with her ever since he had returned to France. But his interest in her irritated him, considering the open hostility she had shown him. Still, he could not keep her from his thoughts. He could not forget the taste and the softness of her mouth. Maybe he would finally be able to rid himself of her image after seeing her again.

Rafe shook his head to clear his mind and moved to the ship's railing. The deck was sparsely populated with couples seated under the black velvet sky who seemed to enjoy the soft music that drifted from the salon. Rafe recognized the song the band was playing, and the vocalist's soulful tenor rode on the evening breeze: *"Still to us at twilight comes love's old song, comes love's old sweet song."* When the melody ended, Rafe turned and walked toward his stateroom.

Kacey absentmindedly toyed with her scrambled eggs and toast. Her stomach was in a turmoil, and food was the last thing she wanted right now. But Sarah had insisted that she eat breakfast, and she didn't want to offend the dear woman the day before she and her father planned to leave. The housekeeper declared that Kacey barely ate enough to keep a bird alive anyway.

Even the beautiful bouquet of pink tea roses that Sarah had placed in the center of the table did nothing to soothe Kacey's troubled mind. Her father had informed her just last night that Rafael Assante would be accompanying them out west. He had tricked her. If only he knew how the rogue piqued her, she was sure he would not have asked him to join them. Why, just the thought of the man had her seething. Spending a whole month in his company would be unbearable. How could her father have done such a thing?

Kacey stopped the brown study of her plate and looked at the object of her thoughts. "Father, I wish you had discussed the prospect of inviting Rafael Assante with me.

If you really knew the man, I don't think you would have asked him to join us.''

"Kacey, dear, I do know Rafe, and he is a fine young man. Why, he took care of his father's estate while the old fellow recovered from his illness. He's like you, Kacey. He cares for his family. Any young man who'll give up time to help his parents deserves our respect.''

"Oh, pshaw, Father. He probably can't wait to inherit the family fortune. And you've asked this . . . this fortunehunter to go with us.''

"Dear, I fail to understand whose fortune he is hunting. I certainly don't have one and, well, I believe he is well set himself. When he turned twenty-five last year, he inherited his grandmother's estate. According to Rafe, that in itself is worth a fortune. No, dear, you're barking up the wrong tree.'' Colin picked up his cup of coffee and took a sip before reaching into his coat pocket to retrieve his gold pocket watch. The watch had been his father's, and he never looked at the timepiece without thinking of the grandson he hoped someday to bestow with the precious heirloom. He opened the embossed covered face and saw that if he were to meet Rafe at the dock on time he would have to hurry.

As he started to speak, Kacey countered Colin's defense of Rafe with her own declaration. "Don't you see, Father, he could easily have made all that up. Why, it would be like taking a drink of water for him.''

"No, I don't think Rafe's like that. And deep down I don't believe you think so either. Are you sure you don't want to go with me to meet him? His telegram said he should arrive today.''

"No, I still have much to do before tomorrow. What hotel are you taking him to?''

"Why, I wouldn't dream of taking him to a hotel when we have plenty of room here.'' Colin saw his daughter's distressed look and added as he rose from his chair, "Everything will work out all right, dear. You'll see.''

Kacey would not be put off. "But maybe he would rather stay at a hotel."

"I've already asked him to stay here, and he has accepted. I didn't do all that before clearing everything with Sarah."

"So, she has known about this all along and didn't tell me?" Kacey narrowed her eyes, and from their corners she saw Sarah start through the door from the kitchen then step back when she heard Kacey's statement. Now Kacey realized the actual plotting that had gone on right under her nose without her knowledge. What were they up to? she mused. She turned her gaze to her father, and his innocent countenance was shattered when he shifted his eyes away from hers. But how could she be angry with those two? They were both the sweetest creatures on the face of the earth. She just shook her head and once more turned her wrath toward the absent Monsieur Assante, who, she believed, certainly had her father fooled.

"Well, I must be going, dear." Colin walked to where Kacey sat at the other end of the table and placed a good-bye kiss on his daughter's cheek. "We should be back in time for supper, but if Rafe's passage has been delayed, don't worry."

"Well, do take care, Father, and I . . . I'll try to be civil to our houseguest. You can count on that," she said as she returned the affectionate gesture.

"I know you will, dear. Good-bye." Colin patted his daughter's shoulder, then turned to walk to the front hall, where he picked up his hat and umbrella. He was looking forward to meeting Rafe and making the journey west.

Kacey heard the front door close and knew that when she saw her father again, Rafael Assante would be with him. The man was a womanizer, and she wanted no part of him. His astounding arrogance mortified her. But she had promised her father that she would be civil to him, and she always kept her promises. Even the ones to herself.

She stood to clear the table, and the hem of her ivory-colored lawn dress fell in soft folds to the carpeted floor. Suddenly she decided the table could wait; she walked softly to the kitchen door and peeked through to where the housekeeper stood beside the cookstove.

"Sarah?"

The woman turned but would not meet Kacey's chiding gaze. She continued about her business of scraping food from a porcelain pan and answered, "What is it, darlin'?"

Kacey strolled farther into the room before she spoke. "Oh, I just want to know—how long?"

"How long what, darlin'?" The woman pretended innocence as she moved about the kitchen.

"You know what I'm talking about, Sarah. How long have you known that Rafael Assante is coming here to our home?"

"Why, I thought your father told ya. You mean you didn't know?"

"You know perfectly well I didn't know. As far as I'm concerned, we can stuff him in the attic."

"Now, now, darlin'. You know you don't mean that. I'm sorry I didn't mention it to ya, but your father seemed to think it best not to."

"Yes, Father was right," she fumed. "Now it's too late to do anything about it. I'll just have to make the best of the situation."

"Don't you think you're makin' too much out of it?" Sarah said as she tried to console the young woman she had helped to raise.

"You just don't understand, Sarah. That man is insufferable. You'll find out when he gets here. Just remember I told you so."

Sarah merely nodded her head and looked forward to meeting the young man who had Kacey in such a state of agitation.

Three

Boston Harbor
May 22, 1887

Rafe made his way down the wide gangplank beside the other passengers. He wore a light-blue suit and a white, flat-topped boater hat with a darker blue band. Boston Harbor was a beehive of activity, and the sounds of the dock elated him. He was happy to be in the United States once again, and his lively footsteps echoed that feeling with a forceful rhythm on the planks. Dock workers yelled their commands for unloading wooden crates of various goods, while families and friends greeted loved ones back home with fervid hugs and kisses. But the welcome sights and sounds were interrupted by a shrill voice from behind. He pretended not to hear as Mary Carlisle's vocal cords grated on him like claws down a washboard.

"Ra-aafe. Oh, *Ra-aafe*. Yoo-hoo!"

He speeded his steps and refused to turn around. All the while, he strained to see the professor through the crowd ahead of him, but to no avail. "*Ah la vache.*" Damn, he muttered to himself. The woman was a curse, and she had her sights on him. He had to get away. What if the professor wasn't here? He'd have no excuse but to entertain the maddening woman.

Rafe experienced déjà vu as he searched for an opening in the crowd. There was none to be found, and he knew he had to face the coquette. As soon as he came to that realization, he felt a hand touch his coat sleeve. His gaze followed the length of the limb latched onto him, and his eyes came to rest on Mary Carlisle's pleased face.

"Surely you weren't leaving without saying good-bye, monsieur." As she spoke, she opened and closed her eyelids so rapidly that Rafe thought she possibly had an affliction.

"Ah, but of course not, Madame Carlisle." He raised his hand and tipped his hat as he lied. At that moment Rafe looked up to see Professor O'Reilly standing at the bottom of the gangplank. The expression on his face was one of humor, but Rafe saw no humor in the situation. He seized the opportunity to escape. "I'm truly sorry to have to leave you like this, but there is someone I have to meet." Once again he tipped his hat and turned to leave.

The woman called after him in a high-pitched whine. "I'll be staying at the Marlborough Hotel until next wee-eek."

Colin looked past Rafe at the woman who was shouting and waving a handkerchief wildly in the air, as if its movement would help to carry her urgent message.

"Well, Rafe, I see you're still popular with the ladies."

"I don't know what you mean, Professor, but let's get out of here." Rafe pretended ignorance as a smile formed on his lips in greeting.

When he saw the astonished look on Colin's face, he explained, "It's not what you think. But believe me, we have to go before she descends on me again."

Colin saw the cornered look in Rafe's eyes. "You don't know what I'm thinking. But if you say let's go, then stop wasting time and let's go." He put his arm across the younger man's shoulder and led the way to their carriage.

"Have you taken care of your baggage?" Colin asked as he stepped up into the hired vehicle.

"*Oui*, Professor. I had it sent to your home address. But I still have to go to the immigration center just around the corner."

Kacey worked to fill the centers of the flaky pastry with the creamy confection that Sarah had concocted. At one time Sarah had worked in a bakery, and she was an expert at preparing delicious desserts. Her matronly figure attested to the frequent tasting that was needed when preparing such delicacies. At the moment Sarah was stirring a hollandaise sauce at the stove, and she could not leave the mixture to chance. Sarah knew that the secret was in the stirring and did not allow anyone else to do the chore. But out of the need for more hands, she allowed Kacey to spoon the mouth-watering custard into each pastry cavity. Sarah had planned a special evening meal for the young Frenchman who was to stay the night at Professor O'Reilly's home, and it was nearly time for his arrival.

The housekeeper looked at the Regulator clock on the kitchen wall and pushed back an errant strand of hair. "Would ya be looking at the time, Kacey, m'love. Are you almost through puttin' the filling in?"

"Yes, Sarah, just one more to go." Kacey glanced at the older woman and saw how anxious she seemed and how flushed her cheeks were. "Now, don't you be nervous. We've had guests before, and it never put you in such a dither. Everything is going to be just fine. You always outdo yourself, Sarah." Kacey finished the last cream puff and laid it on the platter next to the others before spooning herself the last morsel of filling from the bowl. When she had swallowed the custard, she added, "Mmm-mm, it's absolutely delicious as always. And if Monsieur Assante doesn't like it, then that's too b—"

Kacey cut off her words as she looked at the doorway

and saw two men standing there: her father and Rafael Assante, the latter looking as assured and confident as she remembered him. His black hair shone like a raven's wing, and the mocking smile that played about his lips sent her pulses racing. She absently looked down at her spattered apron and reached to straighten a loosened hair that she was sure had escaped from its coil on top of her head before she reached behind her to untie the soiled apron.

Sarah did not miss Kacey's attempt to better her appearance and smiled to herself as she saw the smudge of filling on her right cheek.

Colin was the first to speak as he introduced Rafe to the older woman. "Sarah, this is Rafael Assante, our houseguest from France."

Rafe moved toward the housekeeper and bowed. "*Bonjour,* Madame Sarah. I am pleased to make your acquaintance."

Sarah was immediately smitten by the charming young gentleman, and she smiled. "I'm happy to meet you, too, Mr. Assante."

"Ah, please call me Rafe, madame."

Colin nodded toward his daughter with the smudged filling on her cheek. "And you remember Kacey?"

"*Oui. Bonjour,* Kacey." Rafe bowed once more, but his mocking gaze never left Kacey's face.

By now Kacey had removed the apron and placed it on a chair beside her. She had promised to be civil to their guest in front of her father. But she and Rafael Assante both knew that that was as far as it went. The arrogant rogue would get no sweetness from her. He had his dues coming. But for now she feigned politeness and said, "Good day, monsieur. I trust you had a pleasant voyage?"

Rafe recognized the animosity behind the cool words and instantly knew where he stood with the beautiful mademoiselle. The niggling bit of remorse he felt for the way he had treated her when he was last in America deserted him. *Mon Dieu,* but the woman had a way of annoying him. She got under his skin like a burr under the saddle of Huguenot, his favorite stallion.

Rafe's eyes glittered, and his nostrils flared. "*Oui*, mademoiselle. A *bon voyage*."

Colin broke the stilted atmosphere. "Now, if you ladies will excuse us, I have some things I want to show Rafe in my study before dinner."

"Go ahead, Father. I'll call you when dinner is ready."

Kacey's voice took on a different quality when she spoke to her father. The softening of her tone was notable to Rafe, and unaccountably the fact left him feeling deprived. That fact irritated him. Why should he care if the sharp-tongued shrew liked him or not? Plenty of other females liked him extremely well, had proven it to him again and again. Rafe's reverie was broken by Colin's voice.

"Come along, lad. I'll show you Dunning's letter." Colin had turned and started through the doorway, and Rafe followed him.

The masculine voices trailed off to a murmur, and to Kacey's annoyance she found herself straining to hear the conversation. What was wrong with her? she thought. She didn't make a habit of listening in on others' conversations. But she transferred her annoyance with herself to Rafe. The man had a way of bringing out the worst in her.

Kacey could imagine her disheveled appearance and turned to the older woman. "Sarah, if there's nothing else you need me to do, I'm going to freshen up a bit before dinner."

"Of course, darlin', you go on. I can take care of everything. And don't forget to wipe the custard off your cheek." Sarah smiled at Kacey and winked when she saw the wide-eyed look of dismay on the young woman's face.

Kacey rushed from the kitchen and made her way to her upstairs bedroom. She was grateful that she did not have to pass her father's study on the way. Her chamber was located next to the guest room at the end of the upstairs hall, and at the moment she was not thrilled at the prospect of spending the night in the room next to Rafael Assante. She knew she was being ridiculous, but the proximity of the man set her pulse racing at a speed she did not like.

She opened the door to her spacious room, which was decorated in a pale cabbage-rose wallpaper. But the muted pink tints of the large roses that lay against a cream background enhanced the loveliness of the room instead of overpowering it. An ivory eyelet spread covered the gleaming brass bed, and a bouquet of pink roses that matched the ones in the dining room rested on a lace doily atop a light-oak chest. On top of the matching dressing table was arrayed an assortment of fashionable combs, bottles of various sizes, and a tortoise-shell mirror set.

Kacey moved across the carpeted floor to the door of her water closet and went inside. She stood before the mirror over the basin, gazing at her reflection. Sure enough, custard had dried on her cheek. She didn't have time for a bath before dinner, but she reached for a washcloth and soaked it under the faucet. She scrubbed her face until she had rid herself of the custard remnants, then walked to her wardrobe to choose a suitable dress for the evening.

The ivory day dress she wore would have been fine under normal circumstances, but she she did not want to be at a disadvantage in the presence of Rafael Assante. She riffled through her clothing until at last she found something presentable to wear. The simple elegance of the dinner dress pleased her, and she smiled as she started to unbutton her clothing. She hurriedly moved about the room as she undid the buttons and glanced in the dressing-table mirror at her hair. It, too, needed something done.

Drat! She had not allowed enough time to do all the things that earlier had not seemed important. Why hadn't she taken the time to have a leisurely bath and style her hair? Kacey was thoroughly put out with herself. Oh, well, she thought, she would just have to make do. Hastily she realized that she usually did not get this agitated over guests who came to dinner, especially young men. Kacey pushed the thought to the back of her mind and pulled on the blue velvet dinner dress. Blue was her favorite color, and it seemed to enhance her coloring.

She fastened the tiny pearl buttons down the front of the ensemble, then moved to sit at the stool in front of the dressing table. She uncoiled the length of titian tresses and began to brush vigorously. When she had thoroughly brushed her hair and used her fine-toothed comb, she then arranged the shining coppery mass atop her head in a popular Psyche knot. Kacey thought the style flattered her oval face, which she felt was too long. She turned her head from side to side and decided to use some of the face powder she had recently purchased. With that applied, she pinched her high cheekbones to give her pale face more color, then stood to go downstairs.

She felt guilty at having deserted Sarah in the kitchen, but she told herself that Sarah was an accomplished cook and that everything would be fine.

Kacey reached for the doorknob. Suddenly she felt a stirring of nerves as she realized how Rafael Assante affected her. Why couldn't he have stayed out of her life? It had become predictable and . . . calm. She went out occasionally with gentlemen, but most of them had stopped trying to win her hand in marriage. She felt comfortable with them. Not so with Rafe. He set her pulse racing, and that disturbed her. She realized she had used the more familiar version of the man's name, which startled her. He had wanted her to call him that when last they met, but she had declined to accommodate him. Now the name fell from her lips without a thought. Kacey refused to admit the ease with which she had shortened Rafael's name. The name "Rafe" seemed to sound so intimate to her ears, and she had no intention of becoming . . . familiar with any man, much less a scoundrel like Rafael Assante.

Kacey's cheeks burned at the direction her ruminations had taken. She glanced toward the guest room and wondered if the object of her thoughts was there. Once more

she aimed her irritation with herself at Rafael Assante and
turned to go down the hall toward the stairs.

Rafe nodded at the professor's words and smoked his cheroot as he sat on one of the cushiony wingback chairs that
flanked the fireplace. At this time of year there was no
blazing fire, but a cool breeze filtered through an open
window of the study, and the two men enjoyed the early
evening air. Rafe listened carefully to the professor, but he
could not get the sight of Kacey out of his mind. Seeing
her again had certainly stirred his blood. *Mon Dieu*! She
was even more beautiful than he remembered. A muscle
in Rafe's jaw jumped as the object of his thoughts spoke
from the open doorway.

"Excuse me, gentlemen. Dinner is ready."

Colin and Rafe turned at the same time to see Kacey
standing in the doorway. Colin stood as he said, "Thank
you, dear. We're coming."

Rafe stood, and with Colin motioning for him to go
ahead, he trailed Kacey to the dining room. His eyes bore
into her straight back as her full velvet skirt swished back
and forth in a graceful rhythm. With her plentiful upswept
hair and slender neck, she was a vision of loveliness, and
Rafe swallowed hard as her beauty hit him head-on.

Kacey felt sure Rafe was staring at her back. Hard as
she tried to ignore it, every nerve in her body tingled at
the thought of his maleness. She straightened her spine and
raised her chin, in defiance of her pulse.

When she came to the dining-room door she turned and
forced a smile as she indicated a seat. "Monsieur Assante,
please be seated there next to Father's place." Then she
took her own chair at the opposite end of the table.

After Colin had seated himself, he looked at Kacey and
said, "Dear, I'm sure our guest much prefers to be called
Rafe. And we'll all be sharing such close quarters in the
near future that I think we should dispense with formali-
ties." He looked at Rafe. "Don't you think so, lad?"

"Ah, *oui*, Professor. I heartily agree. I would hope that Mademoiselle Kacey will call me Rafe." He looked at her and pointedly nodded his head as he reached for his glass of wine. "And I would like to *porter un toast* to our journey." Colin picked up his glass of wine and waited for a hesitant Kacey to do the same. Rafe continued as he and the professor stood. "May our journey be successful and all our wishes come true."

The two men waited for Kacey to stand, then they all reached to the center of the table to touch goblets in the age-old ritual.

Kacey felt like a reluctant pawn in a game of chess. Here she stood drinking a toast with the devil himself. The man's dark virility disturbed her in every way, and she would feel relieved only when he once more returned to France. She had no time for the errant emotions that invaded her body.

Sarah came into the room and served the entrée. After that everything fell into place, and dinner passed without incident except for the tension between Rafe and Kacey. When the meal ended, Colin insisted that Kacey join him and Rafe in the parlor.

While Kacey was thinking that she would just as soon finish her packing, she discovered that she had become ensconced on the sofa beside Rafe. She found the nearness of the man somewhat disturbing and yet . . . exciting. She felt she had to get away. All her past reserve seemed to be deserting her. She suddenly found herself wanting to get closer to the man's masculinity, wanting to reach out and touch his dark head. By all the saints! The man *was* a devil, and he had cast a spell on her body. She cursed inwardly and swore to herself never to let him know that he attracted her in any way.

Kacey willed her pulse to slow to a normal rate. She had no intention of permitting herself to fall under his spell again, nor would she allow herself to be distracted by romantic notions. She had made a vow to herself to dedicate herself to her father, and she had no intention of changing her plans. With that in mind, she shrugged and settled back into the deep red cushions while Rafe and her father discussed the preparation for tomorrow's departure.

Colin's words cut into Kacey's reverie. "Kacey, dear, what time can you be ready to leave in the morning? We need to be at the station by nine o'clock."

"Oh, whenever you say, Father." His question was a perfect opening for her next words. "And that reminds me, I still have some packing to do tonight. I regret to leave you but I must say good-night." Kacey stood, and Rafe immediately did the same.

He bowed low and said, "*Bonsoir*, mademoiselle. I hope you have pleasant dreams, and I will see you in the morning, *n'est-ce pas?*"

Whether she imagined it or not, the tone he used to speak to her always seemed to have a seductive quality, and Kacey wished to goodness that Rafael Assante would please stay out of her dreams. She answered with reserve and a slight smile of defiance. "Thank you, monsieur. You're very kind. I'm sure I will, as I haven't had a nightmare since I was eight years old." With that she turned and walked to the parlor chair where her father sat, then bent to kiss his cheek. "Good-night, Father. I'll see you at breakfast."

Kacey walked from the room and made her way to the kitchen to speak to Sarah before she went to her bedchamber to finish packing. She found the housekeeper still at the sink finishing the dishes.

"Sarah, I should have helped you with the dishes. You would already have been finished."

"Now, you didn't want to go spoilin' that pretty dress, did you, darlin'? Besides, I am finished. Now, you go along to bed 'cause you have an early start in the morning and ya need to be lookin' your best."

Kacey hugged the woman's ample waist, then backed away. "I'll miss you, Sarah. You be sure to take care of yourself while we're gone, and I'll post you a letter whenever possible.''

"Don't you be worryin' about me, darlin'. I'll be fine. It's you I'll be worryin' about, what with those wild Indians out there lookin' to do in a pretty head of red hair.''

Kacey couldn't keep the smile from her lips. "Oh, Sarah, they don't scalp people anymore. You can stop worrying about that.''

"It wasn't your scalp I was worrying about," Sarah pointed out as she raised her eyebrows.

"You can quit thinking about any bad thing that's going to happen to me. Believe me, nothing awful is going to happen. Good-night, dear.'' Once more Kacey hugged the woman, then kissed her cheek and turned to go upstairs.

Kacey made her way to her bedchamber and closed the door. She began to unfasten the buttons on her dress as she whirled around in a lighthearted attempt at the waltz. Kacey was excited about the trip out west, and she refused to let Rafael Assante put a damper on her spirits. She would finish her packing, then get into bed and have a most wonderful night's sleep. She stepped out of the velvet ensemble and hung it in her steamer trunk along with shirtwaists and skirts that she planned to carry on the trip.

After washing her face and donning her nightgown, she turned out the light and scrambled into bed. She lay against the soft white sheets and listened to the sounds that came from her open window. She heard horses' hooves clopping against the cobblestone streets and the humming of voices as couples walked in the moonlight. She also heard a bump that came from the guest room. She thought she heard a muffled curse. Then she imagined that Rafe must have stubbed his toe, and she laughed quietly as she mused inexplicably how he deserved it and much more.

Finally sleep came to Kacey, and she swirled through an abyss of spiraling color. A figure stood at the end of the vortex and seemed to wait for her arrival. She fought against the impending meeting and struggled to turn around and go back the way she had entered. But a man's voice called to her through the distance; it was Rafe's low, seductive tone, and her mind was in an uproar. She denied that she really wanted to go to him, to do his bidding. Her own voice could be heard disclaiming her physical wants. Eventually she was pulled through to the other side, and when he reached to touch her, she trembled and awoke in a cold sweat. She lay silently in the night as the entire dream raced through her mind.

After a few moments she reached to turn on the lamp beside her bed, and light flooded the room. She shielded her eyes as she looked at the banjo clock on the wall, its pendulum clicking a steady rhythm. Three o'clock in the morning. She pushed the cover back and stood beside the bed. Her mouth was so dry she had to get a drink. She padded to the basin in the water closet and ran water into a glass. She drank its contents, then went back to bed to try to get more sleep. Maledictions to Rafael Assante, she fumed, why couldn't the man leave her alone? Now he invaded her dreams, or rather nightmares, which she'd told him she hadn't had since she was eight.

Kacey turned in the bed and tried to find a comfortable position. Finding that impossible, she raised herself and began to fluff her pillow by beating it on the ends. Then she put the pillow back on the bed and let her head flop against it in frustration. After what seemed like hours she eventually slept once again.

Rafe and the professor had decided to call it a night at an early hour, and Rafe walked toward his room at the end of the hall. The professor had gone into the room across the hall, so he decided that the room next to his must belong to Kacey. His footsteps paused momentarily in front of the door. He could not keep thoughts of her from his mind. He tried to picture the kind of nightgown she would wear. Amused, he thought it probably had a very high neck and long sleeves. The kind his mother wore. He shook his head and once again tried to convince himself that she was not his type . . . yet there were times when he thought that she was attracted to him. He knew he had not been wrong the one time he had kissed her, when her lips had softened under his own. But she adamantly refused to admit that it was so. *Mon Dieu*, he thought with exasperation, but she was *une femme qui me rend fou*, a maddening woman.

Rafe continued the short distance down the carpeted hall toward his own room. He reached for the doorknob and went inside. The room was bathed in darkness, and before his eyes could adjust, he walked toward where he knew the bedside table stood. He had not calculated his trunk standing on the floor, however, and his shin found it before he remembered its location. "*Ah la vache*," damn, he muttered. The oath slipped from his tongue as pain shot up his leg. When the ache had eased, he reached for the bedside lamp and pulled the chain. Light filtered through the silk-tasseled shade, and the coziness of the room surrounded Rafe. The brass bed and fluffy blue coverlet looked inviting. Like the rest of the house, it was modern in its decoration but still comfortable. He mentally applauded Kacey for her good taste, because he was sure she had been the one to choose the decor. Always back to Kacey, he thought. How could he get the woman off his mind? As if in answer, he bent to scoot the trunk out of the pathway before he began to doff his attire.

Rafe looked forward to sleep, and as soon as he had rid himself of his clothing he switched off the lamp and slid under the covers. The soft sheets felt good to his roughened skin. Almost as good as a woman, he mused, as muffled voices from the street below came through his window with the breeze. A horse whinnied, then silence once again. He closed his eyes, and in the muted night he heard what sounded like soft moans coming from the room next to his. She had said she never had nightmares. Rafe wondered what was causing her distress. Momentarily he longed to comfort her if she was distraught. Then on the other hand, he felt certain she did not want him to soothe her. *Mon Dieu*, he thought as he shifted his weight in the bed, all women were curses, and he was going to try to ignore the one in the other bedchamber. With that, Rafe tried to free his mind of the bothersome Kacey and attempted once more to sleep. Eventually he did drift off, but he could not keep the woman out of his mind, even in his sleep.

Four

Kacey shifted her weight and settled back against the plush seating of the Pullman railroad car. Her father had booked passage for the three of them on the New York Central line, which took them from Boston to Albany. There they had changed to the Atlantic Coast Railroad, which would take them to Philadelphia. Her father had explained all the different switches they would make, but Kacey did not want to have to think about them all. She had a window seat and she just wanted to enjoy the beautiful scenery along the way.

The eastern countryside was breathtaking in its spring finery—greenery dotted occasionally with bits of color from fields of wildflowers. Lavender, yellow, and red splashed the landscape like oils on an artist's canvas. Kacey loved the outdoors and sunshine. She also loved the feel of soft rain against her cheeks.

Occasionally her thoughts were interrupted, and she would glance across at the Frenchman seated just opposite her. She also gazed around the interior of the car at the many faces she saw. So many people going so many places. Her eye was caught by a man who looked to be in his early thirties. He smiled at her, and she immediately returned the friendly gesture. He had a kind face, she decided, and he was quite handsome. She returned her gaze to the scenery out the window as the train moved along at its steady pace. Rafe had pulled his hat down over his eyes and seemed to be asleep, while Colin focused his attention on his notes.

A baby's cry interrupted Kacey's absorption with the landscape, and she looked in the direction of the plaintive wail. A young woman seated across the aisle was trying to soothe a distraught infant, but without success. Being an only child, Kacey had never been around young children, and when she looked at the unhappy baby her heart went out to the mother and child. Without thought, Kacey stood and nearly lost her balance as the train lurched sideways. Quickly she reached for the back of her seat and caught herself just before she would have fallen into Rafe's lap. She refused to look his way, but from the corner of her eye he appeared not to have noticed, and the hat was still draped across his eyes. With a disgusted sound she regained her balance and made her way toward the young mother.

When she stood beside the woman, she said, "May I hold your darling baby for a while and let you rest? He seems to be restless, and I would be more than glad to help."

The mother looked at Kacey with amused and appreciative eyes. "Oh, could you? *She's* been so restless since we got on the train. I'm on my way to meet my husband in St. Louis, and it's been more than I bargained for what with the baby and all." The young woman, who looked to be no older than eighteen, handed Kacey the child.

Kacey held out her arms and took the bundle. "Oh, my, she's an armful. How old is she?"

"She'll be nine months old tomorrow."

Kacey saw the mother's eyes sparkle with pride as she

spoke of the chubby blue-eyed child with soft ringlets of honey-colored hair.

"You don't mind if I take her to my seat, do you? I'm just sitting across the aisle." Kacey nodded toward her seat.

"That'll be fine, and it's very kind of you to offer to help. She's awfully sweet, but she gets a little heavy to hold at times. If she gets to be too much for you, just say so. Oh, and her name is Amanda."

"That's a lovely name." Kacey shifted the child to one arm and held out her gloved hand to the woman. "My name is Kacey O'Reilly."

The woman took Kacey's proffered hand. "And I'm Libby Hawkins."

The child was fascinated with Kacey's red hair and stylish hat. Her huge blue eyes stared at Kacey's own, and her small lips curled into a toothless smile as she reached with chubby fingers to touch the fascinating plume attached to the headpiece.

With the introductions finished, Kacey said, "Libby, try to get some rest while Amanda and I get better acquainted."

Kacey was amazed at the softness of the chubby child, whose skin was fairer than her own. She carefully made her way back to her seat across the aisle and seated herself once more next to the window. The baby chattered in a language of her own and made a semblance of talking to Kacey. Kacey removed the hat from her head and gave the child what she seemed to want. She placed the hat on Amanda's head, and once again the baby grinned from ear to ear while deep dimples creased her cheeks.

Colin looked at the child, and a deep longing filled him. For a long time now he had not thought of grandchildren, but the sight of the child in Kacey's arms rekindled the old thoughts. "My dear, what have you got there? Looks like a real treasure."

Amanda moved her gaze to Colin and honored him with

the toothless smile that seemed to captivate whomever she favored with it. Then she jumped and waved her arms in the air as she tried to talk to him, too.

"This is Amanda, Father. Her mother looked as if she could use some rest, and I did want to hold her. Isn't she adorable?"

"Yes, dear, she reminds me of you when you were her age. You know, children grow up so fast that sometimes it seems as though they were never little at all."

"I think she wants you to hold her, Father."

Colin reached for the child, and she readily went to his arms where he bounced her on his knee as he had done with Kacey so many years before. Fond memories came to his mind.

Soon Rafe was the object of Amanda's attempted conversation. He straightened from his slumped position and removed the hat from his eyes to see what all the commotion was about. He thought he was still dreaming when he looked across to see the cherub sitting in Colin's lap.

"You're holding *un enfant*." His incredulous tone seemed to request affirmation instead of making a statement.

"Yes, I've been known to hold a baby from time to time." Colin chuckled at Rafe's tone.

"Forgive me, monsieur, it's just that I was not expecting to see such a sight on this trip."

Kacey's amusement was evident in her voice. "Isn't she precious? I wanted to hold her, but she has taken up with Father, and I don't think I'm going to get her back. She's fascinated with his pocket watch. See how she talks to him? I believe she has him beguiled with those big blue eyes. It's amazing to see a grown man taken in by such a small bundle of coquetry." Kacey teased her father, but he seemed undaunted by the act.

"That's all right, dear, the little lady knows quality when she sees it, and so do I. We get along just fine, don't we, Amanda?" Colin turned his attention back to the baby, and she jumped and cooed in answer to his question. Her eyes sparkled as she daintily toyed with the watch draped from his pocket.

The railcar moved along at a steady speed, and soon Amanda tired of her new toy. She raised her arms to return to Kacey when the hat that Kacey had replaced on her own head once more became the object of her attention. Rafe took in the situation with feigned indifference. The sight of Kacey holding the baby both amused and intrigued him. This was a new facet to her personality of which he was unaware. Unbidden, his thoughts turned to the kind of mother Kacey would make. But his mind failed to put her in that role. All he could picture was the efficient archae-ologist and daughter. But there she was—holding a baby and enjoying it. At that moment, Amanda tired of Kacey's hat and reached with chubby fingers toward Rafe. He looked at the professor and Kacey as if to ask what to do.

Kacey answered his mute question. "Monsieur, it seems that Amanda has chosen your company for a while. Are you going to hold her?"

Rafe hesitantly took the child and stiffly sat her on his lap. She looked at him with drooping eyelids and snuggled her small head into his chest before taking her thumb into her mouth. Sleep soon overtook her, and Rafe relaxed his hold as he decided that holding a baby was not so bad after all. He looked at the tiny child cradled in his arms and wondered what it would feel like to hold his own child this way. The idea was foreign to him, but he did not toss it aside. Maybe someday when he had done everything and seen everything he wanted. Rafe realized having a child was a huge responsibility and something that one did not take lightly. His thoughts had taken too serious a turn, and he willed his mind to return to saner musings. He shuffled uncomfortably in his seat and casually glanced at Kacey, who seemed to be holding him with some strange regard.

"Is something wrong, mademoiselle?"

His cool voice broke into her reverie, and she started.

"Oh, no, monsieur." Her incredulous tone filled with sarcasm as she spoke. "I didn't realize you had such a way with females of all ages. I thought your expertise was with older women."

"There are many things you do not know about me, mademoiselle. But I would be happy to show you sometime."

His voice, deep and sensual, sent a ripple of awareness through her, and she realized she was treading on thin ice. She looked for a way out. "I'm sure you would, monsieur, but I hardly have the interest or the time." She was pleased at how nonchalant she sounded.

"*C'est comme vous voudrez*, suit yourself, mademoiselle, but you might find me more interesting than you think." His eyes captured hers, analyzing her reaction.

He was mocking her again, and Kacey snapped in a low voice, "I doubt that. I'm sure you overrate yourself, monsieur. Why else would you feel the need to conquer every woman you come in contact with?"

"But you are mistaken, mademoiselle. I don't need to conquer any woman. And that's a strange word you use, conquer. I would prefer to call it, shall we say, mutual admiration." Rafe nodded at the babe in his arms and goaded her further with a trace of laughter in his voice. "As you can see, they just fall into my arms."

The man's audacity inflamed Kacey, and just as she started to speak, the train stopped suddenly, causing her to lurch forward. Her hat was thrown askew as she did all she could to keep from landing in Rafe's lap along with the baby.

Rafe held on tightly to Amanda as he saw what was happening, but there was nothing he could do to help Kacey. Luckily she was able to hold on tightly to her seat, as was Colin. When Rafe saw that Kacey was still safely seated, he quickly lifted the child and put her into Kacey's lap as he said, "I'm going to see what's wrong. Maybe I can help."

Kacey did not have time to answer before he was gone, and she cuddled the still-sleeping child in her lap. She looked up to see Libby standing beside her.

She asked as she took the child, "Is my baby all right?"

"Yes, Rafe was holding onto her, and she never knew anything happened." Momentarily Kacey realized she had used the man's first name again, and the knowledge did not console her.

"Is Rafe your husband?" Libby asked innocently.

"Heavens, no, Libby! He is just traveling with my father and me to Colorado." Her voice was incredulous that anyone could even think that Rafe was her husband.

Colin's voice cut into the conversation. "So you're Amanda's mother. That's a charming daughter you have. Such a sweet little thing."

"Thank you, she is sweet, but she can be a handful sometimes." At her words Rafe came down the aisle and stood beside the threesome. He addressed his words to Colin.

"A heavy tree has fallen across the tracks. Probably from a storm last night. I'm going to help them try to remove the debris." Then he shifted his gaze toward Kacey as he spoke. "It might take a while, so you ladies might want to go outside and rest beside the lake."

At his words Kacey immediately looked out the window at the large body of water, then said to her father, "Let's do go outside for a while and enjoy the lovely weather."

Colin said as he stood, "You and Libby go along, dear. I'm going to see if I can help the other men clear the tracks."

"All right, Father, but please be careful." Kacey turned to Libby. "Do I need to get anything from your seat for Amanda before we go outside?" The baby still slept in her mother's arms as the commotion went on around them.

"Yes, please. There's a valise on the floor with her things in it. If you can get that, I would appreciate it.

Maybe we can put a blanket on the ground, and she won't
be disturbed from her nap.''

Kacey retrieved the bag and the two women went along
the aisle of the railcar to the outside platform, where they
descended the steep steps to the grassy area surrounding
the lake. When they came to a shady spot near the water,
Kacey took a blanket from the bag and spread it on the
ground for Amanda. Libby lowered the sleeping child onto
the soft coverlet and lovingly patted Amanda's bottom to
lull her back to sleep. The two women then moved a short
distance away to be able to converse without disturbing
the sleeping infant.

Libby was the first to speak. "You know, Kacey, I'm
so glad we met. I don't make friends easily and I'm glad
to know you are on this train with me. It'll make the ride
more pleasant to have you to talk to.''

"Why, thank you, Libby. I'm sure it must be difficult
for you traveling alone except for Amanda. But the trip
will only last a few days before you meet your husband
in St. Louis, and we'll be here all the way if you need
us." Kacey continued as she tried to reassure the young
woman, who obviously had never traveled far from home
before. "You'll soon see your husband and everything will
be fine.''

"Yes, I'm sure it will. It's just that Charles hasn't had
this job very long, and oh, Kacey, life is so uncertain. He
went to St. Louis to work as a journalist, but he's had to
start out as an errand boy, and I just hope everything works
out. But at least Amanda and I will be with him.''

Kacey could see the fatigue and worry in Libby's eyes.
"Of course you will, dear. Now try to stop worrying.
Everything is going to be all right. I'm sure of it.''

At that moment Libby turned her gaze a short distance
away to the blanket where Amanda had been sleeping only
moments before. A look of horror came upon the woman's
face as she saw her child toddle over the bank into the
water. She screamed, and Kacey followed her gaze as

Libby seemed unable to move, only to look at the horrible scene taking place before her eyes.

Instantly Kacey realized what had happened as she heard the splash. She stood and ran to the spot where Amanda had fallen into the water. Not seeing the baby, she dove into the lake and went down, down, forcing her eyes open in the burning abyss. Thank God, the water was not muddy. At last she saw the baby and reached to grab hold of her. She knew that seconds mattered and she made sure she had a firm grasp of the child before starting to the top of the water. After what seemed like forever, Kacey surfaced, quickly pulling the toddler to shore before looking at her. With the baby limp in her arms, she did not give Amanda to her mother. Instead she laid the unconscious infant on the ground and began to try to purge her lungs. At first try, Amanda reacted. She sputtered and coughed up the water. Kacey closed her smarting eyes in a prayer of thanksgiving as the child seemed to come alive.

She was oblivious to the small crowd that had gathered until she heard their cheers when she picked up a crying Amanda. Immediately Libby rushed toward her baby, and Kacey relinquished the bundle.

Kacey had not yet realized that she was soaked through. But everyone, even the men who were clearing the tracks, had joined the throng of cheering onlookers. To Rafe's eyes, the thin material of her dress seemed to be invisible. Her undergarments were clearly visible through the skimpy material. He moved to her side and offered her his suit jacket.

"I'm not cold, monsieur," Kacey said refusing the offer.

"But, mademoiselle, I did not assume that you were cold. Your, ah, dress . . . is no longer doing its job of covering you."

She looked down at the flimsy, soaked material and, refusing to meet his eyes, silently took the coat.

"That was a very brave thing you just did, mademoiselle." Rafe spoke in a tone filled with awe and respect.

"It wasn't a brave thing at all, monsieur. I swim very
well." Kacey turned and moved to stand beside Libby,
who was holding her baby so tightly that she wondered if
the baby could breathe. But a soaked Amanda was
breathing and rubbing her eyes with small chubby fists as
if the day's events had exhausted her.

Libby threw her free arm around Kacey and cried, the
sobs of joy racking her thin body. "Kacey, I'll never be
able to repay you for saving my baby's life."

"You don't owe me anything, Libby. Just seeing you
two together is all the payment I need." After a moment
Kacey remembered her drenched clothing. "Now, dear, if
you'll excuse me, I'll go change into dry things."

Libby let go of her friend. "Of course. And, Kacey,
you'll never know how grateful I am. I couldn't move.
Just seeing her fall into the water . . . I-I couldn't move.
She's never walked before."

"I know, dear, but she's all right now. Let's put it behind us." Kacey hugged Libby and turned to leave. The
crowd had dispersed somewhat, and she made her way to
the baggage car to retrieve a piece of her luggage before
heading to the necessary room to change her clothing.
Leave it to Rafe, she mused, to notice a woman's clinging
clothes. At that moment, she had an odd sensation of
warmth rush through her at the knowledge that Rafe's coat
hugged her body. She had firsthand experience at what its
owner felt like, and unwanted thoughts of Rafe's embrace
rushed her mind. As it had many times before, the carriage
ride filled her thoughts. But she willed them away. She
didn't have time to dwell on such foolishness. And the
man was a pest. Annoyed with herself for entertaining such
thoughts, she continued on to the railcar.

After Kacey had changed into a light-blue shirtwaist and
deeper-blue skirt, she returned to the dining car to find that
Libby and Amanda were nowhere to be seen. She carried
her wet things in a bundle and went along to the outside

of the train to see how much longer they would be delayed. She found that the tree was a large one, and its removal was going very slowly. She decided to take her wet things to a bush and let them dry. She made her way to the spot where she and Libby had sat earlier, knowing there was a suitable area there where she could spread out her drenched clothing without the other passengers having witness to her undergarments.

Libby had evidently taken Amanda inside the train; she was nowhere in sight. Kacey thought she could take this time alone and relax once more beside the lake while her garments and her hair dried. The temperature was warm, and there was a nice breeze to hurry the drying process. After she spread the clothes on a limb she settled down on a cushiony green spot and leaned against a weeping willow. She pulled the combs from her mass of hair and used one to remove the tangles from the sodden strands. The wind blew against her head, leaving tendrils of copper floating about her face. Kacey closed her eyes and reveled in the cooling breeze.

The crew had finished sawing the last bit of downed tree, and the men were finishing their removal of debris from the tracks. Rafe and Colin stayed until the last bit was removed, then headed for the railcar. When they had returned to their seats and saw that Kacey was not there Colin glanced across the aisle to see Libby seated and holding Amanda. He called to her, "Libby, have you seen Kacey? I think we're about ready to start rolling again."

"Why, no. I haven't seen her since she went to change clothing. Do you need me to help look for her?" Concern sounded in her voice.

"Oh, no, Libby, I'm sure she's all right. We'll find her." At his words Colin turned, and immediately Rafe spoke.

"Monsieur, I'll look outside."

Colin answered, "Fine, lad, I'll check the other cars."

Rafe hurriedly went down the steps to the outside, then looked both ways before looking straight ahead at the lake. He followed up on his theory and headed toward the water. Soon, a wall of women's clothing caught his eye, and he followed its lead. A willow bent and danced in the wind, and from its uppermost bow a songbird cheerily sang a trill. Rafe's gaze followed the line of the tree to its base, where an area of blue that was not consistent with nature's coloring held his gaze. The figure was unmoving, and he stared at its tranquillity momentarily before heading in its direction. Rafe stopped just inches from where Kacey lay sleeping. The tranquil beauty of the young woman stirred him. Dark eyelashes rested softly on creamy cheeks, and her lengthy titian tresses drifted about her shoulders. Full lips were slighty parted, and Rafe was hesitant to wake the sleeping vision. What if . . . The thought bloomed fully in his mind, and he acted on it before he had time to consider the consequences. He stooped beside her and leaned forward slowly to kiss the inviting delicacy.

Kacey was in a land of white crystal, floating in a sea of azure. She had seen something that came close to this place in Cambridge when the sun had shone after an ice storm. Its beauty almost took her breath away before something nice and warm brushed her mouth. The taste was pleasant, but she couldn't quite put her finger on what exactly it reminded her of. The warmth of tea against her tongue? No, that wasn't right. It wasn't quite that warm. The warmth of—no, it couldn't be. Kacey fought through the sluggishness of sleep, and her eyelids sprang open. She stared headlong into dark eyes that met her own only inches away. Alarm swelled up inside her. The bittersweet of his lips caused Kacey to pause in her assessment of the situation. But when she was fully alert, she pushed him back and said in her most hateful voice, "What on earth do you think you're doing, monsieur?" Her reaction seemed to amuse him.

"Am I on earth, mademoiselle? I thought surely I had gone to heaven and that you were an angel." His voice was low and seductive as he continued. "How stupid of me. Now I can see that you are not an angel. You have no wings."

His attempt to find humor in the situation and his rakish perusal of her inflamed Kacey. But even so, she felt an unfamiliar arousal at the man's boldness as she said, "Monsieur, I am not one of your playmates that I'm sure you find in every town you visit."

"I did not assume you were, *ma chérie*. I only wanted to wake you, and it worked. The train is ready to go."

"Wh-why didn't you say so?" Kacey glanced around at her garments.

Rafe followed her eyes and rose to retrieve the clothing for her.

Realizing what he intended to do, Kacey quickly came to her feet and commanded in a shrill voice, "I'll get those."

Rafe merely stood aside for her, his expression openly amused. "I've seen women's clothing before, mademoiselle."

Kacey hastily pulled the garments from the limbs. "I've no doubt you have, monsieur, but if you don't mind, I'll carry my own, thank you."

Rafe followed her the short distance and sighed with exasperation. "You know, Kacey, one day some man is going to come along and squelch that biting tongue of yours."

"Well, don't you worry about it, monsieur. I'm sure you won't be there to see it." With her clothing bunched under her arm, she turned to walk toward the train.

Rafe followed and said in a husky whisper, "Don't be too sure, mademoiselle. Don't be too sure."

Five

The trail of smoke that spewed from the giant locomotive looked like a large black serpent as the engine roared along the tracks. Inside, passengers busied themselves with reading, knitting, or conversation. Kacey had taken her window seat, but darkness was approaching, and a lovely twilight spread across the land. Porters were busy lighting the interior as the approaching darkness swallowed the landscape.

Colin was the first to break the growing silence. "Are you two about ready to eat? I think we should go along to the dining car. How about you, Rafe?"

"*Oui*, monsieur, I am very hungry." He lazily swung his gaze toward Kacey.

Kacey answered quickly to avoid Rafe's dark eyes. "Yes, I suppose I could eat a bite, Father. And what about Libby? Just let me ask her to join us." She stood and made her way across the aisle, where Libby sat holding a sleeping Amanda. Libby also appeared to be napping, and Kacey decided not to disturb her. The events of the day seemed to have exhausted them both. She returned to her seat next to her father and looked toward the mother and

infant as she spoke. "Those two are sleeping so soundly
I didn't want to bother them."

"Well, then, let's go along to the dining car. I'm famished. It's been a long day." Colin stood, as did Rafe and
Kacey, and the threesome made their way to the dining
car with Kacey in the lead.

After they were seated, Kacey mused that the first day
of their journey had been quite out of the ordinary. They
had not made very good time because of the delay with
the tree, and she couldn't get the thought of Amanda's
near-drowning off her mind. She felt relieved that the child
was all right. It would have been a terrible disaster if . . .
Kacey's thoughts were broken by her father's words.

"What will you have, dear?"

"You order for me, Father. I'm not very hungry this
evening." Kacey seemed plagued by the events of the day.
One thought led to another, and she soon replayed the
scene where Rafe had kissed her. Her gaze swept his face,
and she felt blood rush to her cheeks as his eyes caught
hers, as if he knew what she was thinking. *Drat the man!*
He was certainly making life difficult for her.

"Aren't you feeling well, mademoiselle?" Rafe asked
in a tone that seemed to convey concern. But his mouth
curled as if on the edge of laughter.

He did not fool her for a minute. "Why, yes, I feel fine.
What about yourself, monsieur? You've also had quite a
busy day." Kacey was equally taunting in her tone.

"All in a day's work, Mademoiselle Kacey."

Her name fell from his lips in a way that would have
made a schoolgirl swoon, but Kacey was no schoolgirl,
and she had no intention of coming under the spell of
Monsieur Assante. She had to admit, though, the man was
persistent.

He pulled something shiny from his pocket. "I would
like to give you something, mademoiselle, that I bought
on the ship. I almost forgot about it."

He held the tiny silver and mother-of-pearl box in front

of her, almost as if in offering. But for what? Kacey had to admit that the box was lovely. But she did not reach for it as she said, "I couldn't possibly take anything so lovely."

Rafe persisted. "Please, mademoiselle, I have no one else to give it to. And I did buy it for you."

Kacey was speechless. Why would he have bought it for her when he seemed to hold her in such contempt? The man was a mystery. She slowly reached for the box, for she didn't like to hurt anyone's feelings, even a womanizer like Rafe. She had seen the wounded look in his eyes when she refused the gift.

"Wh-why thank you, monsieur. But you shouldn't have bought such an expensive gift," Kacey said as she admired the lovely box. She opened the lid to find a lining of white satin. Kacey raised her eyes and found that Rafe's expression made him look like a little boy. "It's very beautiful, thank you."

"*De rien*, you're welcome. I just ask one thing, mademoiselle. Please call me Rafe." His expression changed and became almost somber.

Kacey hesitated too long, and her father cut in. "Of course, dear. We'll all be working so closely there won't be a place for formality."

"I didn't know it meant so much to you, monsieur. I'll try to remember."

"*Merci beaucoup*, mademoiselle."

At Rafe's words a waiter appeared to take their orders. Kacey placed the box to the side of the table, as she was having second thoughts about accepting the gift. The man had made everything very awkward. She scolded herself for her moment of weakness. She should not have taken the box, but there was no way now to return it graciously.

As Kacey mentally berated herself, a waiter brought their food. Colin had ordered a light meal of baked halibut and cucumbers for himself and Kacey, and Rafe had ordered roast beef. The three ate their meal as Colin and

Rafe carried the bulk of light conversation. Kacey's reverie was interrupted as Colin addressed her.

"My dear, you seem to be miles away. Isn't your meal suitable?"

"Yes, it's fine, Father. I'm just not very hungry. I'm actually very tired. I think today's events were more exhausting than I realized. I believe I'll go along to see if Libby has awakened from her nap, if you and Rafe will excuse me." Kacey nodded at both men and pushed her chair back to stand. Rafe stood as Kacey did.

Colin replied, "Of course, dear, you go ahead. Rafe and I will be there shortly. We should be coming into Philadelphia before long, where we'll be changing over to another line. Today's event caused us quite a delay."

"I'll check on Libby and let her know, in case she's still asleep." Kacey turned and disappeared through the vestibule that separated the train cars.

She soon stood by Libby's seat and leaned closer to the young woman to waken her. Amanda was quietly leaning against her mother, still sucking her thumb, but she was wide awake. Kacey called softly, "Libby? Libby?" When she failed to respond, Kacey gently shook her shoulder and tried once more. "Libby?"

Libby slowly opened her eyes, and as they half-focused on her friend's figure, she answered in a tenuous voice, "Kacey, is something wrong?"

"No, Libby, it's just that we'll be coming into Philadelphia before long. I thought you would want to know. Are you feeling all right? You seem a little groggy."

"I do feel a little weak. I'm so hot."

Kacey looked at Libby and saw the flushed appearance of her face. Then she said, "Would you like me to take Amanda for a while? I'm sure you're just tired."

"Well, yes, if you can. She has been so good all afternoon, bless her heart."

Kacey reached for the baby, and Amanda readily went to her arms. Kacey was concerned about Libby. She appeared to have a fever and she was in no shape to be tending a child. Kacey rummaged through Libby's bag for something in the way of food for the child but found nothing. Then, leaving Libby, she went to the dining car once more and found her father and Rafe still seated.

"Well, well, you've brought little Amanda to entertain us, dear. But I thought you were tired."

"Libby seems to be more tired than I am. I think she may have a temperature, poor dear. With Amanda to look after, she's going to need help. I'll get Amanda fed, and then maybe you can look after her while I see about Libby." Having no idea what a child of Amanda's age would eat, she merely guessed at what to order for her. Later, she decided that she must have guessed correctly because Amanda ate everything that was offered her, especially the creamed potatoes, and once more blessed her audience with a toothless smile as bits of her meal plastered her face.

Kacey took a napkin and dipped it into her water glass, then wiped the child's face and hands as she said in a soft tone, "Poor little dear. Maybe your mother will feel better tomorrow." She hugged Amanda to her then slackened her hold as she continued. "You've had quite an ordeal today, haven't you, darling?"

Amanda seemed to understand as she looked wide-eyed at Kacey and tried to speak in her usual sputter and coo. Then she turned large blue eyes toward Rafe and began what appeared to be conversation. When he failed to respond, she leaned against Kacey and once more stuck her thumb into her mouth.

Kacey said, "Father, would you hold Amanda while I check on Libby? I hope she feels better than she did earlier."

"I hope so, too, dear." Colin reached for the child.

"I should be back in a few minutes. And don't give Amanda any more to eat. She'll probably have a stomachache now." Kacey's gentle laughter rippled through the air as she stood and left the table.

She was unaware of the captivating picture she made, and Rafe's blood pulsed at the musical quality of her voice. His dark eyes watched her movement as she made her way toward the vestibule.

When Kacey once more stood beside Libby, she saw that the young mother was in no condition to care for the child. The seat beside her was empty, and Kacey sat down before attempting to speak to her. "Libby?"

At Kacey's question, Libby opened her fevered eyes and admitted, "I feel very weak, Kacey. Where's Amanda?"

"She's with Father and she's having a ball. Don't you worry about her. We'll see to it that she's all right. But we're close to Philadelphia, and it'll be time to change over. Do you think you can do that?" Kacey asked with concern in her voice.

"I have to, don't I? I can't go back now. Charles is expecting me, and I can't let him down." Libby gasped, then asked softly, "Kacey, can you get me a drink of water?"

"Of course, dear. I'll be right back." Kacey went to the necessary room at the end of the car and came back shortly, holding a cup of water.

Libby took the container and sipped its contents. "Kacey, I'm not sure if I can stand. How will I get off the train if I can't?" A note of hysteria crept into her speech.

As Kacey was about to speak, Rafe's heavy French accent came from behind her. "Do not worry, madame, we can get you off the train."

The words seemed to calm Libby, and she sank back further into the seat and closed her eyes.

A porter's voice rang out. "Next stop, Philadelphia, Pennsylvania. Ten minutes."

Kacey looked at Rafe, and he returned and held her gaze with dark unfathomable eyes. For a moment it was as if they were the only two on the train before he spoke.

"Your father is bringing Amanda now. I will carry Libby if you can see to her baggage and have the porters bring it along."

His authoritative voice did not provoke Kacey. She knew he was trying to help, and she readily accepted his offer. She tried to speak to Libby once more to find out about her luggage. Libby's voice was garbled, and as far as Kacey could tell, Libby had one trunk in the baggage car besides her valise under the seat.

Soon the train came to a halt, and a porter announced their location while some passengers stood and others remained in their seats. As soon as the aisle cleared, Rafe lifted the ailing woman into his arms, and Kacey grabbed her valise. Colin still held Amanda, and the troupe made their way into the enormous train station.

Inside, Colin took Libby's valise and gave Amanda over to Kacey before he went to one of the many station clerks seated behind caged booths. Rafe deposited Libby in a seat and sat down beside her. Kacey and Amanda also sat next to Libby.

She opened her eyes and said in a weak voice, "Is everything going to be all right? I've got to get on the train, Kacey. Charles will be waiting, and I don't want to worry him."

"Yes, Libby. Father is taking care of all the arrangements. But do you think we need to find a doctor first?" Kacey suggested.

Her words seemed to agitate the young woman. "Oh, no, I'll be all right if I can just get on the train. It'll take me straight to St. Louis. I'm sorry to be such a bother, Kacey, but I know it's just a little fever, and the least bit always puts me under. Besides, there's probably a doctor on the train if I need one."

Kacey took a deep breath and raised her gaze to Rafe. The shadow of a beard was forming on his square jaw, making him appear even darker. But the strength that em-

anated from his strong features gave Kacey assurance as
she looked back to Libby and said, "All right. We'll see
that you get on the train if you promise to let me look
after Amanda until we get to St. Louis. You'll need all the
rest you can get."

Libby's pale lips forced a smile. "Thanks for being so
kind to me." Pausing, she turned her attention to Rafe,
then continued almost shyly, "And you, too, Mr. Assante."

Kacey thought she saw the young woman blush as she
offered her gratitude to the darkly handsome Frenchman
who had carried her from the train.

At that moment Colin came toward them, and Amanda
began to bounce up and down on Kacey's lap at the sight
of him. He stopped in front of them and said to no one in
particular as he reached inside his pocket for his watch,
"The train should be here shortly. Of course, we were
delayed so long that the one we should have been on left
hours ago. But, no matter, this one will be just as good."
Then he looked at Kacey and asked, "How's our patient?"

Libby opened her eyes and answered, "I'll be all right,
sir."

Kacey interrupted her and said, "She's still pretty weak,
but she wants to go on to St. Louis. She's agreed to let
me look after Amanda."

"Why, of course, dear, we'll all help."

As soon as Colin said the words, a locomotive whistled
on the tracks, and he realized that their train had arrived.
Other passengers began to rise from their seats and walk
in the same direction as they made their way onto the
passenger car, with Rafe once again carrying Libby. Kacey
thought to herself that Rafe must be very strong. He was
not even short of breath, and carrying little Amanda
seemed to be all she could handle. The thought piqued her
as she walked up the steep steps behind him onto the vehicle that would take them to St. Louis. Colin was right
behind her with bags in tow.

Inside the car, Rafe found a seating area where the four could sit together. As soon as they were settled, Kacey gave Amanda to her father and rose to find the porter. Shortly she came back and said, "The porter is preparing sleeping berths for Libby and me." She paused momentarily before continuing. "Rafe, I'll take Amanda if you'll bring Libby."

Rafe nodded in agreement, and Kacey reached to take Amanda, who seemed to be squirming in Colin's lap. Colin said matter-of-factly, "I think we have a problem, my dear. I think you'll find she needs to be changed."

Immediately Kacey noticed the odor. "Oh, my. She probably does. What do I do, Father?" Kacey showed her disbelief in the tone of her voice.

"I'll bring along Libby's bag, dear, and I'm sure you'll figure it out." His mouth quirked with humor at the thought of his daughter changing a diaper.

Amanda looked at Kacey and made a face with a half-wrinkled nose. Her lips seemed to form something between a frown and a smile. Kacey stared at the cherubic countenance, and a smile formed on her lips before she rallied. "Of course, we will, won't we, Amanda?" The child seemed unsure whether she shared Kacey's confidence.

Kacey turned and walked toward the vestibule of the car; she went all the way through until she came to the hotel car, where a porter had made bunks ready for Libby and herself. Colin followed, along with Rafe, who once again carried the infirm woman.

Rafe deposited Libby on a bottom bunk, then straightened to stand back. Still holding Amanda, Kacey moved closer to stand beside him and offered her appreciation. "Thank you, you've been very kind to help Libby."

"I'm more than glad to help, mademoiselle. If you need my assistance further, please ask."

His dark eyes seemed to smolder as they bored into Kacey's. Even in the seriousness of the situation, his maleness pressed into her sensuality, and she was unable to cast it aside. To lighten the situation, which was fast becoming a study in her ability to think straight, she replied, "Well, have you any experience in diapers?"

An arched eyebrow indicated humor as he said, "*Non*, mademoiselle, I leave that to your expertise as a woman."

Kacey took the bait and replied in a silky voice, "There you go, monsieur, taking the male role and relegating mundane chores to a female. Does your conscience ever bother you?"

"*Non*, mademoiselle, and I thought you were going to call me Rafe from now on?"

At that moment, Amanda started to move in Kacey's arms, reminding her that the child needed attention. "As you can see, I don't have time to discuss it right now, monsieur. Good-night." Kacey dismissed the man and turned away.

"*Bonsoir*, Mademoiselle Kacey." Rafe inclined his dark head and left the car.

Colin had been talking with the porter during Kacey's conversation with Rafe. As Rafe left the car, Colin said to Kacey, "Can you manage by yourself, dear?"

"I don't see why not. If Libby can do it, then I can."

"All right, I'll retire to the smoking car for a while. If you need me, just send a porter."

Kacey looked at Amanda and teasingly said, "He thinks we're helpless, darling."

Amanda crinkled her nose and seemed to delight in Kacey's conspiratorial tone. She beamed a shy smile as she brought the back of her tiny, dainty hands together at her chest.

Colin was not immune to the delightful ways of Amanda, and he smiled as he said, "You two are anything but helpless. Pity the man who tangles with either of you. I'll leave you now to your own devices." At that he walked out of the hotel car.

Kacey found Libby's bag and picked it up before laying Amanda on an empty bed. She rummaged through the valise to find a diaper, then set to the task of changing Amanda. She found a wet cloth wrapped in oilskin and another piece of the waterproof material in which to contain the soiled diaper until she could deal with it later. When she was finished with Amanda, she picked her up and moved to Libby's lower berth to check on her. There she put the child beside her mother before loosening the neck of the sleeping woman's shirtwaist to try to make her more comfortable. She did not know where Libby's nightclothes were, but it was not feasible to try to change her clothes in the closeness of the berth.

Kacey looked around at the other berths readied for sleep. The hour was still early, and many bunks were yet empty. Those with sleeping passengers had curtains pulled. Kacey reached for Amanda and closed the curtains to Libby's bunk. Maybe a good night's sleep would do her a world of good. Kacey hoped so as she held the helpless child in her arms.

"Are you ready to go to sleep, young lady? I think it's time that you and I went to bed also, don't you?" Amanda merely looked at her with large drooping eyes.

They made their way to another car, where they found a porter to retrieve Kacey's night bag. When he brought it to the sleeper car, Kacey joined Amanda in the berth above Libby and settled the child against the wall so she would not fall off the bed during the night. She then readied herself for sleep in the close confines of the curtained berth by changing into a cool cotton nightgown. Shortly, Amanda cuddled against her, and with thumb in mouth, she soon slept. Kacey had never been responsible for anyone else in her life, and the feeling both concerned and thrilled her. She found sleep nearly impossible as the thought of the child falling from the berth played on her mind. And dark mahogany eyes haunted her thoughts. Eyes that reached inside her and toyed with newly awakened senses.

• • •

Rafe left the hotel car and went to the rear of the train to stand on the platform. He reached into an inside coat pocket and pulled out a cheroot and match. He lit the slim cigar as the cool night air helped to fan the flame. The distant roar of the engine blocked the sounds of the evening, sounds that Rafe loved to hear. But, no matter, he had but one thought on his mind. Kacey. His mind replayed the kiss beside the lake and the way her creamy neck had looked in the sunshine, draped with copper strands. *Mon Dieu*, if she only knew how much he wanted her, from the first time he met her. She was different from most women he had known. She was not interested in him and made it very plain that she had no intention of becoming involved with him. His long masculine fingers unconsciously brought the cheroot to thinned lips as he thought of the haughty attitude she seemed to reserve for him.

His reverie was broken by the opening of the door. He turned to see Colin stepping outside.

"Enjoying the night air, are you, Rafe?" Colin asked.

"*Oui*, Professor. The air inside was getting stuffy."

In the light streaming through the windows Colin noted the young man's subdued expression, but did not press the issue.

"Well, we should be in Durango in four or five days. There'll be all the open air you'll need. I'm not used to being confined to a train either. Makes me edgy." Colin shrugged as he continued, "Oh, and Rafe, you shouldn't pay too much attention to Kacey. She tends to keep young men at bay. She has this notion that I need taking care of for the rest of my life. But if the right young man were to come along, I think he could convince her otherwise."

"Don't be too sure, monsieur. Mademoiselle Kacey is very strong-willed. I think if she sets her mind to something, she follows through with it."

"Why, yes, she is, but I wouldn't want her to be any other way. And I don't believe any man worth his salt would either."

"You are probably right, monsieur." Rafe thoughtfully puffed at his cheroot, then continued. "Mademoiselle Kacey is very beautiful. I'm sure she has had many suitors of admirable qualities."

"Well, you have to understand Kacey. She lost her mother at an early age, and, well, she grew up quickly. She never seemed to be interested in boys, as other girls her age were." Colin paused a moment before going on. "I think a good deal of you, lad, and, well, if something were to develop between you and Kacey, I would be very pleased."

"I am honored, Professor, that you feel that way, but you need to know that mademoiselle has refused every advance I've made. I'm sorry to disappoint you."

"Well, lad, as Persius once said, 'He conquers who endures.' "

"I will remember that, Sir."

Six

Kacey awoke from her light sleep to find Amanda still snuggled against her side. The soft sound of rain against the roof was soothing to Kacey, and she lay for a long while listening as water trickled down the exterior of the car. She knew she needed to check on Libby, but Amanda was sleeping so soundly she hated to disturb her.

From her curtained berth she could hear the whispered sounds of other passengers as they rose from sleep. She reached to pull the drape aside slightly and peeked through the crack. Many of the passengers had risen, and their berths had been converted back to empty seating. The empty berths made her feel that she had been lazy, and she decided that she must check on Libby. But she did hate to wake little Amanda. She eased the child further toward the paneled wall and then sat up in the close quarters of the berth. She reached for her clothing at her feet and, eyeing the corset, she made a face. There was no way she could put the thing on in such a small space. Besides, she felt sure no one would notice its absence anyway. She decided against trying to don the corset, then removed her nightgown and pulled on the chemise that lay folded atop her dress. As soon as she got the chance she could go to the necessary room and wash and put on proper clothing. A rebellious smile formed on her lips at the thought of defying convention even for a little while. Besides, the dratted corset was terribly uncomfortable. She had often threatened to throw hers away, but each time she mentioned the idea, Sarah had nearly gone into apoplexy, ranting things like "dear departed mother . . . God rest her soul . . . ," and "in all her life she'd never . . . ," and so on.

Kacey finished dressing and combed and arranged her hair before she slowly opened the curtains so as not to awaken Amanda. She slid from the bunk and opened the drapes below her own. Libby still slept, and Kacey reached to touch the other woman's forehead with the back of her palm. Thank goodness, she thought, realizing the woman's temperature had fallen a great deal. She gently closed the curtains and looked in her berth once more at Amanda. The child was sitting up and rubbing her eyes with two tiny fists. Suddenly she stopped and looked at Kacey. Her small but perfectly formed mouth curled into an open-mouthed grin as she saw the familiar face.

Kacey returned the greeting with a grand smile, and Amanda came toward her, reaching to be taken. Kacey was grateful that she had thought to use some of the oilcloth as a covering for Amanda's diaper. When she felt through to the cloth, she discovered that it was soaked, but the bed was mostly dry.

"Hold on just a minute, Amanda. Your diaper needs to be changed," Kacey laughingly said in a soft whisper. She did not want to disturb the few remaining sleepers or Libby. With one hand she held on to Amanda to keep her from falling, while with the other she retrieved a diaper from the small stack she had placed in her bunk.

After changing the baby, Kacey held her and decided to go to the dining car for breakfast. She felt certain that that was probably where she would find her father . . . and Rafe. She would bring something back for Libby to eat.

Kacey carried the child toward the dining car. But before she came close, she spotted Rafe coming toward her from the other direction. For no reason she could fathom, her pulse lurched. In an instant she took in his shining dark head, his clean-shaven face, and his impeccably tailored suit of navy wool. Suddenly she felt annoyed with his good looks. She had not even washed her face yet, but he looked as if he had just stepped from a bandwagon. Momentarily she wanted to turn around and go in the other direction. But pride quickly surfaced, and she refused to be put at a disadvantage by the devilish man. She raised her chin and nodded across the distance as she continued on her path.

Rafe had spent much of the previous night enjoying the cool air from the rear of the train after Professor O'Reilly had gone inside. After much reflection on what the professor had said, he had finally retired to one of the berths in a sleeping car just before the rain had started. As much as the professor tried to encourage his attraction to Kacey, it was foolish, he felt, to continue to try to win the admiration of a woman who obviously found him repugnant. Even after going to bed, he had spent much time ruminating on the subject before finally drifting off to sleep. He had awakened early in the morning and joined the professor for coffee. When the professor had mentioned Kacey, he had offered to go and bring her back, so they all could enjoy breakfast together.

Now he was staring at her, and instead of all the reasons he had counted last night for ignoring the woman, once more he gasped at her beauty *ravissante*. Even at this distance he could see that she still had the telltale touch of sleep about her eyes, and at the moment she looked very vulnerable as she held on tightly to the small child. Rafe returned her nod and continued down the aisle, all the while not taking his eyes from her.

When Rafe at last stood face-to-face with Kacey in the narrow aisle, he swallowed hard, then said in his heavy

French accent, "*Bonjour*, Mademoiselle Kacey and *la petite* Amanda. I have come to find you. Your father is in the dining car. He waited to have breakfast with you."

Rafe's eyes darkened with emotion as he spoke, and his maleness once again threatened Kacey in the closeness of the aisle. He was too close, and she felt that she had to put distance between them as she said, "Thank you, monsieur. We're on our way there now. I hope he hasn't been waiting long?" Kacey hoped Rafe would take the hint and turn around to lead the way. She didn't want to have to pass him in the narrow aisle.

But he didn't budge as he said, "The professor and I have been enjoying coffee while we waited, mademoiselle. And how is Madame Libby today?" Rafe asked with concern in his voice.

"Libby's fever has dropped a great deal, I believe. She is still sleeping. I thought I would take her something later."

"A good idea." He stood aside for Kacey to pass him and gestured with his hand. "Please allow me, mademoiselle."

Kacey refused to let the man see her discomfiture, and she attempted to slide past him. But one of the laws of nature prevailed—what is too large to fit in one space will either be compacted or will not fit. As she and Amanda tried to go past Rafe, she would have sworn that he was not doing anything to help. It was inevitable that their bodies would touch. But when her corsetless breast momentarily brushed his coat out of the way and she felt hard, muscled chest through the thin material of his shirt, her senses reeled, and she silently cursed the man while wondrous feelings enveloped her body. Feelings she had no time to consider at the moment. But her erratic pulse did not care that she did not have time. It continued anyway, causing a stir in her usually normal equilibrium. Against her wishes, her head swayed toward the man blocking the aisle. She tried to readjust Amanda on her hip, but that was impossible.

Rafe's eyes widened at the knowledge that Kacey evidently was not wearing a conventional corset. His body refused to budge from the exquisite softness of her breast pressed against him. He sought her eyes, but she refused to look at him as she kept her head averted. He could feel the change in her breathing. Her breath came in short erratic spurts that seemed to increase the pressure of her full breasts pressed against his chest. He stiffened when he realized what was happening to him. The stress he felt below his belt quickly manifested itself, and he longed to take her in his arms and kiss the soft mauve peaks that he knew existed beneath the straining material of her dress.

Kacey quickly recovered from her lapse and slid the rest of the way past Rafe, the journey playing havoc with her senses. When she was beyond him, she turned slightly and heard her own voice, stifled and unnatural. "They are making these aisles ridiculously small, evidently at the expense of the passengers."

Rafe's voice sounded thick and unsteady. "*Non*, mademoiselle, it was no bother to me." His dark volcanic eyes bored into her back as she turned and headed toward the dining car.

Kacey, Amanda, and Rafe found their way to where Colin was seated, and soon they all were enjoying breakfast. Little Amanda seemed to enjoy the fare the most as she giggled and bounced with each mouthful of tasty pancake smothered in rich maple syrup.

Rafe played the aisle scene over and over in his mind, and each time his abdomen ached in a way that felt as if he had been kicked full in the stomach. He found that his gaze kept coming to rest on Kacey as she held Amanda on her lap.

Abruptly he said, "I've nothing else to do, mademoiselle, if you would allow me to look after Amanda. I'm sure her mother would like something to eat. The professor and I can surely entertain such a small one while you check on Madame Libby.''

"I did intend to take Libby some breakfast. That's very kind of you, monsieur. I'm sure Father would help.'' Kacey's next words were aimed at the child. "Amanda, darling, will you be a good girl for Kacey and stay with Father and Monsieur Assante while I check on your mother?''

Immediately Amanda started to sway back and forth as she stretched her small arms toward the air and spoke, "Ma-ma, ma-ma.''

"Yes, darling, mama.'' Kacey watched with dismay as the child began to screw up her face as a prelude to crying.

Rafe stood at that moment and took the child before she had the opportunity to start a full-blown cry. She merely whimpered and rubbed her eyes as she leaned against Rafe's welcoming shoulder before sticking her tiny thumb into her mouth.

Rafe turned to Kacey. "See how it is done, mademoiselle? And please call me Rafe in front of the child.''

The man's arrogance never ceased to amaze Kacey, but she had to appreciate the fact that he was willing to help care for Amanda. She let the remark that teetered on her tongue slide by while her eyes flashed scathingly toward Rafe's.

"Yes, you are quite amazing, monsieur. It's almost beyond belief,'' Kacey said as she covered the remaining pancakes on the platter and stood. "I'll take these to Libby now, Father.''

"Yes, yes, dear. You go see about her and tell her Amanda is fine.''

Kacey made her way to the sleeper car and found Libby's curtain still closed. She pulled the drapery aside and sat on the bed beside her. Gently she shook Libby's shoulder, and the woman slowly opened her eyes.

"Well, hello there, sleepyhead. I thought you could use some breakfast. How about it? I've brought pancakes smothered in syrup.''

"Oh, Kacey, you're such a sweetheart." Libby attempted to come to a sitting position while Kacey reached behind her to stuff another pillow there. "I'm feeling much better today. But still pretty weak. Where's Amanda? Is she all right?"

"Of course she is, dear. She's with Father and Rafe," Kacey assured the concerned mother.

"Oh, Kacey, I don't know what I would do if anything happened to her."

"Nothing is going to happen to her. Now stop worrying about it and eat. That's an order." Kacey teasingly coaxed Libby into eating the breakfast.

"Since yesterday I've had this awful feeling that something is going to happen to my baby."

"No, it's not. I promise you. You've just had a traumatic experience that was no one's fault. Amanda is fine, and she is going to stay that way. Now, eat your breakfast so you can gain strength to take care of her."

At Kacey's words Libby smiled as the tension of the previous day seemed to disappear from the woman's face.

Some time later Kacey opened the door of the ladies' room, and with valise in hand she moved to the washbasin. She had spoken with the porter, and he had allowed Libby to use the berth for the remainder of the day. Even though Libby had protested, Kacey had persuaded her to stay in bed and rest.

This late in the morning, Kacey had the room to herself to freshen her appearance and put on a change of clothing. After her encounter in the aisle with Rafe, she definitely intended to put on her corset. The man was insufferable. The way he had blocked her! Kacey's cheeks burned at the knowledge that Rafe probably had *known* she was not wearing her underthings. Well, she thought, she wouldn't be caught that way anymore in the close confines of the train. But when she reached the Dunning ranch, there was no reason she had to be confined to the dratted thing. All she had to do was stay out of his way, and that shouldn't be too difficult on a wide-open ranch or a dig site. Kacey smiled as she thought how she had outwitted the Frenchman. She simply refused to be another in his long line of fawning females.

Kacey looked into the mirror and smiled again as she said to the absent man, "Yes, Monsieur Rafael Assante, this is one female you won't see vying for your attentions. And you can go to . . . where it doesn't snow."

After Kacey had said the words with more conviction than she was feeling, she began to rub her face heartily with a wet washcloth, as if to wipe out the memory of certain mahogany eyes that seemed to penetrate her soul.

When she had finished with her morning ablutions, she donned corset, chemise, and a fine linen shirtwaist the color of silver maple leaves before a storm. She pulled on the matching skirt and set about to arrange her mass of copper hair with its shining gold highlights.

Kacey studied her reflection in the mirror, and all in all she seemed content with what she saw. She put her things away and went out to face the world.

And face the world she did. As she hurriedly stepped from the ladies' room, something hard and solid hit her head-on. Kacey looked up to see a man quickly regain his stance and reach to assist her in doing the same. When she gazed closely at him, she recognized him as the attractive man who had smiled at her when they had first boarded the train in Boston.

He was smiling broadly as they started to speak simultaneously. "Please excuse—" Kacey began.

"I beg your pardon, m—"

Kacey started to laugh, and the man followed suit while he shuffled from one foot to the other and removed his dark Stetson hat.

"I do beg your pardon, ma'am. I hope you're not hurt?" he asked, the concern apparent in his voice.

"Oh, no, just a little shaken. Do forgive me for barging out of there without looking."

Logan Connor knew an opportunity when he saw it, and he never passed one by. "It's all my fault, and I won't forgive myself unless you agree to have lunch with me." The tall blond man took his watch from an inside pocket and looked at it. "It's eleven o'clock now. May I escort you to the dining car, ma'am?"

"Well, actually, I'm on my way to find my father, but you're more than welcome to join us for lunch, Mr . . . ?"

"Connor. Logan Connor, ma'am. But please call me Logan. And your name is?"

"Kacey. Just Kacey, er, Logan."

"Well, Miss . . . Kacey, please allow me." Logan bent at the waist and motioned with an outstretched arm for her to fall into step in front of him in the narrow passage. He replaced his well-worn Stetson as a smile played around his lips.

Colin and Rafe had each held Amanda for a time in Kacey's absence, and the younger man now took his turn. Rafe sat at the dining table and held Amanda on one leg. She had begun to fuss, and the two men had agreed that she was probably hungry, so they had gone to the dining car. Colin had ordered creamed potatoes and green peas for the child, which was apparent because she and Rafe had a substantial amount of the food on them both. As Rafe would offer her a bite of food, she would take it into her mouth and just as quickly put her fingers in also.

Kacey stood at one end of the dining car and spotted her father seated at the table near the opposite end. There, also, she saw Rafe holding Amanda. What she saw next caused her to have to hold back an outright laugh as she brought her hand up to cover her mouth. Rafe looked as if he had been dappled with green and white paint. The green was the awful color of avocadoes after they had been smashed.

When she had composed herself, she turned to address the man who had come to stand beside her. "I see my father, if you want to follow me, Logan."

He answered in a slow teasing drawl as he once again removed his hat. "Ma'am, I would follow you to the ends of the earth." Then he flashed a smile that seemingly reached to his eyes, which appeared to be accustomed to the gesture. "Just lead the way."

Kacey recognized the banter for what it was and smiled as she stepped toward the other end of the railcar.

Many passengers had filtered into the dining car, and it quickly filled to capacity. Rafe momentarily looked up from feeding Amanda and saw Kacey coming toward them. He never failed to notice her aristocratic carriage, from her straight back to her raised chin, and he forgot about his spattered appearance as he drank in her loveliness.

Rafe paid no attention to the man directly behind Kacey until he stood alongside her at their table. Then, with the keen sight of a hawk, Rafe's eyes narrowed, taking in every visible aspect of the man, from his handsome polished boots to his freshly trimmed hair topped with a cowboy hat. An alien feeling rushed over Rafe, and the hair on his skin bristled as the man stood close to Kacey.

Colin looked up from his attempt to assist Rafe in feeding Amanda. "Why, there you are, dear."

Kacey began introductions as Colin and Rafe stood. "Father, Monsieur Assante, this is Logan Connor, whom I have invited to join us for lunch."

Colin immediately held out his hand to the stranger, and they engaged in the age-old ritual of handshaking while exchanging greetings. Rafe was still holding Amanda, but he managed to free one hand, the one that just happened to be the messiest, he gladly observed. He followed suit and shook the man's hand—leaving a trail of green in the man's palm.

"Oh, my, what a mess you two have made." Kacey

gently laughed as she took a napkin and began to mop Amanda's face and hands. In reply, Amanda giggled and jumped in Rafe's arms. When the child was somewhat cleaner, Kacey handed her to Colin, then the four adults sat down. "Monsieur, I hope your suit is not ruined."

"*Non*, mademoiselle, I am sure it can be cleaned. It is of no importance. The *bébé* is no longer hungry, and that is all that matters."

"Why, that's very kind of you, monsieur. I know Libby is very grateful." Kacey turned her attention to Logan, who was seated next to her. "Libby is the child's mother. She's resting today while we three look after this adorable child."

Before Logan could respond, Colin said, "So, Mr. Connor, what brings you east? One doesn't usually find your accent this side of the Mississippi. Texas, I believe?"

"Right on the nail, sir. I've been to visit my sister in Boston. She recently married, and I was unable to attend the wedding. But she was busier than a cranberry merchant, and I didn't stay too long. Now I'm just lookin' the country over." Logan's eyes drifted to Kacey, then back as he continued, "And I might say that there's some awful pretty country out this way."

Kacey could not keep her eyes from briefly scanning Rafe's darkened countenance, and she thought he seemed to glower at the man across from him.

"Where in Texas are you from, Logan?" Kacey enjoyed using the man's first name in front of Rafe. The Frenchman seemed to think he was the only man in the world that women fawned over. She would show him. Let the arrogant man fume. He had no hold on her, nor was he ever likely to.

"Well, ma'am, I'm from a little place called Olmstead, but I do a lot of traveling. Right now I'm on my way to St. Louis."

Colin noticed that Kacey was openly flirting with the

cowboy, and a slight smile came to his lips as her voice sounded a bit too high-pitched.

Rafe broke into the conversation. "And what do you do in your travels, monsieur?"

"Well . . . let's just say that I do a lot of speculating, Mr. Assante."

"So, monsieur, you are ashamed of what you do?" Rafe's voice was hard and defiant.

Logan bristled in his seat. "No, I'm not ashamed of what I do. It's what I am. I'm a gambler."

Kacey spoke to break the stifling silence. "How exciting. You must meet many memorable characters. I've never met a professional gambler before."

Colin cleared his throat. "It's got to be interesting, to say the least, lad."

Logan answered in his Texas drawl, "Well, yes, sir, I guess you could say that."

At that moment a waiter came to the table, and after Amanda's dirty dishes were whisked away, the adults gave their orders. Soon the food came, and Kacey attempted to keep the conversation light to keep Rafe from further insulting Logan. The two men seemed to have actually locked horns. Even though Kacey delighted in anything that agitated Rafe, she did not want the two men to come to loggerheads.

Colin still held Amanda, but he managed to eat his meal with one arm as she slept in the comfort of the other. Rafe's mood seemed to have gone from dark to darker.

Mon Dieu, but the woman was a study in sanity, he thought. She refused to call him by his given name, but a stranger she just met she could easily call by his first name. The thought fired Rafe, and once more he deemed to put the femme fatale from his mind. She could have the cursed gambler for all he cared. Why, she just sat there so calm and regal, while men attended her every wish.

"Monsieur, I am no novice myself in games of chance, and I'm wondering just how good you are." Rafe's statement seemed to hold more than one kind of challenge as the two men glared at each other.

"Well, Mr. Assante, it'd be real easy for you to find out, now, wouldn't it? Unless . . . maybe you only wager a sure thing. If that's the case, sounds like you may be ready for a rocking chair in a quiet little place somewhere."

"I assure you, monsieur, I am not ready for a rocking chair. Shall we continue this conversation later in the smoking lounge over a game of cards?" Rafe paused, then continued with meaning. "Oh, and, monsieur, we'll have the porter bring a new deck."

"As we say in Texas, Mr. Assante, the pleasure will be all mine."

Seven

Kacey excused herself from the table to take Libby something to eat. To her relief, Libby seemed even better than she had that morning, but Kacey urged her once again that it was for the best that she remain in bed. Moments later, she found her father and the child seated in the passenger car without Rafe and Logan. She breathed a sigh of relief that the two men were nowhere in sight. Right now she did not want to have to deal with Rafe's immature behavior toward her new acquaintance. The man was incorrigible to have spoken so rudely to Logan.

"Hello, Father," Kacey said as she seated herself beside him, "and Amanda, darling." She gave the child a bright smile and reached to take her from her father's lap.

"You know, Kacey, she's a precious little thing. I could get used to having her around."

"Yes, she is at that." Then Kacey teasingly added, "But I don't think Libby would give her up."

At that point Amanda beamed a big smile toward Kacey that could have won over the most reluctant heart.

"No, I don't expect she would, at that." After a pause Colin added, "Do you think you can manage all right for a little while? Much as I enjoy being in the company of two lovely ladies, I'd like to go to the smoking car for a spell.''

Kacey feigned irritation as she looked at Amanda. "There you go, Amanda. So much for the plight of women to be forever deserted by men while they go have their fun.''

"Kacey, darling, I just cannot picture you with a pipe in your mouth.''

Kacey made a face. "Oh, Father, heaven forbid! Women have more sense than to stick those smelly things in their mouths.'' She eyed him sideways, then continued the banter. "But I'll bet other, more exciting things go on in smoking cars.''

"Well, dear, could be. Could be. I'll go find out for us.'' He winked a conspiratorial eye at Amanda and stood.

"Amanda and I will be waiting for your report, won't we, darling?'' Kacey hugged the child to her as she toyed with the large pearlized buttons on Kacey's shirtwaist.

When Colin entered the smoking car, he immediately spotted Rafe and Logan sitting at a small round table cluttered with ashtrays and playing cards. The gambler maintained an amused look, giving the appearance that he held the hand he wanted. Rafe also sported a confident air as he puffed on a cheroot. Colin went toward the pair, pulled a chair to their table, and seated himself without appearing to distract the two young men.

"I will call you, monsieur, and raise you a double eagle,'' Rafe's voice was cool and steady as he picked up the twenty-dollar gold coin from the stack in front of him and pitched it onto the money mound in the center of the table. He boldly eyed his opponent in an effort to read his thoughts, and if Rafe read him correctly, the man was superb at bluffing.

Other men began to gather around the table to watch

the high-stakes game. Colin cleared his throat and sat back to enjoy the entertainment.

Logan answered Rafe's challenge by adding two gold eagles to the ante before laying his cards on the table.

"You've called, Mr. Assante. Can you beat it?"

Rafe eyed the other man's four queens but did not lay his cards down. "*Non*, monsieur, you have won this hand. Until next time, *n'est-ce pas*?" Rafe turned his attention to Colin. "Professor, would you like to take my place?"

"No, no, lad. I never partake in games of chance. It's bad for the wallet, wouldn't you say?"

"*Oui*, monsieur, it can be bad for the wallet, but as I am sure Monsieur Connor can tell you, it can be good for the winner, eh?" Rafe stood and nodded to his opponent. "Until later, monsieur. I need a breath of fresh air. *Excusez-moi*, gentlemen."

Rafe made his way to the upper-level observation deck and was surprised to find Kacey and Amanda seated on a bench there. They were alone on the platform. She had wrapped a scarf around the child's head, and they both seemed to be enjoying the wind whipping in their faces.

Kacey had her back to Rafe and did not see him until he came to sit beside her on the bench. Her pulse surged at the nearness of the man, and as always her body's re-action to him nettled her, instantly turning her into a ter-magant.

"Why, monsieur, I'm surprised to see you. I thought the two of you would have gobbled each other up by now. You know, like the gingham dog and the calico cat." Much as she tried, she could not keep the irritation from her voice.

"I have no idea what you are talking about, mademoi-selle. If you are referring to Monsieur Connor, he is still very much alive." Slightly under his breath, he said, "And, I might add, much richer than before."

Kacey glanced at Rafe's dour expression as his last

words trailed off unheard before he continued.

"I came out to sit in the air for a while. I trust that I am not . . . disturbing you, mademoiselle." Rafe suddenly felt wicked and reckless as he looked ahead to see a railroad tunnel in the distance.

"Why, certainly not, monsieur. I hardly give you a thought."

Rafe mused how the irritating woman hardly gave him anything. Not even the time of day. Suddenly the thought fired him as the train readied to go into the darkened tunnel. He plotted his course and proceeded.

Kacey was distracted by Amanda, and she did not see the tunnel coming fast toward her, nor in its darkness did she see Rafe move closer, grasping her by her upper arms before his all-consuming lips took her own. The quickness of his actions gave her no time to think. No time to refuse. Only when his lips touched hers did she have time to feel the exquisite pleasure of his mouth pressed hard against her own. At first his lips were fierce and demanding, but in an instant they softened, and Kacey's softened also, allowing him entry into her moist, satiny recess.

The train quickly came out of the darkness into the light, and Rafe's lips still held Kacey's captive, refusing the parting that had to come. Amanda squirmed beside Kacey, bringing her back to reality, and she quickly pulled away from Rafe, her senses hating to give up the rapturous moment, her mind refusing to acknowledge her pleasure. She ineptly tried to look aghast at the man beside her, her cheeks flaming.

"Monsieur, what were you trying to do?"

Rafe's voice sounded thick and husky. "Mademoiselle, I was not *trying* to do anything. I think the attempt was a complete success." He continued to observe her discomfiture. "If you would only admit that you liked it, too."

"That'll never, never happen, monsieur. I don't see why you persist in your barbarous displays."

"Mademoiselle, I notice you didn't deny that you did

enjoy the . . . 'barbarous display.' You merely said you would never admit it.'' Rafe leaned close to her ear and took in her sweet aroma, his voice becoming lower. "But never is a very, very long time, *ma chérie*."

The low, seductive quality of his voice sent tiny flames throughout her body, but she was saved by a familiar Texas drawl from behind.

"I hope I'm not intruding on an intimate conversation, ma'am."

Kacey turned to see the gambler, and her face lit up as she welcomed the perfect foil for her previous moment of weakness.

Rafe's lips thinned as he saw the welcoming light in Kacey's eyes and the smile on her lips for the big Texan. Once more the jealousy came over him, so much so that the emotion began to feel quite familiar.

"Of course not, Logan. Please join us. Amanda and I are enjoying the sunshine and air. Monsieur Assante was just leaving." She turned her gaze pointedly to Rafe. "Weren't you, monsieur?"

"I've changed my mind, mademoiselle. I think I will enjoy the air a while longer myself."

The intensity of his gaze and the challenge in Rafe's eyes chilled Kacey. Inexplicably, the man had the ability to stir her beyond her normal threshold of arousal and reasoning. To occupy her wandering emotions, she turned her attention toward the blond man.

The gambler moved to stand facing Kacey and leaned on the iron railing as he addressed the Frenchman.

"Oh, by all means, keep your seat Mr. Assante. Don't let me disturb you. Besides . . . the view is much better from here." His smooth voice came through curled, smiling lips as he gazed at Kacey, who looked up at him, mirroring the gesture.

The scene was almost more than Rafe could stomach: the gambler smiling at Kacey, Kacey smiling at the gambler. But *ah la vache*, damn, he thought to himself, he absolutely refused to leave the man alone with Kacey. Why, he mused, the woman acted as if she had no sense, taking up with the stranger. If not for her sake, then for his friend, the professor, he would see to it that she was not taken in by this womanizing gambler. The professor seemed to dote on his *l'idiote* daughter.

"Mademoiselle, don't you think the *bébé* needs to go in out of the cool air?"

"Why, yes, she probably does need to go in for a while. Thank you, monsieur, for offering to do that."

Rafe had backed himself into a corner, and he watched, unable to speak, as Kacey lifted the child into his arms.

"Mr. Assante, if I am ever in need of a nanny, I'll sure know where to look."

Logan's lazy drawl irritated the Frenchman, and the look Rafe shot him before his egress was unmistakable as it hit its mark.

From the corner of her eye Kacey watched Rafe's departing back. She smiled to herself as she recalled the startled look on his face when she pretended to misunderstand his intentions. She looked back to her companion as he seated himself in Rafe's vacant spot on the bench.

"I do love the outdoors, don't you, Logan?"

"Well, yes, ma'am, I do . . . if someone as lovely as you are is sharing it with me. Otherwise it's just a lot of grass and dirt, or mud when it rains." He looked sideways at her in a teasing manner.

Kacey continued the banter. "My, my, Logan, you do know how to turn a lady's head. Why, I just know you have scads of young ladies waiting for your return."

"Could be, ma'am, could be. But none of them are as pretty as you. The way the sunlight reflects off your hair, like gold dust splashed across a field of copper, why, it just goes right straight like an arrow to a man's heart, ma'am."

"You really do have that line down pretty good, don't you?" Kacey laughed lightheartedly as she spoke.

"Why, Kacey, you wound me." Logan feigned a hurt look as he grinned a devilish crooked grin and continued. "Could it be you've already given your heart to someone else?" Logan was serious now as he looked her full in the eyes.

"You don't know what you're talking about, and no, I have not given my heart to someone else. My heart is my own, and I intend to keep it that way."

"Have it your own way, then. I'm glad to hear I'm still in the running."

"There is no 'running.' I'm not a prize to be given to the winner."

"Whatever you say, ma'am."

"I say let's go in. I need to check on Libby."

Rafe was seated in the passenger car holding Amanda while she slept when Kacey and Logan came through. He did not fail to notice how closely the gambler stayed by Kacey as they made their way down the narrow aisle. Colin was still in the smoking car, and Rafe tried to take his gaze off the couple but could not. Kacey turned to say something to the man, then went through the vestibule alone.

Kacey found Libby sitting up and feeling much better. She had insisted that the porter undo the sleeping berth and convert it back to a seating area.

"I'm so glad you're feeling better, Libby. But I have to warn you—Amanda is having a great time. I know this is going to hurt, but I don't believe she has missed you."

When Libby looked at Kacey, who was trying very hard to look serious, both women burst out laughing at the badinage.

"Oh, Kacey, you are so good for me. And I really am feeling much better. By the way, how is the light of my life?"

Kacey described how Rafe and Colin had fed the child

lunch, and she delighted in describing Rafe's appearance with the food on him and his clothing.

"I wish you could have seen it, Libby. The arrogant Monsieur Assante, all covered with mashed green peas." Kacey laughed once more at the memory.

Libby laughed, too, before she said, "You know, Kacey, you really are too hard on Mr. Assante. I think he is a fine gentleman."

"Oh, you do, do you? Well, I could tell you things that would change your mind and might even curl your hair."

"Oh, I doubt that. You forget, Kacey, I'm a married woman. And it's all too clear what he thinks of you. I see it in his eyes every time he looks at you."

"You see what in his eyes? Lust?"

"Lust, love, there's not much difference when it comes right down to it."

"Oh, Libby, Libby, Libby, you may be married but you certainly don't know Rafael Assante. You know what they say about Frenchmen."

"No, what do they say?"

"Well, you know."

Libby looked blank as Kacey tried to put into words her opinion of Frenchmen, especially a mahogany-eyed, dark Frenchman who caused her skin to prickle with excitement every time he came near her.

"Well, never mind. I can see he has made another conquest." Kacey feigned disgust as she looked at her friend and shook her head.

Libby smiled. "Well, now that we have that settled, I would like to go get washed up a bit. Do you have time to help me?"

Kacey nodded agreement, and the two women made their way to the ladies' room.

Kacey was glad that Libby seemed to be feeling much better as the two of them joined the others that evening in the dining car. Logan Connor also joined them, and the meal passed with Rafe paying an undue amount of attention to Libby and Amanda, while Logan occupied most of Kacey's conversation as he sat next to her at the table. Rafe sat across from Kacey, but he refused to look at her, and she at him.

Above the noise in the dining car, Kacey's words drifted to Rafe's ears as he ineffectually tried to listen to what Libby was saying.

"So you'll be leaving us in St. Louis, Logan?"

"Yes, the train should be there by Thursday." He paused, then said under his breath to Kacey, "But you know, ma'am, I sure will hate to leave you."

Rafe watched and strained to hear the gambler's words as Kacey returned his smile.

"I'm sure the wound will heal very quickly," Kacey said in an attempt to be light, "I know someone will be waiting for you there."

"No, ma'am, I haven't been to St. Louis for some time. I'm going there now to enter the annual riverboat gamblers' play-offs." Logan looked at Libby and added, "Kacey tells me you are getting off in St. Louis, also, Mrs. Hawkins."

"Yes, my husband is there waiting for me. I'll be so glad to see him, but I'll miss the new friends I've made on this trip. They've all been so wonderful to me and Amanda." Libby's grateful gaze passed over Kacey, Rafe, and Colin.

"I'm sure they have, ma'am." Logan's gaze moved back to Kacey. "Would you join me for a bit of air on the observation deck, ma'am?"

Kacey saw this as an opportunity to prove her independence to Rafe. She quickly replied, "I'd love to, Logan. When you are ready."

The gambler stood and helped Kacey with her chair as she rose. "Please excuse us, Father, Libby, we won't be long." She purposely omitted Rafe's name.

Kacey and Logan made their way to the observation

deck and seated themselves on a bench. The western sky was filled with shades of mauve surrounding the remnant of a large sinking globe of orange brilliance. The scene was breathtaking, and Kacey's sense of wonder took over.

"Oh, Logan, isn't that sunset lovely? Did you ever see anything so beautiful?" Kacey's face was animated as she stared at the evening sky in wonder.

"Well, ma'am, I could say yes, I have, and that I'm looking at her right now, but I don't think you would like it, so I won't say it."

"Now, Logan, be serious," Kacey scolded halfheartedly.

"I'm always serious, ma'am. I may not always tell the truth, but I am always serious." Logan's gray eyes sparkled with mischief.

"Will you teach me to play poker?"

"Well, now, I've seen some mighty good quick-change artists in my life, but I do believe you're right up there with them. You can change a subject quicker than a rattler can strike a toad."

Kacey laughed at the man's colorful language, then tossed her head sideways.

"Well? Will you?"

"Sure. I can teach you to play poker. When do you want to start?"

"How about right now? Do you have a deck of cards?"

"I wouldn't be without the little treasures. They've come through for me many a time." He reached into an inside coat pocket and took out the cards. He shuffled them expertly, then began to deal, dropping Kacey's cards into her lap.

She spent the remainder of the early evening light learning about royal flushes and other ranks of hands. She was enthralled by the game and hated to quit when the last ray of light blended into the landscape.

"I think it's time for me to go in, Logan. Libby may need some help."

"I'm right behind you. Just lead the way, ma'am."

In the near-darkness, Kacey and Logan carefully strolled back into the well-lit passenger car to find Colin holding Amanda and seated beside Libby. Rafe sat facing them in an otherwise empty seat. When Kacey stood beside the others, she turned to the gambler and held out her hand.

"I almost forgot to thank you for the lessons, Logan."

Rafe's body stiffened at her words as the man reached to take her hand.

"Anytime. Anytime at all."

Rafe thought the man held her hand way too long, but he refused to look straight at the couple. He continued to look from the corner of his eye as Kacey let go of the man's hand and made her way over Rafe's feet to the window seat beside him, facing her father.

Logan tipped his Stetson and went down the aisle to find a seat in the crowded railcar.

Colin and Libby were absorbed in Amanda's antics, and Rafe used the opportunity to speak privately to Kacey.

"What kind of lessons did Monsieur Connor give you, eh?"

Kacey bristled at the taunting tone of his voice.

"Why, that's really none of your business, is it, monsieur?" Kacey spoke under her breath, as did Rafe.

"*Non*, you are right, mademoiselle, it is none of my business. But I have the deepest respect for your father, and I don't want his daughter to make an idiot out of herself."

"Well, monsieur, if that happens, please don't hold yourself responsible. And, I might add, the lessons were quite enjoyable. I now feel that my education in the school of life has been very much enhanced by my association with Logan." She raised her eyes to his and flashed a defiant, pleased look.

Rafe's countenance darkened at her words, and for an instant she thought that she had gone too far in taunting him. She knew a minute portion of the passion he was capable of and how that passion affected her. Her cheeks burned as she recalled his kiss from that afternoon and how her senses had reeled from its intensity.

Rafe mistook the reason for her reddened cheeks. In his mind he pictured Kacey's lips ravished by the big Texan in the twilight and her enjoyment of his kisses.

"You really should be locked away, mademoiselle. And I may just be the one to do it."

"Don't even think it, monsieur. I don't know about France, but it would be illegal in this country."

"They would have to find you first, mademoiselle, something about habeas corpus, eh?"

"So, your sadistic side comes through after all, monsieur. I knew it was just a matter of time."

"Mademoiselle, I assure you I am not nearly so well trained in the powers of sadism as you are."

"I don't know what you are talking about, monsieur, and this conversation has turned bizarre. I refuse to continue it."

"I believe you do know what I am talking about, *chérie*. You return my kisses but you refuse to admit it. Do you know how that makes me feel?"

"I really couldn't care less, monsieur, how you feel."

"Ah, *oui*, I make my point, *chérie*, you are the best."

Kacey ignored the Frenchman's last words, and in an effort to put him from her mind she looked toward Libby, who seemed to be feeling much better, even though her cheeks still showed signs of a fever. Kacey marveled at her recovery as the woman smiled at her daughter, who bounced in Colin's lap.

"Libby, I'm so pleased that you're better. I know you'll be glad to see your husband when we arrive in St. Louis, but we will miss you and Amanda." Kacey's voice conveyed the sincerity she felt. "I think Father has truly enjoyed Amanda as much as I have, haven't you, Father?"

"Why, yes, dear, she is delightful. I will miss her."

Colin looked down at the small cherub-faced child as she toyed with his pocket watch once again.

"I will always remember your kindness." Tears came to Libby's eyes as she gazed at the trio who had helped her and her child. "I don't know if we would have made it without you."

"Why, of course you would have, Libby. You're much stronger than you know." Kacey paused, then said, "Your husband is very lucky, and don't you forget that."

Libby smiled at Kacey. "I'll be so happy to see Charles. But I'll still miss you."

At Libby's words the foursome settled back in their seats, and each one became absorbed in private thoughts as the railcar moved through the evening.

Eight

St. Louis, Missouri
Thursday, May 26, 1887

The St. Louis depot was bustling with activity as the locomotive of the Pennsylvania Railroad slowed to a stop at Union Station. Steam hissed from the engine like a giant dragon in the warm afternoon. Porters took their assigned positions by the steps as they waited for passengers to file from the train.

"Now, Libby, we won't leave you until we're sure Charles is here to meet you. We'll probably have to wait for the next train anyway," Kacey said as the two women prepared to leave the passenger car.

"Oh, he'll be here. I'm sure of that, Kacey." Even as Libby spoke, she stooped to look out the window toward the station, her eyes searching for the familiar figure of her husband.

Rafe held Amanda while the women gathered their personal belongings from the seating area. Then the troupe hastily made its way outside to the station, where Libby would meet Charles and the others would ready to board the Atchison, Topeka, and Santa Fe railroad line.

Kacey was dressed in a light-blue traveling suit and matching hat. Her coppery hair was swept high under the stylish headpiece. She looked around in search of Logan to say good-bye, but he was nowhere to be seen. Then she caught sight of him coming toward her through the crowd.

Rafe saw her searching gaze and felt a stab of jealousy when his eyes came to rest on the man in the distance. Her friendliness toward the Texan for the past few days had been an ordeal for him. He couldn't bear watching Kacey and the gambler in their closeness. All she seemed to hold for *him* was contempt. He was not sorry that the gambler would be staying in St. Louis. The thought seemed to comfort him.

Kacey flashed a large smile at the tall blond man who came toward her. She had become extremely fond of Logan during their time on the train. He was almost like the brother she never had. She felt at ease with him and enjoyed the light conversations they engaged in. She moved toward him on the platform as he removed his large hat.

"Good-bye, Kacey. I'll miss your lovely smile."

She extended her gloved hand toward him.

"Good-bye, Logan. I'll miss you, too. And remember, we expect to be at the Dunning Ranch near Durango for at least another month. We'd love to have you come to our dig site." Kacey laughed. "We can never have too many helpers."

"I might just do that, ma'am. I haven't been that way for a spell."

Colin had come to stand beside his daughter, and the Texan offered a friendly handshake to him.

"It's been a pleasure meeting you, sir, and I hope you find what you're looking for in Colorado."

"Thank you, lad, I believe we will."

"Father, I've invited Logan to come to Mr. Dunning's ranch."

"Of course, dear, that's a splendid idea." Colin

switched his gaze back to the man. "By all means, come if you can, Logan. We can always use an extra digger."

Kacey laughed. "That's what I told him, Father. I hope we don't scare him off before he gets there."

Libby and Rafe reached the trio in time to hear the gambler's words.

"Oh, I think I could develop a liking for archaeology, Kacey, if you're going to be the one teaching me."

Logan's Texas drawl was as slow as syrup on a January day in Boston. His white teeth and light hair were enhanced by the bronze of his skin, and he looked very tall and handsome standing there smiling down at Kacey. She was not immune to his good looks, but he did not stir her as Rafe did.

"I'd be delighted. I think you would find it as exciting as I do." Kacey's gaze moved to his strong, slender hands, the backs of which were covered with silky, light hairs. "You seem to have capable hands for archaeology, Logan."

Rafe, who still held Amanda, had moved closer to Kacey, and she heard something that sounded like a snort as she spoke. She cast an irritated glance at the arrogant Frenchman before returning her attention back to the blond man.

"Why, thank you. I'll keep that in mind if Lady Luck ever deserts me."

Logan nodded toward Libby. "Good-bye, Mrs. Hawkins. You take good care of Amanda."

"Good-bye, Mr. Connor, I wish you luck here in St. Louis."

"Thank you." The gambler paused, then continued. "I must be going now." He nodded to the four, replaced his big hat, and turned to go as he said to Kacey, "Maybe I'll see you in Colorado."

Kacey waved to the big Texan and then turned toward Libby.

"Have you seen Charles, Libby?"

"No, I haven't, but I know there's nothing to worry about. He'll be here." She turned to Rafe as she reached for her baby. "I know you must be getting tired, Mr. Assante. Let me take Amanda. I really don't know what I would have done if you all had not been so kind to me."

"It is nothing, madame. You are too grateful."

"Just the same, I will always remember all of you." When she had Amanda in her arms she turned teary eyes toward Kacey and the professor. "Please don't worry about me now. You need to catch your train."

"Nonsense, my dear girl, we wouldn't think of leaving you and Amanda here alone. We'll wait until your husband arrives." Colin was adamant as he tried to make the young woman feel better.

"Libby, there's a man coming toward us now who looks as if he might know you."

The young woman quickly followed Kacey's gaze to a man wearing a brown derby hat and a smile as wide as the Mississippi River they had just crossed. She seemed to leap toward him, and when they met, they came together in a tight hug with Amanda squeezed in between them. Kacey smiled to herself, knowing that everything would be all right now with Libby and her family.

Charles Hawkins seemed to be a capable young man, and Kacey breathed easier when she left Libby and Amanda. The woman and her child had found a place in Kacey's heart, and she wanted to see them taken care of. She believed they would be, if she could trust her intuition.

Libby and Charles made their departure, and Kacey turned to her father.

"They are a lovely couple, don't you think so, Father?"

"Yes, my dear, Charles seems devoted to Libby and Amanda both. You can stop worrying about them now."

"I wasn't exactly worrying about them, Father."

"Now, Kacey, I know how you are. You're just like your mother used to be." He paused a moment and added,

"It's an admirable trait, though, to care about others. I'm sure they will be just fine."

"I think so, too, Father."

"Good, we can carry on with our plans now." Colin swept his hand in front of him. "After you, my dear, and Rafe."

The trio headed toward the grand station to prepare for the next leg of their journey to Colorado. As Kacey walked along, keeping pace with Colin and Rafe, she turned slightly to speak to her father, and she did not see the deep dip in the boardwalk. From that moment everything seemed to move in slow motion. She pitched forward while a searing pain wrenched through her ankle. The pain was so great that she could not keep the agony of it from showing on her face.

Rafe was beside her in an instant, and just as suddenly he grasped her around the waist to keep her from falling to the ground. He watched helplessly as she bit into her lower lip.

"Are you all right, *chérie*?" He could see that her face was white as she held to him, and when she did not answer, he swept her the rest of the way into his arms as he looked around for a bench.

"P-please, p-put me down, monsieur. I-I'm sure I can walk," Kacey protested through her pain, her face as white as alabaster.

"My dear, let Rafe carry you to a seat." Colin's voice cracked and betrayed his concern.

Rafe paid no attention to her protests and continued toward a bench near the station.

Pain continued to shoot through Kacey's ankle and up the side of her leg, but even though she was racked with pain, she could not keep her heart from racing at the touch of Rafael Assante. As the man held her against his hard chest, the solid strength that emanated from him generated traitorous feelings that spread throughout her body—feelings that felt like fire licking along her veins, creating heat waves that seemed to consume her. Kacey did not like what was happening to her, yet she could not deny the exquisite warmth and heady sensations that enveloped her from his touch.

Then, just as suddenly as she was in his arms, she was deposited onto a bench. She immediately felt the loss of his strength and warmth, the pain in her ankle once more taking precedence.

"Kacey, what happened to you?" Her father's voice broke through her thoughts.

"I think I've just turned my ankle. I'm sure it'll be all right."

"Maybe we need to take a look at it, dear."

"No, Father. Just let me sit here for a while."

"Mademoiselle, you are very stubborn. You should let your father see if it is all right."

"I-I'll be f-fine."

Colin tried to humor his daughter. "Well, dear, while you sit for a while, I'll go and see about our train tickets. Rafe, you stay with her."

"*Oui*, monsieur, I'll make sure she is all right." His dark gaze moved to Kacey's face as if to dare her to say otherwise.

When Colin had moved away, Rafe said to Kacey, his voice husky and low, "Mademoiselle, you are the most stubborn woman I have ever met. What if your ankle is broken and needs to be set?"

Throbbing pain seared Kacey's ankle like the blow of a sledgehammer, but she refused to give in and accept help from Rafael Assante.

"I-I'm sure it will be fine, monsieur."

Rafe wanted to take her by her arms and shake her. He felt helpless as he watched her try to conceal her agony. *Ah la vache, but this woman is exasperating.* Why couldn't she admit her pain like most people and accept help?

Kacey felt relief when she looked up to see her father returning.

"How are you, my dear?"

"I think it may be better, Father."

"Do you think you can walk on it? It seems our train is running on schedule and leaves in five minutes." Colin looked at Rafe, the tension showing on his face.

"I'm sure I can." Kacey slowly brought herself to a standing position, but when she put her weight onto the injured leg, the pain was unbearable, and she dropped to the bench.

Rafe looked at Colin, and the professor returned his gaze.

"Professor, I can carry mademoiselle. That is no problem." He moved his gaze to Kacey. "She is not heavy." Rafe recalled how she had felt in his arms earlier. Her voluptuous figure was misleading. She had seemed featherlight in his embrace.

"You certainly will not, monsieur. I won't be carried through this crowd of people like some sort of invalid."

"Now, dear, that is the only mode of transportation available at the moment. If we miss this train, there won't be another one for six hours. I think you need to reconsider Rafe's kind offer."

"I'll walk." Kacey attempted to stand once more, trying to keep her weight on one foot. When she moved to take a step, she reached for her father as the pain increased.

Rafe saw instantly what was happening, and once more he stooped to sweep Kacey into his arms. Her protest fell on deaf ears as he continued through the throng of people.

"Monsieur, put me down!"

"Mademoiselle, much as I would love to . . . discard you, you heard your father. We need to catch a train, and this is the only way I know." His voice became low as he continued. "Is my touch so repulsive, *chérie*? Why can't you act a lady, as Madame Libby did when she had to be carried aboard?"

"That was different."

"*Oui, chérie*, that was different." The tone of his voice

conveyed perfectly what he meant as he followed Colin toward the westbound train.

In Rafe's arms Kacey almost forgot about her throbbing ankle. His low voice did strange things to her usually normal equilibrium, and her head seemed to sway as she realized she was not immune to his dark good looks, as she usually tried to pretend. The man put her routinely peaceful emotions in an uproar. Her face was too close to his neck now, and she could see the shadow of a beard forming on his chiseled jaw. Much as she fought it, she wanted to reach out and touch his face, to feel the hard line of his features. She wanted to stroke his raven hair, which almost appeared blue in the sunlight. Kacey was not used to these emotions. She could see a pulse throbbing in his neck and remained fascinated by it as she tried to gather her unruly thoughts into a semblance of order.

Rafe followed Colin toward the railcar. The softness of the woman in his arms was playing havoc with his senses. He clenched his jaw and refused to let his feelings surface. She treated him as though he had a plague, and he'd be damned if he would whine for her attentions like a lovesick puppy.

Rafe tightened his hold on Kacey as they came near the passenger car, as if his body were resisting the inevitable moment when he would have to put her down. He easily carried her up the steps and placed her in an upholstered seating booth inside the car.

Fleetingly Kacey felt deprived of his warmth and masculine scent. His musky aroma was heady, and she breathed a sigh of relief as she put the discomforting thoughts from her mind when he put her down. Even though she missed the comfort of his arms, she was relieved to be able to think coherently now.

Colin sat beside his daughter. "How is your ankle, dear?"

"It feels fine at the moment, thanks to Monsieur Assante." Kacey met Rafe's gaze and registered his surprise, while her own eyes felt like liquid warmth, unable to look away.

Kacey's gracious appreciation jarred Rafe, for it was the last thing he expected to hear from her. "You are quite welcome, mademoiselle." Then he continued recklessly while she seemed to be in a reasoning mood. "Are you ready for your father to look at the injury?"

"I-it really is feeling much better at the moment. . . . Maybe if I stay off it for a while longer it will be all right, monsieur."

"Now, dear, don't wait too long. You know if it is broken it will need to be set soon." Colin's concern was once more apparent in his voice.

"I realize that, Father, but I don't think it is broken." Even as Kacey spoke, she did not feel the conviction she tried to convey.

Rafe studied Kacey's previous words of gratitude. Had the woman actually softened toward him? Did he mistake the velvet of her eyes just moments ago? When the train started to move, Rafe moved to the seat facing Kacey and her father and sat down, stretching his long sturdy legs to within inches of Kacey's skirt.

She refused to look at Rafe. The pain in her ankle continued, and she knew that soon she would have to consent to having her ankle examined. She could feel the swelling stretching the soft leather of her shoe and knew that to delay inspection could be a mistake if there were broken bones. Finally she realized the time had come to take a look.

"Father, I think maybe we'd better look at my ankle after all. It does seem to be swelling."

"Yes, of course, dear. I'll try to find a doctor—maybe there's one on the train." Colin stood and looked around. "Now where's the porter when you need him? I'll be right back." He strode down the aisle of the railcar.

"Mademoiselle, I know something about such injuries. The animals on my father's estate required attention from time to time, and often I assisted the veterinarian.''

"Monsieur, I don't doubt your expertise with farm animals, but I believe I would prefer the opinion of a people doctor in this case.''

"As you wish, mademoiselle. But . . . there might not be a doctor until our next stop.''

"Well, then, I'll wait.''

"That may not be possible, mademoiselle.''

Colin returned, and his expression showed his concern for his daughter.

"Dear, there's not a doctor on the train.''

"Professor, I was just telling Mademoiselle Kacey that I know somewhat about dealing with bone injuries. I would be willing to assist.'' Rafe paused and looked at Kacey. "If mademoiselle is agreeable.''

"Father, I don't think Monsieur Assante's experience applies to people.''

"Nonsense, dear. If Rafe has any experience at all, it's more than I have. Let him take a look and see what he thinks.''

Kacey could not ignore the pleading in her father's eyes. He actually thought that the Frenchman knew what he was talking about. She had no recourse but to do as her father wanted.

"Very well, but . . . can we find a more private car?'' Even as Kacey said the words, the look she gave Rafe showed her reluctance.

"Of course, dear.'' Colin swung around and went toward a porter a few feet away. After a brief discussion he returned with the man by his side.

"This is Elijah, and he is going to take us to a salon that is deserted this time of day.''

Quickly Rafe stood and lifted Kacey into his arms once again, even as she protested in his ear.

"Monsieur, I'm sure I can walk now if you will put me down. People are staring.''

"*Non*, mademoiselle, if you could walk you wouldn't

need someone to look at the ankle, *n'est-ce pas*?'' Rafe turned and followed Colin.

Kacey hated being at the mercy of anyone, especially Rafael Assante. She had hardly been sick a day in her life, much less unable to walk. She did not like the feeling of being dependent on another to go from room to room. She prayed that her ankle was not broken as she scorned the idea of Rafael Assante being her only means of conveyance the rest of the journey. Poor Libby. Kacey had not realized the embarassment of her situation until now.

Before she knew what was happening, Rafe had placed her on a daybed and looked at her now as he spoke.

"I assure you, mademoiselle, I won't hurt you.''

Kacey looked toward her foot and eased her skirt a modest distance above her ankle. Rafe smiled inwardly at her withdrawing attitude, thinking all the while how her normally biting tongue seemed incongruous to her reticent behavior. He untied the lacing of her hightop shoe before carefully removing it. For a moment he glanced up to see her expression as she bit her lower lip.

"I'm sorry, mademoiselle, if I have hurt you.''

"No, monsieur, you haven't hurt me, but I want to be prepared.''

"I see you do not trust me.''

"Let's just say that people and animals are different, monsieur.''

"Bones are bones, mademoiselle, and they are repaired the same way for man or beast.''

"He's right, dear. Just let Rafe do what he thinks best. I'm confident he knows what he is doing.''

"You will need to take your stocking off, mademoiselle.''

Rafe's matter-of-fact tone irritated Kacey, and she started to protest as she looked at her father, but his expression told her that he was in complete agreement.

"I certainly won't take it off in front of you, monsieur. You'll have to turn around.''

Rafe's lips curled as a smile played around them at the woman's sense of decorum in such a situation.

"*Oui*, mademoiselle." Rafe turned away from the day-bed, as did Colin.

He was laughing at her, and she knew it. Drat the man! He had a way of making her feel childish and unsophisticated. But she had no intention of making a show of her legs to someone who affected her the way he did. The man was positively rakish, and she felt he had no scruples where women were concerned. That was what infuriated her so, that her body reacted so foolishly to his touch and even his nearness.

She was able to remove the dark stocking without much trouble, and once again lowered her skirt to a proper level just above her swollen ankle.

"You can do whatever it is you do to bones now, monsieur, but I really don't see how you can tell if it is broken or not."

Rafe turned around and stooped in front of Kacey. He gently felt and probed the bruised ankle before he came to a conclusion.

"You have some swelling, and although it appears not to be broken, it is difficult to tell for sure in a situation like this. I would suggest you stay off it for at least a day to see if the swelling goes down any. And keep it propped up."

Kacey was aghast at the man's declaration as she sputtered, "But, monsieur, you haven't told me anything I didn't already know."

Colin patted his daughter's hand. "Now, dear, try to relax. Rafe's advice sounds good to me. We'll watch it, and if necessary we'll get off at the next stop to see a doctor. You lie here with it propped up, just as Rafe suggested. I'll be back shortly to check on you."

Kacey nodded, and in an effort to calm down, she closed her eyes. The Frenchman was a phony, and her father was in league with him. The thought did nothing to relieve her, and she tried to focus on more pleasant musings as she heard the men leave. One thing she knew for sure: The pain was atrocious when she attempted to stand on her left foot. She tried to comfort herself by saying over and over that her ankle was not broken. But she knew that saying it did not necessarily make it so. She prayed again that her ankle was not seriously injured.

Soon she slept and drifted off to another world where the only people there looked exactly like Rafael Assante, with raven hair and mahogany eyes that seemed to search deep into her soul.

Nine

Kacey was awakened by someone calling her name. She was being pulled back from another world and she fought against it. Slowly her eyelids fluttered, and she roused enough to hear her father.

"Kacey, dear, I've brought you a plate from the dining car. Rafe and I have already eaten."

"Thank you, Father. I must have drifted off without realizing it."

"Yes, you did, but you needed the rest. The conductor has allowed us to use this car temporarily. How is your ankle?" Colin pulled a small marble-topped table nearer to where Kacey was seated and placed a tray there before seating himself on a plush sofa nearby.

"It seems to be feeling much better, thank you." Kacey paused, then asked, "Where's Rafe?" She easily used the man's given name without thinking. After the words were out of her mouth, she was thankful for his absence.

"He's in the smoking lounge, I believe. Do you need something, dear?"

"No." In an effort to hide the fact that she missed his presence, Kacey lifted the lid from the plate, and a heavenly aroma met her nostrils. "If this tastes anything like it smells, it'll be delicious."

"Must be the yeast rolls. They were excellent. I didn't know I'd miss Sarah's cooking so much."

"She is the best, isn't she?" Teasingly she added, "You don't suppose someone will try to steal her away while we're gone, do you, Father?"

Colin played along with Kacey's conspiratorial tone. "Well, I don't know. Do you suppose we should rush back home just in case?"

Kacey feigned the thought process. "No, I don't think so. We've come this far, and I believe we have a pretty good hold on Sarah."

They both laughed good-naturedly as Kacey cut into a juicy chicken filet.

She soon finished her meal, and to her surprise she ate most everything on her plate.

"Seems you were hungrier than you thought, my dear."

"I must have been famished. It was delicious, though." Kacey placed the tray back on the table. "I think I'll try to get up now, Father, before Rafe comes in. He won't let me try on my own, and I know I can walk."

"Now, dear, Rafe just wants to help. He's a fine young man, in case you haven't noticed." Colin cast a sideways glance at his daughter as he sang Rafe's praises.

"Hmmph." The sound had barely rolled from Kacey's tongue when the door to the salon burst open. Rafe came toward the two with a swiftness that startled her, and he did not stop to speak until he had lifted Kacey into his arms.

She had no time to protest before he swept her into his strong embrace for the third time that day, and the frequency unnerved her. His nearness disturbed her senses in a way that nothing else ever had.

"Professor, we must evacuate this car immediately. There is a fire in the kitchen, and a crew is trying to extinguish it now. As a precaution, we will exit when the train stops." He nodded toward the rear of the car as the train slowed to a halt, and Colin quickly followed his lead.

"Monsieur, put me down! I will walk."

"Be quiet, *chérie*. There is no time to talk. We must get outside."

Kacey saw the futility of her demands and allowed herself to be carried from the salon to a grassy knoll several feet away from the train where Rafe gently but swiftly deposited her onto a thick carpet of new grass.

A steady swirl of smoke came from the windows of the dining car, and men worked to unlatch the smoke-filled car from the rest of the train. Passengers stared in awe as the railcar became enveloped in a darker smoke that soon turned into an incendiary glow in the approaching twilight.

The rest of the train had been saved, but the dining car was on fire and burning rapidly with no hope of saving it. The sight unfolding before Kacey reminded her of a long, segmented reptile that had been separated and whose middle was fast disappearing. She realized that if Rafe had not acted when he did, she could very well have been trapped inside the salon, which was near the burning car. Her father stirred beside her.

"Well, dear, looks like this might be a long night. How is your ankle feeling?"

Kacey let out a nervous laugh. "Why, I had almost forgotten about it. I guess that means it's better." She looked around to see where Rafe stood, but he was nowhere in sight. "Where did Rafe go? I want to thank him."

"He took off toward the train right after he brought us here. I'm sure he meant to help."

Kacey said almost to herself, "Yes, he would do that."

"I'm sorry, dear, what did you say?"

"Oh, nothing important, Father."

Kacey watched from the safety of the knoll as the glow from the burning railcar soon faded to dying embers. Darkness swept over the landscape, and the only light came from lanterns swinging from the hands of porters trying to calm distraught passengers. Her father had gone to see what plans were being laid, and she jumped as she heard someone drop beside her on the grass. Even before she recognized the face in the dim light she identified the male scent.

"Rafe, you startled me. I-I wasn't expecting you."

"Forgive me, mademoiselle. Who were you expecting?"

Kacey ignored the question. "Rafe . . . I want to thank you for everything you've done and . . . to say that maybe I've been wrong about you." She turned to face him as she extended her hand in friendship. "Can we be friends?"

Rafe took her hand, and his gaze darted to her own. "If that is what you want, mademoiselle . . . to be friends."

"Yes, I'd like to try. I mean, we'll be working closely together, and I'd like to think I'm amiable." Rafe was holding her hand much too tightly and too long, and his dark eyes would not let go of her gaze.

Kacey realized the inevitable as she watched Rafe's mouth slowly descend to her own. The tenderness of his lips touched an atavistic urge in Kacey that she did not know existed until that very moment. She longed for something more, but this was not the time to think on it. She slowly removed her lips from his and tried to pretend that the kiss had no effect on her. Yet her breath came in short, quick bursts that matched the rhythm of her heart.

"*Chérie,* I can see that you will make a very good *friend.*"

"Always the Frenchman, aren't you, Rafe? Will you ever learn that all women do not come to heel for you? That kiss . . . was just a kiss."

"If you say so, *chérie.*" Rafe's expression belied his words.

The evening sky had darkened, and on the eastern horizon a full moon began to scale the velvet starlit night, casting an ethereal amber glow larger than life. Kacey felt the magic in the night, magic of which she had no intention of being a part. To her relief, Colin strode toward them.

"The engineer thinks it is safe enough to board the train again. They are going to pull the burned-out car to a side-track just up the way and leave it there. Kacey, dear, are you going to be able to walk?"

"I'm sure I can, Father. My ankle is feeling much better now." She eyed Rafe with her best "I dare you to say otherwise" expression. Colin reached out his hand to assist his daughter in rising.

"Well, then, we better get ready to board. The conductor will be announcing any minute now."

Kacey took her father's hand and pulled herself to a standing position. Her ankle did feel somewhat better, even though dull pains still throbbed there as she put her full weight on her feet. Instinctively she leaned on her father to take some of the weight off her injured foot.

"I'm ready, Father, if I can lean on you."

"Of course, my dear." Colin patted his daughter's hand.

"Mademoiselle, if you are still in pain, please allow me to assist you."

"No, Rafe, I've imposed on you enough for one day. I'm sure I will be fine." With that she started toward the train alongside her father with Rafe right behind her.

Kacey lay in the railcar berth, reflecting on the events of the past twenty-four hours—most especially those involving one Rafael Assante. She was not sure just when it happened, but that it did happen was what she most dwelt on at the moment—"it" being the fact that her complete dislike of the Frenchman had taken such an astronomical turn. Memories of his kiss the night before washed over her in a tide of warmth. She had spent the day resting her ankle and being attended to by her father. The swelling in her foot had lessened dramatically, and she felt great relief knowing that it was not broken.

Either the heat of the night or the heat of her thoughts

was making the close confines of the berth unbearable. She was not sure of the time but knew that it was very late, because most of the passengers had long ago retired to their respective berths. She wondered if she could slip from her bed without disturbing anyone. She decided that she could and she quietly retrieved her robe and slippers from the foot of her bed and opened the curtains. In the near-darkness she silently slid from the berth and made her way along the aisle in the moonlight that streamed through a window.

Kacey walked outside to the observation deck at the back of the car. She stepped to the edge of the railing and took in the scene before her. A silvery full moon gave the vast prairie land a soft incandescent glow that seemed to heighten her awareness of the surrounding beauty. Tucked in the berth she had been warm, but the night air was exhilarating, and she closed her eyes and reveled in the breeze against her skin. She was glad that she was alone in the night and did not have to share this moment with anyone. She pulled her robe tighter around her and leaned on the railing for what seemed like minutes before she became aware of the smell of cigar smoke. She turned sharply and saw the figure sitting on a bench against the rear of the train.

"*Bonsoir,* Mademoiselle Kacey. I see you could not sleep either."

Kacey could see the glowing tip of his cheroot as he pressed it between his lips.

"Why, good evening, Rafe. How long have you been there?"

"Much longer than you, mademoiselle. I have watched the moon travel some distance now."

"Why didn't you say something sooner?"

"Shall we say, I enjoyed watching . . . the elements in their uninhibited state. And I did not want to disturb your enjoyment either."

In the dim light Kacey could see the smile that played

about his lips, and she felt drawn to him. But something kept her rooted to the spot where she stood. That and the fact that she had on her nightclothes, which made her uncomfortable in his presence.

"That's very kind of you, Rafe. It is a lovely night, and I did enjoy my communion with nature."

Rafe stood and moved between Kacey and the passageway.

"Your ankle seems to be much improved, mademoiselle. You don't even appear to limp."

"Oh, yes, it's much better. Much to my chagrin, Father waited upon me all day, and I've had the opportunity to rest the entire afternoon."

"You don't like being dependent on others, do you, mademoiselle?" The words were more a statement than a question.

"No, I don't. And I don't see you as someone who would like that either, monsieur."

"Ah, mademoiselle, I have offended you, *n'est-ce pas?*" He stepped toward Kacey, and his voice became husky. "You know, *chérie,* your hair is very lovely in the moonlight. You should wear it down more often. The length of it shines like liquid copper."

He was standing very close to Kacey now, and she seemed to sway toward him as their gazes locked. They stood as stone for what seemed like minutes, each one drinking in the essence of the other. Suddenly Rafe broke the contact and stepped back.

"Mademoiselle, I believe I am through communing with nature for the moment. Do you intend to stay out here all night?"

At his abruptness, Kacey came to her senses with an odd feeling of loss. She had expected something, had even anticipated something. But his unexpected behavior muddled her mind.

"Possibly. I'm still not sleepy and I don't relish the idea of that stuffy railcar. I much prefer to be here."

"Very well. I will bid you good-night, then. I won't ask you if you will be all right. I don't want to offend your sense of . . . independence."

"You are learning about me, aren't you, monsieur?"

"*Oui,* mademoiselle, I am learning about you." Rafe turned to go. *"Bonsoir."*

Kacey stood alone on the observation deck. Strangely, the exhilaration that she had felt earlier at being alone in the night had deserted her. She still held to that sense of loss that had struck her earlier. *Had she wanted Rafe to kiss her? Had she wanted to feel his arms closed tightly around her?* Those were questions that she hadn't time now to try to answer. She felt that the answers would be long in coming, and that they would be answers she did not want.

Rafe made his way to the smoking lounge and found it nearly deserted. At one o'clock in the morning most passengers were asleep aboard the train. He wished he were one of them, but sleep seemed to escape him tonight. He had had to get away from Kacey before he did something stupid, like kiss her again. She had been insistent that they be friends and nothing more. Rafe cursed his attraction to her. Continuing a platonic friendship with Kacey seemed almost impossible. *Mon Dieu,* but he had to quit thinking about the woman. She wanted no part of him, and why couldn't he remember that? He stood, walked to the bar, and ordered a shot of Scotch whiskey. The bartender served the amber liquid, and Rafe held the glass high as if in toast. With sarcasm thick on his tongue, he muttered, "To women everywhere, may God bless their lily-white necks . . . and souls." Then he downed the fiery liquid, and with his eyes ordered another.

The morning dawned bright and clear, and Kacey was glad to learn that they were nearing their destination of Durango, Colorado. Her mind turned swiftly at the thought of working at a dig again and the possibility of making a find that would contribute greatly to American archaeology. From her father she learned that a buckboard would be sent out from Dunning Ranch as soon as the Dunnings were notified of the professor's arrival in Durango.

Rafe had barely spoken to her this morning. He and her father had conversed over breakfast, but he had merely nodded her way as a means of saying good morning. She now sat across from her father in a window seat, and Rafe had gone off to the smoking salon where, by the looks of his eyes, he had spent most of the night. That was one thing about trains; a person had nowhere to go to escape.

"We're almost there, dear. The conductor says just a few more hours should put us in Durango."

"I'm glad to hear that, Father. I'm ready to be off the closeness of railcars and out in the wide open country. My mind and body are starting to tire of this confined existence."

"Yes, yes, dear. I'm just glad your ankle has turned out all right."

"It seems fine now. I don't foresee a problem with it, and I can't wait to get off this train."

Kacey's thoughts returned to Rafe and how the past few days had changed her attitude toward him. The man was an enigma with his brooding moods. Just when she seemed to soften toward him, he seemed to harden his feeling for her. She fought to put the man from her mind, as she had done all morning.

Speak of the devil! Her gaze fell on Rafe as he walked toward their seat. His eyes refused to meet hers, and she quickly averted her attention back to her father, whose thoughts seemed to be taken by the picturesque landscape.

Rafe seated himself beside Colin, and the older man turned.

"Rafe, my lad, we're almost there. It'll be good to be able to take a very long walk."

"Yes, Professor, I know what you mean. I'm looking

forward to riding again. It's been quite some time since I've been in a saddle." Rafe turned his regard to Kacey.

"Do you ride, mademoiselle?"

"Yes, actually, quite well." Kacey was somewhat perturbed by Rafe's social neglect of her this morning, and she could not keep the bite from her words.

Colin cut into the conversation.

"Kacey has ridden in the equestrian competition in Boston and received many awards for her riding ability. How long have you been riding, dear?"

"Father, if you remember, Uncle Creighton put me on a horse when I was four. I can still see Mother's horrified expression when her favorite brother confided the information to her after my visit to Connecticut that summer."

"It seems that mademoiselle does everything very well, eh, *chérie*?"

"Well, I always try to do my best. Does that bother you, monsieur?"

"*Au contraire,* mademoiselle. I am very glad to hear that you put yourself completely into . . . whatever you are doing."

Kacey felt the unwelcome warmth spread upward to her face at the implication of intimacy that was threaded through Rafe's words and the way his voice had lowered for her ears only. She tried to ignore his meaning as she attempted to change the subject.

"Yes, well, we'll soon be at Mr. Dunning's ranch, and we all will have a chance to prove our worth. Isn't that correct, Rafe?"

"Ah, so now we are in competition, mademoiselle?"

"On the contrary. We will be working very closely for the good of the team. You do know what teamwork is, don't you, monsieur?"

"*Oui*, mademoiselle. I am at my best in . . . teamwork. And I am elated to be on your team, *chérie*."

Once again, his meaning hit home with Kacey, but she feigned ignorance and refused to make a reply. His innuendos were putting a strain on their agreement of friendship.

Durango, Colorado, was a lively town that boasted a train depot, livery stable, various general stores, and the newly built Strater Hotel. The wide, dusty main street was flanked by low brick-and-frame false fronts and surrounded on all sides by high shadowing mountains.

A messenger had been sent to the Dunning Ranch while the archaeology team checked into the hotel to await the arrival of John Dunning.

The first thing Kacey did was to bathe in the large footed tub in the water closet of her room. She and her father had taken separate rooms because a suite was not available. She slid below the water's surface and soaked away the days of train travel that lay behind her. The water felt wonderful; it allowed her to relax her mind and to ready herself for the hard work ahead.

Suddenly a knock at the door to her room startled her from her relaxed state. She opened her eyes.

"Come in, Father, I'll be just a moment." Kacey regretted having to give up the warm, soothing water, but she stood from the tub and dried herself before donning a long chenille robe the color of the clear Colorado sky. When she heard no reply from her father she continued talking as she tied the sash to her robe and stepped into the main room that served as parlor and bedroom. "Are they already here from the ran—Rafe! I-I thought . . ." Much as she wanted to, Kacey refused to bring her hands up to try to cover the robe she was wearing. Not that there was anything wrong with it. Its thickness completely covered her, but she still felt at a disadvantage with Rafe obviously eyeing her from head to foot.

"I apologize, mademoiselle. I did not realize that you were not dressed." Even as he said the words, he stepped closer to her.

"What did you want, monsieur?" Kacey could not keep

her heart at a steady rhythm, even as she tried. He had moved much closer to her, and she could see his eyes darken with desire. There was no mistaking the want in his gaze, and the knowledge worked to weaken Kacey's reserve. A liquid warmth washed over her much like the bath she had just taken, leaving her vulnerable in places she had never known before. The onslaught of his visual seduction did nothing to strengthen her natural ability to keep men at bay. She knew at this moment that if he took her in his arms she would be helpless to resist.

Rafe started to speak, but his voice deserted him as he saw the depth of emotion in Kacey's eyes. She looked like a wide-eyed doe, skittish, yet wanting to experience the wonder of the unknown. That was his undoing. He reached for her and held her slender body in his arms, gently at first, his gaze never leaving hers. His lips took hers as a primitive hunger for something more consumed his body. He was out of control, and her own eagerness fired the flame. His lips traced the white softness of her neck to the gentle swell of her chest, and further to the dusky peak of her breast where he teased the taut flesh until a moan escaped Kacey's lips.

Rafe had pushed her robe aside, and now Kacey stood bared to his hungry gaze. "*Mon Dieu, chérie,* but you are beautiful." He continued to murmur endearments to her as his hand traveled to the silky softness of her thighs.

Kacey had never known, never wanted, the feel of a man's hands on her body. But now the feeling was beyond imagining, and she did not want the moment to stop. She arched her back to get nearer to his body, and in the act she felt his stem of desire. The knowledge inflamed her, made her want to get as close as possible to this man, who evoked passion in her like none she had ever known. She could not get close enough, and the feeling left her with an insatiable desire for more. Kacey's own hands moved over Rafe's clothing, and she undid his shirt, moving her hands to the richness of dark curly hair underneath.

A knock at the door followed by a familiar voice brought them both to a startling halt.

"Kacey, dear, are you there?"

Rafe stared at Kacey, and she returned his gaze.

"Y-yes, Father. I'm just stepping from my bath. I-I thought I would take a nap."

"Of course, dear, go ahead. I'll be downstairs in the lobby."

Seconds later, Kacey and Rafe heard footsteps moving away from the door. She withdrew from his embrace, and Rafe's voice sounded low and husky, betraying his emotion as he saw her look of distress.

"*Chérie*, I should ask your forgiveness, but I am not sorry. You must know how I feel about you."

Kacey's voice was shaky as she turned away. "There's nothing to forgive. It was as much my fault as yours. It seems that the untouchable is not so untouchable after all."

Facing her back, Rafe moved to grasp her upper arms.

"Don't be so hard on yourself, *chérie*, you are merely human after all."

Kacey shook her head. "But you don't understand. I made a commitment not to become involved with anyone. I want to take care of my father as long as he needs me."

"That is very admirable, but I believe your father does not need you as much as you think. Have you ever stopped to consider that your self-imposed propriety is merely a curtain to protect yourself instead of your father?"

Kacey whirled around, her eyes firing electric darts.

"How dare you! Please leave my room, monsieur!"

Rafe looked defeated as he did her bidding and walked to the door.

"*Oui, chérie,* with regret I will leave your room. But will I leave your heart?"

"Why, you arrogant, pompous—ooooh, get out of here before I scream!"

Ten

Kacey sat stiffly in the front seat of the buckboard that had been sent for them from the Dunning Ranch. She winced for what seemed to be the hundredth time as the wagon hit a bump in the road and nearly bounced her off the seat, despite the fact that she held tightly to the iron railing beside her. After the plush seating of the train, the absence of cushioning on the boards was taking its toll.

She almost felt like telling the cowboy to please slow down. One would think that he would have enough sense to know that his passengers were being bounced all over the place. On the other hand, she felt a perverse sense of amusement in knowing that Rafe was taking the same beating. Especially after the incident in her hotel room. *Let the puffed-up peacock suffer. The man's head is way too big. Too bad it's not his head that's taking the pounding!*

Kacey turned her head toward the lanky driver to speak, but stopped herself in time as the words formed on her lips. She could endure if the others could. She seemed to be the only one having difficulty staying on her seat, however. From the corner of her eye she spotted Rafe, who seemed to be having no trouble whatsoever staying seated.

The knowledge made her fume. At that moment she pictured the arrogant man flying through the air to land in the Colorado dust. The thought brought a smile to her lips.

"Mademoiselle, it's good to see you smile. May we share in your humor?"

Kacey had not realized that the Frenchman could see her face. His voice seemed to drip with honey. She turned her head to face him squarely, at the same time letting go of the seat arm.

"Monsieur, I'm afraid you would not find much to smile about. My humor can be rather . . . sordid at times."

"Ah, I see, mademoiselle. A secret."

Kacey had no time for a further reply as she bounced off the seat and onto the hard Colorado dirt, facedown.

The buckboard came to an instant halt beside her as the rugged cowhand jumped to her side. She was shaken to her bones but did not allow that to show. Through a multitude of apologies that sputtered from the man's lips, Kacey allowed him to help raise her to a standing position. She brushed off her clothing, and with as much poise as she could muster, climbed back onto the wagon, allowing Rafe only a parting glance.

"My dear, are you all right?"

"Perfectly, Father. A little fall like that is not going to hurt me."

"It wasn't such a little fall," her father protested.

Her tailored green suit in which she had chosen to meet Mr. Dunning and his family was now almost brown. And she couldn't be certain, but she thought her hair had probably fallen down some. She felt sure that she looked shaken. She knew that Rafe was most likely laughing. But double-curse the man if she would give him the pleasure of seeing her discomfort. She stiffened her back and sat regally on the seat. Thankfully, the driver had slowed significantly.

"How much farther do we have to go, Mr. Finn?"

"About two miles, ma'am. I sure am sorry about you falling off the wagon like that."

"Oh, it wasn't your fault, Mr. Finn. I should have been holding on better." Kacey felt that there were times when lies were appropriate, and this seemed to be one of them.

"Well, ma'am, you're an awful good sport. Most women woulda been giving me what for."

"Nonsense, Mr. Finn. I believe you sell women short."

"Well, ma'am, I know what I know, and there ain't no changing the facts."

Kacey laughed outright at the man's candor. She seemed to have made a friend, and she was glad. Maybe now he would keep the wagon at a decent pace over the rough dirt road. She thought she was beginning to understand Bill Finn. He probably thought to give the "city folk" a thrill, and it had backfired on him. Kacey liked him anyway. The pallor she saw on his face when he had helped her to her feet had most likely matched her own. The strength she had felt in his hands and the frank expression in his eyes indicated to her that he was a man to be trusted.

The melodic tinkle of Kacey's laughter thrilled Rafe. He watched her from the corner of his eye and surmised, once again, that she was the most beautiful woman he had ever met. He could not stop the stab of jealousy he felt as he watched her openly flirting with the rugged cowhand. *Mon Dieu*, but surely she did not know the effect she had on men. Why, she had the man practically eating out of her hand. And it fired Rafe that anyone but him would be eating out of her delicate hand. His thoughts were interrupted by the cowhand's words.

"Is this your first time in the West, ma'am?"

"My first time to Colorado, Mr. Finn."

"Ma'am, if you keep calling me Mr. Finn, why I'll have the bighead so bad that they couldn't stand it at the ranch."

Kacey laughed again.

"All right, Bill, you win."

"So what do you think of Colorado?"

"It's beautiful country, all right. I'm really looking forward to seeing the pueblo that Mr. Dunning found. How soon do you think we can see it?"

"Well, I can't rightly say, ma'am. As soon as the boss can get around to it, I'm sure. There's other visitors waiting to see it, too. He'll probably take you all at the same time."

"Did you say other visitors?"

"Yes, ma'am."

"Oh, I didn't understand that anyone else knew about the find."

"Oh, yes, ma'am. There's been a steady flow of visitors ever since the discovery. Mr. Dunning can't always get off from the ranch, but every chance he gets he takes off for the pueblo, too. I don't find it so interesting as he does, though. He seems to be under some kind of spell, so to speak. 'Course, I don't believe in no Indian curse, but just the same, I'm not hankering to hang around it."

"Why, whatever do you mean, Bill?"

"Ah, nothing I can put my finger on, ma'am. But there seems to be such a strange quietness about the place. The Anasazi, the ancient ones, lived there, and I don't believe in disturbing their spirits, if there are any. Even old Acowitz stays away from the old pueblo. That's John's Ute friend. 'Course, I understand that that sort of thing don't bother you scientists none. Just the same, I'll tend to roping and riding and let you tend to figuring out Pueblo Mesita."

Kacey quietly studied Bill Finn's words before she spoke again.

"You know, Bill, I've experienced that same quietness that you find so disturbing at other dig sites. But I've never found it . . . strange. In view of the fact that the inhabitants have been dead for many years, I find it to be expected and rather peaceful. I always get so caught up in the cataloguing that there's no time to think of anything else. Every artifact must be carefully cleaned and tagged. It's really very time-consuming." Kacey was aware of the excitement in her voice of anticipating being in the field again.

"Well, ma'am, you make it all sound so scientific. But still, I believe I'll stick to ranching." Bill cast her a sideways grin.

Kacey laughed, knowing he was teasing her. "All right, Bill, I can see you're no convert. I know when to quit." She returned his easy smile before turning her attention to the countryside.

The sun was shining brilliantly in the azure sky, and Kacey noticed that the surrounding landscape was now a lush green. An eagle soared overhead, and she caught her breath at the beauty of the land. The scene spread out before her seemed to have changed as much as her own spirits had in the last few minutes. Bill Finn's words cut into her thoughts.

"The ranch is just up ahead. You can see it over the next rise. Mr. Benjamin is the owner, but his oldest son, John, has taken over more and more responsibility recently. I reckon Mr. Benjamin knows he's getting older." The cowhand paused momentarily, then continued when Kacey made no comment. "There's five brothers. No girls at all. But Miz Miriam don't seem to mind. She sets great store by her boys. There's usually some females around anyways, especially with the new attraction."

Kacey finally caught a view of the sprawling ranch in the valley below. A low, rambling ranchhouse was set in a shady grove of cottonwoods. The dwelling faced the barns and corrals, while mountains rose in the distance. Long, neat rows of white, three-boarded fences enclosed the nearest pastures and corrals.

"This is beautiful country. And the Dunning Ranch looks very impressive from this vantage point."

"Oh, it's impressive from any point, ma'am. Mr. Benjamin and his boys have worked hard to make the ranch something special. And Miz Miriam . . . why there's not a better wife and mother in Colorado.''

"Sounds as if you are quite fond of the Dunning family.''

"Yes, ma'am. They have been very kind to me. But that's their way. They're Quakers, you know.''

"No, I didn't. I've never met Quakers before.''

"There aren't finer people anywhere. I'm sure you will agree once you've met them.''

"I'm sure I will, too.''

Kacey and Bill Finn lapsed into silence as the buckboard slowly made its way along the winding road toward the Dunning Ranch in the valley below.

The sun was low in the western sky as Bill Finn stopped the buckboard in front of the Dunning residence. By the time he had dropped to the ground to assist Kacey in her descent, a small, round woman appeared on the front veranda. Her smile was contagious, and all three guests returned her expression. She was joined by an older man who also smiled warmly at the trio as he extended his hand to Colin.

"Welcome to our humble home, Professor O'Reilly. We have looked forward to thine arrival for some time now. I'm Benjamin, and this is my wife, Miriam. Our son, John, with whom thee hath corresponded, will be here soon for supper. I hope thee had a good trip. Please come inside and join our other guests.''

"Thank you, Mr. Dunning.'' After shaking the man's hand, Colin addressed the woman standing near him. "And thank you, Mrs. Dunning, for allowing us to stay with you and your family.''

The smiling woman nodded. "We are honored for thee to be here.''

Colin touched his hand to Kacey's shoulder. "This is my daughter, Kacey.'' His other hand went to Rafe's shoulder. "And this is my friend and colleague, Rafael Assante."

Benjamin Dunning shook hands with Rafe and nodded toward Kacey. His wife smiled even more broadly, acknowledging the two younger people before she led the way into a large parlor where three other women, one older and two younger, sat before a large picture window.

The room had little decoration but was simply and comfortably furnished. A pieced denim quilt that served as a carpet covered the center of the floor. The room seemed cozy and inviting despite its large size.

Benjamin Dunning nodded toward the older woman, who held a small Yorkshire terrier in her lap.

"Mrs. McCracken, this is Professor O'Reilly, his daughter, Kacey, and their associate, Rafael Assante. These are the archaeologists that John invited. We will leave thee to make the introductions." Benjamin and Miriam Dunning left the room.

"I'm delighted to meet you and your young people, sir. We've all been looking forward to your arrival, and to our trip to Pueblo Mesita. Mr. Dunning refused to take us until you arrived." As the lithe woman stood, she cradled the small tan-and-gray dog with one hand and extended her free one toward the professor. "Please call me Victoria, Professor O'Reilly." Not waiting for a reply, she moved her gaze and her hand to Kacey. "My dear, you are lovely." With that she moved to Rafe. "And you, monsieur, are most certainly French with a name like that." She moved her eyes rapidly between Kacey and Rafe.

"*Oui,* madame. Please call me Rafe." With those few words, an understanding seemed to develop between Rafe and Victoria McCracken. He took her extended hand and in the French manner brought his lips to touch the back of her hand.

"Monsieur, I won't keep you to myself." The woman whirled to the young women still seated. "Let me introduce you to Miss Rainey Billings and her sister, Elizabeth, who have come from Denver to see the ancient dwellings also.''

Rafe moved to stand in front of the younger women. Rainey raised her hand to him first, and then Elizabeth followed suit. He kissed each hand respectively.

Elizabeth was the first to speak. ''Everyone calls me Beth, monsieur. Elizabeth seems so stuffy, don't you think?'' Her young eyes seemed to glow with something close to adoration.

''*Non,* mademoiselle, Elizabeth is a lovely aristocratic name.'' His heavy French accent seemed to coat the name with gold. ''But on the other hand, Beth is lovely, too.''

Victoria McCracken's strong voice broke into the conversation.

''Kacey, you look very tired. I'm sure Mrs. Dunning would not mind your resting before dinner. I'll show you to your room. I understand that we'll be sharing, if that's all right with you?''

''Why, certainly, Mrs. McCracken. Miss Billings, Elizabeth, will you excuse me?'' Kacey nodded toward the young ladies and followed the courtly woman from the room.

Just outside the parlor, when Kacey and Victoria were alone in the corridor, Victoria began conversation as she led the way to their room.

''Those are delightful young ladies. Beth is just coming into her right as a woman, and she seems very shy. I must admit, however, I was surprised to see her come out of her shell with Monsieur Assante. Of course, I've only known them a few days, but one can learn much about others in such close quarters. Rainey, on the other hand, is more confident. She seems quite fond of John Dunning, and I believe the feeling is returned.''

Victoria saw the expression on Kacey's face and began an immediate apology as she stroked the terrier in her arms.

''Oh, my dear, I'm sorry if I've embarrassed you. I'm

just a doddering old fool who tends to poke my nose into other people's lives. Please forgive me if I've talked too much. I'll leave you alone now. Dinner is at six." She turned to leave but was stopped by Kacey's voice.

"Mrs. McCracken—"

"Victoria, please."

"Victoria . . . thank you."

Kacey smiled at the older woman, who returned the gesture and swept from the room, leaving a faint scent of lavender to float on the air much the way she did.

Kacey gazed around the room at the simple furnishings. Two small, feather beds covered with colorful Navajo blankets sat against opposite walls. A small dresser stood against the wall opposite the door, and the floor was covered with more denim, pieced together to form a striking pattern. When she stepped onto the carpet, its softness thrilled her. She stooped and peeked underneath the material to find that straw had been placed below the covering. Kacey admired Miriam Dunning's creativity and knack for making a lovely, comfortable home in such isolated country.

She moved to the paned window that framed the mountains in the background. The view was breathtaking, and she stood there a long while taking in the beauty of the landscape before she decided to retire to one of the beds for a short nap. Its softness was inviting, and she fully reclined, stretching her body, then curled into a comfortable position and closed her eyes against the weariness of the trip.

Rafe and Colin were enjoying glasses of cool cider when Victoria came back into the parlor.

"I see that you gentlemen have been taken care of. Mrs. Dunning is such a gracious lady, and her cider is the best."

"It is deliciously cool and refreshing. Much the same as the company of you lovely ladies." Colin was looking directly at the older woman, and he surprised himself with

such a bold comment. It must have been the long train trip
that made him so forward. That and the fact that Victoria
McCracken seemed to bring out thoughts that he long ago
had dismissed.

"Why, Professor O'Reilly, you are kind." Victoria
McCracken's voice seemed to take on the quality of that
of a much younger woman, even though she appeared to
be well past the age of forty-five.

Rafe's eyebrows rose at the professor's statement. He
was startled to hear him use flirtatious words. He realized
he had always—unfairly?—thought of the man as well
past the age of enjoying a lovely lady. He decided to keep
quiet and see what else the professor had to say. As he
made his decision, he smiled profusely at the two young
women whose attention was directed his way.

"I'm not kind at all, just truthful. And Victoria is such
a lovely name. It suits you well, my dear."

"Why, thank you, Professor." Victoria studied the professor's face before she continued. "Are you by any
chance a Sagittarius, Professor O'Reilly?"

"Sagittarius? Why, do you mean as in the zodiac?"

"The same. The Karmic Wheel of Life."

"Why, I don't know. I never studied that sort of thing.
Never believed in it."

"I see. Well, don't you think one must be careful when
one dismisses the ideas of others? Sometimes wonderful
experiences might be overlooked if we discard ideas so
casually. When is your birthday, Professor?"

"Colin . . . please. My birthday is December sixteenth."

"That's amazing. Isn't that just unbelievable?"

"What's so unbelievable about it?" Colin asked with
boylike wonder in his voice.

"That ours would be a one-one acquaintance. A blend-
ing of fire and fire. A one-one relationship is unique. It is
like finding your twin soul."

Victoria spoke with such unrestrained excitement in her
voice that it was impossible for Colin not to feel the same

exhilaration. His heart raced at the woman's vitality and her apparent determination to experience life on every level. This was a woman he would like to know better. Even her voice with its mystical quality enthralled him.

Victoria looked at the other guests in the room.

"Do forgive me. I did not mean to slight you from the conversation, but it's been such a long time since I met another Sagittarius."

Rafe rose to her rescue.

"Do not fret, madame, it's been enchanting . . . and educating." Rafe moved his amused gaze to Colin.

At that moment the door to the parlor opened, and a stocky young cowboy holding a Stetson in his hand entered the room. He momentarily glanced toward Rainey Billings before his eyes came to rest on Colin. He moved forward, a quiet assurance evident in his demeanor.

"Professor O'Reilly?"

Colin stood and offered his hand. "You must be John."

"Yes. I hope our guests have been entertaining thee while we have gone about our day-to-day tasks. I'm pleased that thee has finally arrived, and I'm anxious to learn more of the Anasazi."

"I just hope that we can tell you more."

"At least now I will be able to see excavating done in a scientific manner."

John moved his gaze toward Rafe, and Colin made the introduction while the two men shook hands and instantly made summation of the other.

"My daughter, Kacey, is also with us." Colin turned and admiringly glanced toward the older of the three women. "Victoria graciously suggested that she rest before dinner."

"It is quite a long ride from Durango, but I'm sure she will be rested by supper. I look forward to meeting her." John Dunning nodded at the group as a whole as if to leave, then hesitated, his gaze lingering in the direction of Rainey Billings. "Miss Rainey, would you and Miss Beth care to take a ride before supper? I know how you love the horses.''

Rainey Billings's eyes shone as if a candle were lighted in them.

''That sounds lovely, John. We'll meet you outside in a minute.''

Elizabeth looked at her older sister, then at the handsome Frenchman sitting in the chair next to hers. After John Dunning's exit she made her excuse.

''I don't believe that I'll ride today, Rainey. But you go ahead. I know how you love it.''

''If you're sure, Beth?''

''I'm sure.''

Rafe cut into the conversation.

''Mademoiselle, you would be wise to do as your sister says and go ahead. The sun is fast sinking.'' Rafe smiled at Beth, and the young woman's face turned a bright pink as her sister left the room.

Even though Beth would someday be very beautiful, Rafe could tell that she was still quite young. He guessed her to be about fifteen. Just the age of his uncle's ward, Cecelia. God forbid that she was anything like Cecelia. But she wasn't, because Cecelia hadn't blushed since she was ten years old. His uncle's wife constantly threatened to send her to a convent. But badly as she needed discipline, Rafe wouldn't wish that on his worst enemy.

Colin and Victoria lapsed into their own conversation, leaving Rafe and Beth to their own devices.

''Monsieur, please tell me about France. I hear it's very beautiful and I hope to go there someday.''

''*Oui*, mademoiselle, it is magnificent. Green valleys filled with vineyards for winemaking, and of course Paris, the city for lovers. So many cafes and . . . eh . . . the can-can. By all means go there if you have the opportunity.'' Rafe found his conversation with Beth difficult. Most women he talked with were of an age suitable for flirting. She was too young to discuss the pleasures of Paris and too young to flirt with. But at the moment she seemed to need someone with whom she could talk, and Rafe was that person.

"Cancan, monsieur? I'm not familiar with that." Beth's eyes were wide with childlike innocence.

"The, uh . . ." Rafe cleared his throat before continuing. "The cancan is a stage dance that is done in France, mademoiselle."

"Maybe you can show me how it is done. I love dancing. Mama and Papa sponsor many balls in Denver, and maybe I can introduce it to some of Rainey's friends. They treat me like a child. Oh, I would love to be able to teach *them* something."

"*Oui*, mademoiselle . . . maybe I can show you someti—"

Rafe's words broke off as he raised his eyes to see that Kacey had come into the room, and judging from her expression, she had heard everything he had just said.

Rafe shifted his weight in the chair.

"Why, Rafe, I didn't know that you were such an accomplished dancer."

He recognized the sarcasm in Kacey's voice and saw disdain in her eyes. He realized it was pointless to try to explain the innocent conversation and his description of the risqué dance. With this thought he felt reckless.

"*Oui*, I've been to my share of soirées and would be delighted to teach Beth how the French dance." He smiled at the girl, and she echoed the gesture with obvious adoration.

"I'm sure you would, monsieur. And I'm sure her father would be delighted to know that she has learned the cancan."

"On the other hand, *chérie,* you seem to know much more about that dance than I do. I would be delighted to watch while you teach that one." Rafe hid his smile as Kacey's eyes widened, while Beth's trusting gaze moved to her.

At that moment, Victoria made the announcement that Mrs. Dunning had summoned everyone for dinner and to please follow her to the dining room.

Dinner was an extravagant affair set at a large trestle table covered in a clean white cloth. Mr. and Mrs. Dunning, their five sons, and the six guests sat comfortably around the table, which contained a matching set of slightly chipped dinnerware and huge bowls of steaming food. After the group said grace, the meal passed with pleasant conversation. The Dunning sons—John, Clate, Win, Al, and Richard—were extremely well-mannered and courteous.

After the meal, Benjamin announced that there would be music in the den.

Rafe, who along with the others had stood from the table, made his way down the hall beside Kacey to speak in a low voice. "This is your chance to do the cancan, *chérie.*"

Kacey also spoke low. "Monsieur, you are insufferable."

"*Chérie,* you are back to calling me monsieur."

"I could call you a lot of other things, but that would be very unladylike of me, don't you think?"

"Whatever suits you, *chérie.* You have made your mind up no matter what I would say, *n'est-ce pas*?"

"Now, you are trying to compromise young girls. What else would I think?"

"Beth is not a young girl. She is a charming young lady who wants very much to become a woman."

"Well, I'm sure you will be more than happy to accommodate her, monsieur."

"*Chérie,* you have a very dirty mind. I thought you to be so . . . chaste."

Rafe's mocking tone fired Kacey, and she felt she needed a breath of cool night air. She ignored his last statement and headed for the front door while the other guests filed into a room across from the parlor.

Rafe followed her outside, moving to stand behind her. He stretched his arms toward her, then held back. From the veranda the dark sky looked like a large canvas of black velvet splashed with shimmering diamond dust.

"Kacey, please believe me when I say it was not as it sounded."

As her given name rolled off his tongue like a caress, Kacey's veins seemed to heat up of their own volition. She whirled to face him.

"Now, why don't I believe you?"

"Because you only believe what you want to believe." Rafe moved forward, clasping her slender forearms with his strong hold, pulling her roughly, almost violently, to him. "Don't you see that I—" He finished his statement with a searing kiss, hungrily tasting the sweetness of her lips before releasing her to turn and go into the ranchhouse.

Eleven

Rafe's sudden release and departure left Kacey feeling oddly as if someone had snatched part of her self away. When he dared to touch her, her traitorous body came alive with expectation and desire. Desire for the white-hot of his lips once again brought tears to her eyes and her fingers to her lips as her emotions battled over the man who seemed destined to disturb her in every way.

Light filtered onto the veranda through one of the large front windows, and she could hear the sound of a harmonica. A soft breeze stirred tendrils of hair against her face. But Kacey stood there, unable to move in a vortex of turmoil, recalling the feel of Rafe's hands on her body in the hotel room, and the more recent invasion of her lips.

She turned as the door opened behind her.

"Kacey, dear, you've deserted the rest of us. But I can see why."

For a heartrending moment Kacey thought that her father had seen her tears, but then he continued as he tilted his head to look heavenward.

"This Colorado sky is magnificent, isn't it? Did you ever see such a dazzling display of stars?"

Kacey followed his gaze through mist-filled eyes. "It is beautiful, Father."

"Dear, are you all right? You sound . . . distracted."

"I'm fine. It's just been such a long day that I believe I'll turn in early tonight. I hope the others won't take offense."

"I'm sure they'll understand. I'll make your apologies." Colin continued as he patted his daughter's hand, "You go right along to bed and get plenty of rest for tomorrow."

Tomorrow. What would tomorrow bring? Would it stop the aching in her heart? Would it slow her racing pulse at each thought of Rafe's kiss? Would it make her immune to his rakish charm? She prayed it would.

"All right, Father. Thank you for explaining to the others."

They both turned, and Colin opened the door to the entrance. Kacey was glad for the entertainment in the den. Everyone was in there instead of milling about the hall. She quietly made her way to her room, feeling as if the tumbleweed of emotions that stormed through her senses would never find a calm. All her life she had known what she believed in and why she believed it. Now everything seemed to be so mixed up. She had foreign emotions ravaging her every thought, twisting and turning down every alley of her mind until she seemed to have no rational control of her senses.

Back in the den, Colin seated himself in a straight-backed chair next to Victoria McCracken while Clate and Win played a harmonica duet.

"Colin, is Kacey all right? I thought she looked a little pale at dinner."

"She's just tired, Victoria. But thank you for your concern. The train ride from Massachusetts was something of an ordeal for us all, and it's possible that Kacey is feeling the effects. But she's young and resilient. I expect she'll be feeling much better tomorrow. She has retired for the evening and asked me to make her apologies.''

"She certainly doesn't owe an apology. And if there is anything at all that I can do, please let me know.''

"You are a kind person, Victoria. I hope your husband appreciates that in you.'' Colin's eyes sparkled with admiration as his gaze held hers.

Clate and Win sailed into a rendition of "Barbara Allen" as Rafe and Beth, along with John and Rainey, waltzed around the spacious pine-planked floor.

Victoria glanced at the couples as they spun across the room.

"My husband has been dead for many, many years. We were so young and in love when we married that neither of us could see a fault in the other. Martin didn't live long enough to find fault with me, nor I with him.'' Victoria's voice was soft and hushed as she spoke. "Martin was a Gemini. Total air. So masculine and dynamic, truly a force to be reckoned with. When he came into a room, all the women's heads turned in his direction. But I wasn't jealous because I knew my Martin. We were so in love.'' Her voice momentarily took on a quality of wistfulness but soon returned to its former energetic contralto. "That was so many years ago. But I've never found anyone to take his place in my heart.''

"I'm truly sorry you had to lose him.''

"Karma is not always kind to us, Colin, as you know. But we have a mission to flow through the energy field of life, giving it our best cosmic attempt.''

"That's what is so fascinating about you, Victoria. You seem to have such a vigor for life.'' Colin shuffled in his seat and leaned slightly toward the woman.

She momentarily glanced at Rafe before returning her gaze to Colin. "Monsieur Assante reminds me of Martin to a great degree. He seems to be very taken with your daughter, but look how he is smiling at Beth and making her feel very much a lovely young woman. He seems to sense her need for recognition at this moment, but when he looks at her it is as if he is smiling at a younger sister. Please forgive me for babbling, but I couldn't help but notice this afternoon that he looks at Kacey in a very different manner. He seems to wear his feelings for her on his coat sleeve." Her voice trailed off as she finished, "I wonder . . . I must find out their signs."

Colin laughed good-naturedly. "My dear Victoria, nothing would make me happier than for Kacey to find the right young man. And if Rafe turned out to be that young man, then I would be even more elated. But she seems to think that I need taking care of and that she is the only one to do it. Bless her dear heart, she has been a great comfort to me since her mother's death. But I certainly want her happiness above everything else."

"In these matters, Colin, a horoscope is invaluable." She paused then added, "And there are times when Destiny requires a gentle nudge."

Colin's expression of doubt seemed to amuse Victoria as she lowered her eyelids and cast him a provocative smile, one that dared him to watch her in action.

"I believe it is past my bedtime, Colin. I'll see you in the morning."

Colin bid her adieu, and Victoria rose from her chair. She said her other good-nights and left the room with her small dog in her arms, navigating the dim hallway to the room that she was to share with Kacey. She gently knocked at the door before entering the darkened bedroom.

"Victoria? Is it you?"

Kacey's sluggish speech implied to the widow that she had awakened the young woman. She stood for a moment as her eyes adjusted to the dimness, lighted only by the moonlight cascading through the half-opened window.

"My dear, please forgive me for waking you."

Kacey's voice became more articulate. "You didn't wake me. I was just getting settled into bed myself."

Victoria moved toward the empty bed and released the terrier onto the soft coverlet.

"I know you are exhausted after your long journey. I am turning in rather early myself tonight. It does seem to have been a long day. The others are so energetic and having a lovely time in the den. Monsieur Assante and Beth are such a handsome couple, don't you think so, dear?'' Victoria paused as a grunt rumbled from the direction of Kacey's bed. "Of course, Beth is still so very young, but true love knows no boundaries, and I am such a romantic.''

"Well, I'm sure Monsieur Assante hasn't a drop of romanticism in his blood. He is a dyed-in-the-wool rake, and I think someone should warn Miss Billings.''

"I think you are wrong, my dear. Why, if you could have seen them together . . .'' Victoria sighed before catching a quick breath to continue. "The way he smiled at her, why, there was no mistaking his feelings.''

The small, furry animal jumped from the bed and began to bark frantically, much resembling a barking wig.

"Oh, my, I forgot to take Isis out for her nightly stroll, and she's upset with me. Please forgive the disturbance, Kacey. I'll just take her out for a while, and we'll slip back in as quietly as possible.''

In the ample moonlight Victoria rose from the bed, reached into her skirt pocket, and pulled out a small leash and collar. She soon had the terrier ready for its bedtime stroll, and the woman and dog left the room, leaving Kacey to ponder the revelation concerning Rafe and Beth. Surely Victoria had mistaken the situation. But what if she hadn't? What if Rafe really had been smitten with Beth Billings? After all, she was quite beautiful. Suddenly the room seemed stifling; Kacey threw the coverlet back and sat bolt upright in bed. She needed to get some air. Isis was not the only one who needed to go outside.

She reached for her robe at the foot of the bed and donned the wrapper while slipping slender feet into soft mules beside her bed. She quickly went to the door and opened it quietly, at the same time peering into the empty hallway. She had discovered earlier that the door at the end of the hall was an outside door. She fled in that direction, her long robe flowing as she walked.

Kacey strolled in the moonlight, taking the cool evening air into her lungs. She pulled her robe closer around her as a chill threatened with a sharp breeze. Without realizing it, she had come near the room where music filtered through a window, and she could not resist the overwhelming urge to see inside. She drew closer to the window and mentally cursed the lace curtains that hung over the glass like a spider's web. She strained her eyes to see better, but all she could make out was the outline of two pairs of dancers who seemed to glide around the room.

"Ah, *chérie,* you wanted to go to the dance but were too shy, *n'est-ce pas?*"

Rafe's low, husky voice startled her from behind, making her skin tingle as if a million merciless straight pins had been catapulted at her before the sensation subsided into a weakness that left her knees near the buckling point. She spun to face the mocking voice so near her ear.

"Why are you spying on me?" She fought to keep her tremulous voice hushed.

"It would seem that you are the spy, *chérie.* I am simply out for a breath of fresh air. It is amazing what one can find in the moonlight. Have you ever noticed that, *chérie?*" As he spoke, he moved to stand within inches of her swiftly rising and falling chest. "I certainly never expected to find a heavenly wraith trailing about tonight. But here you are in the flesh. Now, what am I to do with you?" In the bright moonlight Kacey's eyes appeared large and luminous.

"Monsieur, do not concern yourself. You are to do nothing with me. I am not yours to do anything with." Rafe's muscled frame seemed to tower over her, so much so that she felt small and vulnerable in his presence, even as she tried to portray strength with her voice. "As you are, monsieur, I am at liberty to move about freely day or night. So if you will excuse me, I will be about my business.'' She moved to release her body from his gaze and began to retrace her steps toward the back of the house.

Her haughty dismissal launched an atavistic urge in Rafe. His arms snaked out to take what he wanted and desired. In the shadow of the gable he roughly pulled her soft body to him, waylaying her attempts of release. With his superior strength he pressed their bodies together like a vise while his fevered lips plundered the soft mouth of the woman who paradoxically rubbed at his nerves like sandpaper. Never before had he burned so deeply with craving as he did now. Kacey's length had melded to his own, and he felt his manifestation of need press into the softness of her stomach. Rafe kissed her eyes, then moved to shower her hair with a spray of kisses. His hold loosened as he realized she was clinging to him in a way as old as time. Whether she realized it or not, there was no mistaking that she was offering her body to him in this moment of fevered hunger.

Realization hit Rafe like a bottle of champagne at a ship's christening. He mentally pulled back to distance himself for rational thought, at the same time loosening his embrace. An embrace, he mused, that resembled that of a drowning man clinging to a life buoy.

Rafe was the first to speak.

''*Chérie,* why do you make it a habit to run around at night in your bedclothes?'' Rafe's husky voice betrayed his composure.

''There's nothing wrong with my robe. You can barely see it anyway. And why are you always lurking in the darkness?''

Rafe was relieved to hear that the old Kacey had returned. The old Kacey who would not be soft and yielding under his caresses.

''I suppose for the same reason that you are always running around in your bedclothes when we meet.''

''Monsieur, you are a rake of the first degree.''

"You . . . ahem . . . did not seem to think so just a moment ago, *chérie.*"

"Forget a moment ago. I—"

Rafe tightened his hold on her arms. "I will never forget a moment ago, and neither will you." His tone was velvet edged with steel. "I'd better go now before I forget that I am not some primitive man on the prowl for a woman to warm my bed." He paused then added with a possessive desperation in his voice, "But I forgot, *chérie,* you do prefer prehistoric men, don't you? The kind that cannot gaze into your eyes and see the passion burning there. The kind that cannot feel the restrained desire with every kiss."

Rafe's voice seemed edged with control as he released Kacey. Then, turning on his heel, he left her standing alone in the moonlight for the second time that night. Her lips smarted now from his kisses, and her pulse pounded a frenzied rhythm like a drumbeat at an aboriginal ceremony.

She stood there in the moonlight, its ethereal glow casting strange shadows across the tree-studded yard. A breeze rustled the cottonwood leaves, and the movement appeared as ebony apparitions on the ground below. Kacey pulled her lightweight robe closer about her neck as she started for the back of the house. Only moments before, all the starkness of the night had been banished in Rafe's arms. But he had disappeared into the darkness as if he had never even been there beside her, caressing her and kissing her as if they were the only two people on earth. Kacey fought with her errant emotions—emotions that made her feel like a woman who desired a man. The one thing she had never had to deal with before. All other men seemed to pale in Rafe's presence. *Why, oh why, did he have to come into her life at this time?*

Kacey found her way in the moonlight to the entry nearest her bedroom. She slowly opened the door and peered into the hallway. Finding it deserted, she padded to her bedroom entrance and quietly went inside.

Inside the room Victoria had lit a candle, and she sat at

the small dresser in a simple dressing gown, brushing the long length of her light brown hair sparsely salted with threads of silver. Earlier the mass had been swept onto her head in a Psyche knot, adding to her stature and regal bearing. Now, in the soft light, Kacey saw a different Victoria, one who appeared almost girlish.

Isis reclined on a scarlet blanket at the foot of the still-made bed. Her small sentinel ears moved back and forth, adding to her pixielike appearance as her small tongue rolled up like a carrot curl.

Kacey walked toward her own bed and sat on its edge. Her gaze was drawn to Victoria's in the mirror.

"Kacey, is anything wrong? You were almost asleep when I left you, and I was surprised to find you gone when I returned."

"Just had to make a trip to the ... uh ... privy outside." Kacey felt the need for further explanation as the lie rolled from her tongue. "It could have been something I ate." At that her eyes grew larger as she realized the insult to Miriam Dunning's cooking. She continued as she tried to cover the insinuation. "Oh, but I'm sure it was the food at the hotel this morning."

"Yes, I've found that hotel food can be bilious to one's system." Victoria smiled into the mirror. "Almost as bilious as love."

Kacey turned slightly from the woman's gaze in the mirror. "I've never been in love, so I wouldn't know about that."

"My dear, love sometimes comes up on one's blind side much like a bee. And you know what pesky creatures they can be."

Kacey laughed softly at the analogy before Victoria continued in an exaggerated apology. Her voice sounded suspiciously too dramatic. "I hope I didn't upset you by talking about Beth and Rafe."

Immediately Kacey's attention homed in on green eyes reflected in the mirror—eyes that seemed to read through to her soul. "Why, of course not. I think I told you my feelings regarding Rafael Assante."

Victoria lowered her gaze. "Yes, you did. And I'm sure you have a good reason for feeling as you do. Perhaps I shall change my opinion of Monsieur Assante if you feel so strongly about his character."

Too quickly Kacey came to his defense. "Well, I suppose he's not all that bad. It's just that he is such a womanizer."

"How long have you known him?"

"I met him briefly last fall in New York, and of course we have been in each other's company all the way from Cambridge."

"Then you must have seen him behave outrageously to have formed such an opinion."

Kacey thought back on her association with Rafael Assante and could not think of any instance when he had been anything but a gentleman . . . except with her. She lowered her eyelids and felt her skin flush, and Victoria abruptly changed the subject.

"My dear, you should let me do a star chart for you. I do them for all my friends. That is, if you don't mind."

Kacey raised her eyes and with laughter in her voice, she replied, "Sounds like it might be fun, but I have to warn you. I am my father's daughter and I am a trifle skeptical of such things."

"My dear, that's perfectly all right." She stood and moved to a small table where she retrieved a writing pad and pencil, then seated herself beside Kacey. "Just tell me when and where you were born. I need the exact time, as in minutes, and place."

"Oh, my, I'll have to think." She paused. "Mother wrote all that in the family Bible. After she died I used to sit and read it over and over just to see her lovely penmanship. It was almost as if it were a link to her." Kacey turned her head, briefly stricken once again at her mother's untimely death.

"Kacey, I'm sorry if I have caused you grief by asking you to remember." Regret was apparent in Victoria's tone.

Kacey returned her gaze to the other woman. "Oh, no. It's just that sometimes I feel more emotional than at other times. I loved my mother very much. Father, Mother, and I were always together." She gently laughed. "That's why I was born in Costa Rica, and on February 29th of all days, eighteen sixty-four."

"Do you know the exact location?"

"Yes, it was near the village of Upala. I understand that I was nearly a month early, which upset Father's plan to make sure Mother was back at a friend's banana plantation beforehand. She was as much an enthusiast of archaeology as Father and wasn't about to be left behind while he investigated ruins quite a distance from there."

"And what time were you actually born?"

"It was in the afternoon." She looked toward the white-washed ceiling as if the act would help the thought process. "Yes, I remember now from Mother's entry. It was two thirty-three."

"Sounds like your mother was quite headstrong and adventurous, qualities I admire in a woman as well as a man. This will take some time. We'll put it away for tonight. I know you are tired, and so am I." Victoria moved to remove the candle from the dresser and place it on the small table beside her bed. "Are you ready to put out the light?"

"Yes, go ahead. The moonlight is so beautiful streaming through the window."

Kacey lay back on her bed and pulled a light cover over her. In the quietness of the room she tried to gather the skein of thoughts marching through her mind, but the memory of Rafe's hands caressing her body drove all else from her.

Overhead, a mourning dove cooed from the low limb of a cottonwood. Rafe lay next to Kacey on a soft bed of em-

*erald moss. The clear brook beside them trickled an en-
chanting melody as Rafe turned to her and spooned his
body to match her own. His shirt was open to the waist,
and through the thin material of her lawn dress, she could
feel the springy mat of thick hair on his chest. He nuzzled
her neck, and his shadow of beard rubbed against her soft
flesh, sending waves of desire washing over her. She
moved her body deeper into the crook of his. Suddenly he
was kissing her shoulder, the nape of her neck, then tracing a path back to nibble at her ear. Kacey smiled at the
joy of having him so near and doing such wonderful things
to her body—things she had fought against before. But
now it seemed so right in this ethereal place. Kacey moved
to her back and smiled as his lips pressed against hers.*

Suddenly his kisses turned wet against her cheek, and a
brightness filtered through to her pupils. She struggled
against reality, but opened heavy eyelids to find the source
of light that had disturbed her blissful visions. The warmth
of the morning sun covered her face. The brilliant orb
shone through the window in dazzling display, blinding
her momentarily. But when her eyes focused, she fought
against shrieking, controlling herself instead, as the small,
long-haired terrier lapped at her mouth with its tiny tongue.

Twelve

The troupe of professional and amateur archaeologists rode toward Pueblo Mesita. John Dunning had announced at breakfast that he and his brother Clate would be able to lead the party to the ruins, at least a half-day's ride from the ranch. They had bought supplies at Mancos in the morning, and they would all reach the site by nightfall.

Kacey's chestnut mare handled easily as she navigated the rock-strewn path. On the trail ahead, Colin drove the supply wagon, and Victoria sat beside him, her terrier ensconced between them on the seat. Kacey turned her head and saw that Rafe and Beth seemed amused at something as they rode side by side, the girl mesmerized by his wicked charm. She returned her gaze to the trail in front of her while an unfamiliar emotion threatened her peace of mind. The sullen look in Clate's eyes at breakfast told Kacey that he had been the object of Beth's attention before Rafe had arrived on the scene. She remembered Rafe's lips pressed against her own in the moonlight, and fingers of heat brushed across her cheeks at the recollection.

Dark clouds formed in the sky as they reached the

mesa's summit. Kacey's eyes focused on the underbrush ahead. The riders ahead slowed their pace, and she looked closer at the scrub. Beyond its weblike greenery she saw the low, tumbled walls of a structure.

"Pueblo Mesita," Kacey whispered, focusing her attention on the deserted sandstone dwelling that seemed framed in eternity through its veil of underbrush. The others had dismounted, and she did the same. Her light-blue riding skirt and shirtwaist stuck to her damp body as she made her way toward her father, who was assisting Victoria from the wagon.

"Thank you, Colin." Victoria smoothed the long folds of her fawn-colored skirt before reaching for Isis, who barked furiously and spun in circles like a whirlwind on the wagon seat. She wrapped the small dog in the circle of her arm.

Kacey couldn't keep from smiling at the lively Isis, who demanded attention. "I think she's afraid you're going to leave her here alone while you have all the fun, Victoria."

"She would never allow that to happen." Victoria moved her gaze to her canine companion. "Would you, precious?"

At that moment a bolt of lightning struck nearby, sending the occupants on the mesa scrambling to make camp. John and Clate moved quickly, with the older of the two shouting orders. Colin and Rafe rushed in to help. All the women except Kacey took the suggestion to head for the shelter of the canvas covering on the supply wagon. When the downpour came, she was beside her father helping to drive tent stakes into the ground. The deluge continued mercilessly, and Kacey was glad she had taken the time to retrieve her slicker from her saddlebag. Despite the flood of rain, soon two tents stood near the underbrush that partially hid the pueblo. John and Clate moved to stretch a tarpaulin between low trees to make a shelter for the horses.

Colin yelled above the torrent, "Kacey, you'd better get inside the tent!"

"Not until you do, Father!" Kacey shouted back.

"All right, let's go! I think the stakes will hold!" Colin and Kacey ran for cover inside the tent.

As Kacey pulled off her hood from her head, she turned to see Rafe standing just inside the entrance, a Stetson pulled low over his dark eyes. He was holding two cups of steaming brew that he offered to her and Colin. In that instant her opinion of him skyrocketed. The man might look like a devil, but he was an angel. An angel offering hot liquid in the chill of the room.

"Professor, the ladies prepared coffee and heated some tins inside the wagon. I thought that you and . . . Mademoiselle Kacey would like some."

Colin reached for the mugs and handed one to Kacey. "Lad, you're a godsend."

Rafe shrugged. "*Non*, Professor. You would have done the same for me."

Kacey smiled at him. "It was very kind of you, . . . Rafe, to bring the coffee. Thank you."

"You are welcome." Rafe did not move, but continued his perusal of Kacey. His body refused to leave the warmth the woman's smile offered him, while his mind refused to believe what he saw. He stammered as he hadn't done in years. "W-when you are ready, there is warm food at the supply wagon." With those words, Rafe turned on his heel and left the tent.

The only light visible now came from the supply wagon, and he headed in that direction. Lightning flashed to his left, and the rain continued to pound in a frenzied rhythm that matched the racing of his heart. Kacey. The woman was a riddle. Just now inside the tent she seemed . . . almost glad to see him. He could have sworn . . . *Ah la vache,* damn. Rafe shook his head and waded through the mud to the supply wagon. When he stuck his head inside, Beth's easy smile was such a contrast to Kacey's seemingly reluctant one. Hell, he didn't remember Kacey ever truly smiling for him . . . until just now.

Kacey relished each sip of the hot liquid as it made its way to every chilled recess of her body, and was grateful to Rafe for the kindness.

The storm seemed to pound even stronger on the canvas tent. "I've never seen it rain any harder, Father, and I don't believe that it's going to let up anytime soon. I'm going to the supply wagon to see about something to eat and to get my bed linens. Would you like me to bring you a plate?"

"Hold up a minute, and I'll come with you. Just let me finish this last bit of brew," Colin said, drinking the remnants of the coffee. The two pulled their hoods into place and went out into the storm. The ground was saturated and made the going difficult. Kacey held onto her father not so much to steady herself but to make sure that he did not fall. When they reached the lighted supply wagon, she quickly walked up the makeshift steps, then turned to make sure her father was right behind her. He followed her into the shelter as Beth and Rainey scrambled to make room for the new arrivals while they shed their slickers.

The light in Victoria's eyes brightened as she saw her new acquaintances. "I'm sure you're both starving after battling the rain. We've put together a light meal. Let me fix your plates," she offered, and began piling food onto a dish.

"Thank you, Victoria," Kacey and Colin said together, then Kacey added, "You can give that to Father, and I can fix mine. You've done enough already, and it looks grand." As she spoke she reached for a tin plate and began to fill it from the large pot.

Within seconds Victoria handed Colin a plate of food as warm as the smile she wore, then spoke in her cryptic way, aiming her gaze toward Kacey.

"My dear, it sounds like it's raining cats and dogs, as

the saying goes, and this is a fine example of how water and air can be stirred into lashing waves. They don't normally mix at all, you know."

"Well, they're certainly battling it out right now, Victoria. The deluge out there is one of the worst I've ever seen. It's a good thing we're on high ground, or I think we would be wishing for Noah's ark." Kacey's banter brought a smile to Victoria's lips.

"Just the same, dear, it's a magnificent display of the elements, don't you think?"

"I guess if you look at it in that light, it is breathtaking," Kacey conceded before she continued to eat more of her corned beef and cheese while Victoria and Colin exchanged conversation.

Kacey set her plate aside when she had finished eating. "I'm going to the tent, but you ladies will have room in here to sleep. There's no use in your coming out into the storm." Amid a rash of objections from the other women, Kacey found the items she needed and lit one of the many lanterns on hand. "Father, are you ready to make your way to your quarters? We can wade the flood together if you like."

"Of course, dear. Just let me get my cot and blanket, and I'll join the others." He moved to retrieve the items he needed and followed Kacey from the wagon amid a flurry of good-nights.

Kacey had set up her cot and was moving to undress when she heard a noise near the opening of her tent. She turned to hear her name above the din of the storm and made her way to the covered entrance. When she pulled back the flap, Rafe stood at the doorway, and his presence surprised her. As always when she was near him, her heart raced. Unlike before, however, tonight she did not seem immune to his charm. The open invitation in his eyes served to catch her off guard, and momentarily she took a step backward before she spoke, her voice shakier than she would have liked.

"Rafe, is something wrong?"

"*Non*, mademoiselle, I just wanted to make sure that you are all right."

"Of course, I am. But I . . . appreciate your concern."

"May I come inside? The rain is merciless."

Kacey hesitated, then nodded and moved aside to let the Frenchman enter before she turned and walked further into the room. She turned again to face him, her pulse quickening and causing her to rush on. "Monsieur, I do appreciate your taking the time to check on me, but as you can see, I'm just about to settle down for the night, and really I . . . don't think it's appropriate for you to be here."

"You mean you would send me back out into that deluge so soon, mademoiselle? Your shelter looks *so* inviting."

The smile in Rafe's eyes contained a dangerous flame, while the smile on his lips teased her.

"Please go, Rafe. Your presence here just complicates matters." Her breathless whisper seemed to deny her words while Rafe moved to stand within inches of her, looking as though he would reach out and devour her.

"I see. You have told me before that your father needs you. Is that the complication you speak of?" The noise Rafe made resembled a snort. "Have you looked at your father lately? If you would, you'd probably see also that he doesn't need you. Madame McCracken seems to fit that bill very well."

"What is that supposed to mean? Are you insinuating that my father would compromise a lady?"

"I am insinuating that your father is very taken with Victoria McCracken. Whether he would compromise her or not . . . I'm sure that is up to the lady." Rafe reached to pull Kacey to him as he continued almost feverishly. "Open your eyes, *chérie*."

"I do have my eyes open, sir, and I want you to leave

this instant.'' Kacey struggled to pull away from Rafe's hold, but he tightened his grip.

"Do you, *ma chérie,* I wonder? When you're all snuggled into your cozy bed like a proper lady, tell me what you dream at night. Tell me whose arms embrace you.''

When she saw his lips descending on hers, she felt panic rioting within her. His searing lips were more persuasive than she cared to admit, and she closed her eyes to revel in his touch. When his kiss deepened, she realized the path her emotions were taking and she pulled away. Her chest rose and fell while she demanded breathlessly, "I asked you to leave. Will you do so now?''

"*Oui,* as you wish, mademoiselle.'' Rafe paused, his eyes ablaze with desire. He ached to sweep her proud form into his arms and hold her until she admitted her attraction to him. But instead he merely declared, ''Sleep well, *chérie.*'' Sarcasm was heavy on his curled lips as he bowed, then turned and walked into the rain.

The morning dawned with a pale light filtering through the canvas. Kacey stretched the kinks from her body and looked around the otherwise empty tent. She pushed the blanket away and got up, gently pulling the tent flap back. The sun had barely begun to make its ascent above the horizon, but a few wispy clouds and the brightening sky created a lovely display of mauve and gold, with not a trace of last night's storm.

Kacey could wait no longer to see the ruins. She had always loved an adventure and she felt in her bones that this was going to be a great one. She dressed in a khaki split skirt and white shirtwaist and went outside. The camp was quiet, and she did not want to disturb anyone this early. Actually, she was glad the others had not yet awakened. Seeing the pueblo alone would give her the opportunity to sense the mystery of it all and to get a feel for the lives of earlier inhabitants. She relished that feeling. She would like her father to be there, too, but she couldn't

wake him without disturbing the others. With that thought,
the image of a certain Frenchman formed in her mind. The
memory of his dark, overpowering eyes seemed to increase
her heartbeat. Drat the man! Would she forever be haunted
by his arrogance? She tossed her head to shake the image
and walked softly toward the ruins.

The sun was higher now, and in the bright morning light
the dwelling seemed to be waiting for its inhabitants to
come alive and start their morning rituals. But the fact was
that the true story of the previous occupants was lost forever in the ruins unless someone could piece together its
past from the relics that Kacey hoped to find. She remembered Bill Finn's words about an Indian curse, and seeing
this place for herself, she could almost believe it. The stillness was suddenly almost stifling. She decided that now
would be a good time to get a photograph and started toward camp to get the camera and equipment. As she
turned, a loud hissing stopped her in her tracks. Not three
feet in front of her, a rattler dared her to move. A voice,
low and deliberate, reached her ears.

"Don't move, Miss O'Reilly. Just close your eyes and
don't move, whatever happens."

Kacey started when the gunshot vibrated through her
ears. Instantly she opened her eyes and saw the dead snake
in front of her, its head blown apart from its body. John
Dunning was repositioning his rifle and coming toward
her.

"Are you all right, miss?"

"Yes, thanks to you, John. D-Do you think we'll see a
lot of snakes out here?"

"Yes, ma'am, I 'spect so. Just be on your guard and
you should be all right. They're pesky creatures for sure,
scaring the living daylights out of everybody."

The shot brought the rest of the group from camp. Colin
rushed to his daughter's side.

"Kacey, are you hurt?"

"No, Father, thanks to John. I don't believe that snake

was going to let me pass.'' Kacey tried to lighten the moment, but her gentle laugh did not conceal the concern in her voice.

Rafe stood near Kacey, and the fact that she had been in danger shocked him. He wanted to go to her and hold her, but he knew from past experience that his attentions would be unwelcome. Instead, he clenched his fists at his side and fought the wave of protectiveness that came over him. From now on he would keep an eye on her himself. The Dunnings might not always be around when they were needed.

Soon the crowd dispersed, and Kacey went to the wagon to retrieve the camera. By the time she got back, the others had begun to explore the ruins with Rafe's lead. She had to ask them to step aside long enough for the picture to be taken. She wanted the ruins to look as they did the first time she set eyes on them—deserted, except for the spirits of those gone before. After she took the photo, she asked the others to be a part of another picture. She put in another plate and bent behind the camera, putting the covering over her head. She looked through the lens at Rafe and the others standing beside him. Even upside down, the contrast of his height and darkness beside them was startling. Her senses reeled at his rugged good looks, and she took longer than was necessary to snap the picture.

''Kacey, are you having trouble with the camera?''

''No, Father, I'm ready now,'' she mumbled from underneath the cloth and took the photo.

Rafe came walking toward her, and she immediately removed the cloth from her head and stood straight.

''Mademoiselle, why don't you and your father step into the picture, and I will take it for you?''

Colin spoke up before Kacey could answer. ''That's a splendid idea, Rafe. Come along, dear.'' He led his daughter to the rest of the group and came to stand beside Victoria. The action did not escape Kacey, and the discovery hit her full force. Her father *was* smitten with Victoria McCracken. A multitude of emotions whirled through Kacey: happiness for her father, sadness for her mother, and an unexplainable sense of loss for herself. She suddenly felt isolated in the midst of the crowd.

When Rafe finished taking the picture, Kacey's eyes widened to see an old man in full Indian attire standing far behind Rafe, looking toward the camp. His skin appeared dark and wrinkled, and a folded cloth that served as a headband covered his brow. His straight black hair hung in braids down his chest. A colorful blanket was draped over one shoulder, and he looked like a spirit come to life. Kacey swallowed hard while John Dunning moved in his direction.

"Acowitz, I see you found us, friend."

"And I see you did not heed my warning. It is not good when you disturb the spirits of the old people, the ancient ones. The young are foolish in many ways."

"Acowitz, no trouble is going to come. I've asked these scientists to come here to tell us more about the Anasazi."

Colin walked toward them, and John introduced him.

"Professor O'Reilly, this is my friend Acowitz. He is the one who told me this place existed. . . ." John paused and lowered his head momentarily before he continued. "Without really showing me where it was."

Colin offered his hand, and the Indian took it with a firm grip.

"I'm glad to meet you, sir. John has spoken highly of you in his letters. I assure you we'll do as little damage as possible to the pueblo." Colin turned and motioned for Kacey and Rafe to come forward before turning back to the Indian.

"Let me acquaint you with my associates." The professor indicated each one with his hand. "My daughter, Kacey, and my friend, Rafael Assante."

The old Indian nodded, then turned once again to John Dunning. "When you disturb the spirits of the dead, then

you die." After the solemn words the man walked with
noble bearing toward the mesa brush.

Kacey was the first to speak. "My, he seemed upset,
didn't he?"

"Acowitz is an old man. He is just relaying what he
believes to be true. The Indians here are very superstitious
where their dead are concerned." John turned and walked
toward the camp.

Colin removed the hat he wore and brushed the hair
from his brow. "Well, my dear, it's now or never. Let's
get started."

"I'm ready, Father. I'll get the trowels and brushes
ready." Kacey left Colin and Rafe standing together in the
morning sun.

Colin talked in a low voice to the Frenchman. "Lad,
it'll be to our benefit to keep our eyes and ears open, don't
you think?"

"*Oui*, Professor. I am much more suspicious of the living than the dead."

The morning's work advanced without further incident. A
dig site had been established, and the three archaeologists
worked tediously, slowly, and carefully to remove the top
layer of dirt from a small, designated portion of the pueblo.
The rest of the party lingered nearby, hoping to help in
some way. Small shards of pottery were found and carefully brushed and catalogued, then carted away by John
and Clate for safekeeping. The midday meal was served
at the site by Victoria, Rainey, and Beth. This allowed the
workers minimal lost time in their endeavors.

Kacey found a complete piece of pottery, and as she
held the ancient artwork in her hands she delighted in its
simplistic beauty, taking in the delicate painted lines that
the artisan had worked. While she cleaned its surface with
extreme caution, she was distracted by something from the
corner of her eye. She looked up to see in the distance
another Indian, much younger and seemingly more threat-

ening than the one she had met earlier that morning. His
countenance seemed a mask of stone, with a cold, contorted expression. She shivered at the sheer savage appearance of him, then scolded herself for allowing the
man's demeanor to intimidate her. Putting him from her
mind, she returned to her slow, significant task.

Thirteen

Digging was easier because of the rain, and Kacey found numerous items of interest just below the soil surface. Beth and Rainey wanted to be a part of the expedition, and Kacey had put them to work cleaning, matching, and gluing shards of ancient pottery. Colin had taken Victoria under his wing, and he was instructing her in the science, while Isis roamed nearby. John and Clate, eager to learn about archaeology, stayed close to Rafe. Pueblo Mesita had once again come to life as the professionals and amateurs worked side by side.

Kacey could not keep the old Indian's words from her mind as she dug in the soil. "It is not good when you disturb the spirits of the ancient ones." She unconsciously shivered as Acowitz's words reverberated in her brain.

The spell was broken by Rainey Billings's voice.

"We've put together two very beautiful pieces, Kacey, if you'd like to come and look at them."

"All right, I'll be along in a minute. Thank you." Kacey watched the young woman turn and retrace her steps. Then her eyes moved toward her father, who along with Victoria seemed to be completely absorbed in his work. Kacey

knew she was being foolish to feel the emotions that
surged through her. She recognized the jealousy that swept
her mind and was ashamed. But she had always been close
to her father for as long as she could remember, and the
idea that someone else might possibly take her place
caused her serious thought. She tried to brush the feelings
aside and to think of Victoria as she might if her father
were not involved. She realized that if she were honest
with herself, she would admit that she liked Victoria very
much.

Putting those thoughts behind her, she stood and proceeded to the area near the camp where the potsherds were
displayed. The morning's work had afforded several broken shards of Anasazi pottery, and the two complete pieces
that Rainey had spoken of were also there. She walked
toward the artifacts and stooped to get a better view. Not
wanting to disturb the glue, she did not touch the pieces
but admired their artistic and historic value.

"Quite a morning's work, mademoiselle. We seem to
be doing very well."

At once Kacey recognized the French accent behind her.
She stood and turned to face the man who always managed
to put her on edge. Without a word, she allowed Rafe to
continue.

"John has told me about another pueblo not far from
here. About an hour away, he said, due east. I think I will
investigate it. Do you care to join me?"

"Does anyone else know you are going?"

"*Non.* Everyone else seems to be quite occupied here.
Is mademoiselle afraid to travel alone with me?" Rafe
arched his brows in silent challenge.

Feeling quite reckless and alone, Kacey flung the words,
"Monsieur, I'm not afraid of anything, especially you."

"Very well, come with me."

"I'll meet you at the horses. I don't want Father to
worry."

She and Rafe were soon riding east. It was midafternoon, and Kacey was relieved that the sun was behind them. Sweat formed around the band of her wide-brimmed hat, making tendrils of soft curls against her neck. The same liquid that curled her hair trickled in the cleavage between her breasts, and Kacey fought the urge to wipe at the perspiration that felt too much like an insect against her skin. She focused on the journey ahead, acutely aware of Rafe's presence beside her. Never before had she noticed the fit of a man's pants. Never before had it played havoc with her senses. His khaki pants were snug against his thighs, and his matching shirt fit across his chest with the same tailored style. Kacey started when Rafe spoke.

"Have you always been interested in archaeology, mademoiselle?"

"Yes, always. I suppose it's in my blood. When I was five I was asked by a visitor, 'And what do you want to do when you grow up, Katherine?' I counted off on my fingers, 'I want to dig for buried treasure, and explore among the Indians, and paint pictures, and wear a gun, and go to college.' "

"And have you done all those things?" Rafe's voice was low and husky from the radiant picture Kacey's face made when she answered. He found it difficult to make small talk, as the night before frequented his memory like a long-awaited treasure.

"I've never worn a gun." There was a trace of laughter in Kacey's voice as the easy conversation served to lighten her mood. Suddenly, and without warning, the mare she rode limped, then stopped its steady walking gait. She looked toward Rafe to speak, but he was already dismounting.

"What is wrong, mademoiselle?" he asked, quickly walking the short distance to her.

"I'm not sure. Could be a stone." Kacey dismounted and walked to stand beside Rafe, who was already checking the mare's hoof.

"I don't see anything that could be hurting her. But why

not ride with me just in case? We will go slow, and she will be all right without your added weight.''

"Don't you think we should head back to Pueblo Mesita?"

"I don't see why. We should be very near the pueblo now if we have stayed on course. When we get there we will let the horses rest. I will mount first, then you come up behind me." Every pulse in Rafe's body surged at the thought of Kacey's body pressed next to his. It would be all he could do to keep his thoughts sane. He steeled himself for the contact and mounted his horse, pulling Kacey up behind him. She held her body away from him, and he sensed the effort she used to keep the small distance between them.

Kacey held to the reins of the mare behind them, and Rafe urged his horse forward, the act forcing her to reach around his waist to have something to hold on to. There was no keeping her distance now. Her breasts pressed into his muscled back as she clung to him to secure her seat on the jostling steed. Kacey prayed that it was not much farther to the Indian ruins. A heat that had nothing to do with the sun seemed to be consuming her. Instinctively she leaned her head against Rafe. Now her whole body seemed to long for his touch and to touch him. She was thankful that he could not see into her mind at this moment. She felt an abandon that frightened her, yet thrilled her at the same time.

"I see the ruins, Kacey. We are almost there."

Kacey did not reply. Rafe's voice seemed to come from far away as it penetrated her thoughts. Yet . . . he, too, sounded strange and . . . distracted. Moments later when he stopped the horse and dismounted, Kacey's relief matched her loss as she was separated from him.

Rafe turned to help Kacey dismount. His heart hammered in his chest. *Mon Dieu*, the woman was an enchantress. Her nearness had him in a state of turmoil and need that was manifest against the material of his trousers.

When she brushed against him as she touched the ground, her eyes met his. His gaze seemed more daring now, and Kacey's grew bolder, seemingly feeding from his. Their eyes locked, and in that minute expanse, she knew. *She wanted Rafael Assante, and he wanted her.* She had never desired a man before, and now she understood the why and how. She watched, enthralled, as Rafe's full lips descended toward her own and claimed them in near reverence.

The kiss started slowly and gently while he wrapped her body in the fold of his arms. He slowly caressed the soft lines of her back in a motion that swept from her neck to her hips, where he paused to gently press her feminine curves. Kacey moved in an effort to mold her length to him, all the while feeling the need to get even closer. Dormant emotions surfaced like an erupting volcano, and she equaled him in the fierceness of their kiss. Rafe reluctantly pulled his head back, and Kacey opened her eyes to gaze once more into his.

Without saying a word, his gaze never leaving hers, he lifted her into his arms and carried her to a sheltered area of the deserted pueblo, shutting out the world around them. He wanted to tell her of her beauty but feared breaking the spell that seemed to bind them together at this moment. He gently dropped to his knees and lowered her to the ancient soil beneath them, following her down as she went. Rafe buried his head in the hollow of her neck and kissed a path to the silky valley between her breasts. The material of her shirtwaist strained to be loosened, and he undid the buttons, but not before gauging her expression. One look at her eyes told him that she was as much under the spell of the moment as he. Rafe unhooked her corset and pushed aside the part of the chemise that kept him from ecstasy. Having undone the barriers to the creamy skin beneath her shirtwaist, he lowered his lips to full breasts that offered rosy peaks of delight.

Kacey cried out with pleasure and brought her hands to

grasp the raven of his hair as a stray sunbeam shone through a hole overhead, giving him the appearance of a dark, underworld god.

"*Mon Dieu, chérie*, but you are beautiful. Your loveliness is like an aphrodisiac." He kissed her again and reached to undo her clothing.

Kacey's voice was low and unsure. "Rafe . . . I—"

"Don't speak, *chérie*. Trust me. I would do nothing to harm you . . . ever."

Kacey seemed to be riding on waves, drugged to the hilt. She knew she was not thinking rationally, but it did not seem to matter. All she needed to know at the moment was that she wanted Rafe to touch her in secret places, and wanted to touch him as she had never touched a man before. She was afire with want and need. She allowed him to remove her own clothing and place her petticoat under her, then watched as he stood to doff his shirt and trousers in the dim light of the ancient room. Kacey marveled at the ripple of muscle and thick mat of black hair that covered his chest and formed a vee down his abdomen. Before he lowered himself to her again he loosened the string of his knit drawers and let them fall to the ground. Kacey's gaze continued to travel to the staff that stood erect like a proud sentinel.

When he dropped to her, he pillowed her head with his shirt. Then he deftly brought one hand to rest against a taut breast before trailing to the silky hairs at the crown of her thighs. Boldly he teased and toyed at her moist opening before tracing his tongue to the spot. Kacey groaned with an emotion that seemed indescribable to her. Never had she imagined the extent of pleasure that could be derived from a man's touch. Nothing she had learned had prepared her for this situation. And yet, everything she had ever done or experienced seemed to pale in this moment. Her body was on fire for more. She knew there was more. She seemed to writhe for more. She had only to look at Rafe's stem of desire and know what awaited her . . . and the wait seemed unbearable.

"P-please, Rafe." He raised his head and brushed her lips lightly. "I don't want to wait any longer." She moved her unsteady hands over the silky hairs of his chest, kneading and pressing as she went until Rafe straddled her and pressed his rigid staff into the moist sheath of her desire. Instinctively her body arched toward him while a sharp pain-pleasure momentarily ran its course. Rafe went still.

"Have I hurt you, *chérie*? Forgive me."

"No, Rafe. Don't stop." She wrapped her arms tighter around him and began to move her hips with a rhythm of her own that seemed bent on relieving her fevered condition. Instantly Rafe matched her movement with his own frenzied thrusting, causing Kacey to cry out again and again in what approached the pitch of a scream.

When relief came for them both, it came on a tide of exquisite release that brought new meaning to the word *ecstasy*. Neither moved for long moments, each basking in the wonder of it all. Rafe was the first to speak after he lightly kissed her lips.

"Are you all right, *ma chérie, amante*?" His thick whisper seemed to woo the very air she breathed.

"Yes." Kacey whispered, still caught in the rapture from their lovemaking.

"I was not sure," he teased her. "You seemed to be so . . . so involved. But then you always give one hundred percent to what you do." His husky undertone belied his taunt, and he nipped at her earlobe affectionately.

"Always," she replied breathlessly. His gaze caressed her, and it seemed as though he would consume her being.

"I'm so glad, *ma chérie*." Rafe began to suckle at a rosy nipple that still lay uncovered, then moved to the other one.

Kacey rode the tide of desire like seaweed, unable to escape the languor she felt. And once again she experienced the stirring between her thighs, and she moaned aloud. This seemed to fire Rafe, and for the second time they made love in the shelter of the dwelling that belonged to long ago. This melding of their bodies was no less volatile than the first, and when the ecstasy of relief came, they lay spent.

Long moments later, Kacey opened her eyes to see that the light around her had dimmed, and she reached for her chemise, holding it across her chest. Now reality closed in like the shadows in the room. Now her mind was working.

Rafe watched her, trying to guess her thoughts.

"I think we should be leaving before it gets any later, Rafe."

He moved to retrieve his clothing and started to dress himself. "Do you want to look at the pueblo before we leave?"

Kacey felt her face flush and began to don her own clothing. "I think I can look at it another time."

"We might not have another chance, *chérie*."

"I really should go on back now, if you don't mind, Rafe."

"As you wish, *ma chérie*."

"Oh, and Rafe," Kacey said, flushing anew at her words as she turned away, "this doesn't change anything between us. I mean . . . please don't get the idea that this will happen again." Kacey knew as she said the words that *everything* had changed between them, and she must be insane to pretend otherwise.

Rafe stiffened as though he had been slapped. The blood seemed to drain from his face, then rushed back in retaliation.

"Why, *chérie*, why would I think otherwise? Did you think I would offer you marriage?" Rafe suddenly wanted to hurt her as much as she had hurt him. "It seems that your original opinion of me is correct." He hoped she did not see through his façade.

"I guess I owe you a debt of gratitude, then." Sarcasm was heavy on her tongue as she changed her approach.

"For showing me all that life has to offer. Taking me to the limits, so to speak. Now I can say I am truly a modern, liberated woman. That's all I ever wanted to be anyway. I don't want someone telling me what and when I can do something."

"I don't blame you, *chérie*. Neither do I want to be told what to do." Rafe continued on a sad note. "But I think that if two people love each other, they should be willing to compromise a great deal, *n'est-ce pas?*"

Kacey conceded with a nod. "Well, I'm glad we've established that marriage is not for us. Let's get back now."

"*Oui.*" Rafe's mouth held a bitter taste that seemed to purse his cheeks.

They both turned and walked outside toward the horses tethered to the mesa brush.

"I would suggest . . . mademoiselle, that we ride back together just to make sure your horse is going to be all right."

"Well, I don't want to hurt the mare, but do you think it's necessary?" Kacey felt almost trapped at the thought of being in close contact with Rafe again. His nearness did strange things to her equilibrium, not to mention her pulse. She must not give herself an opportunity to come under his spell again.

"Yes, it is necessary." Rafe untied the horses and mounted the sorrel stallion that he had chosen at the ranch. He reached to pull Kacey up behind him.

"Very well." Kacey took Rafe's hand and mounted the large horse as she had done earlier that day.

"By the way . . . mademoiselle, for your peace of mind I assure you that what happened . . . in the ruins—and that seems to be quite a suitable summation, *n'est-ce pas?*— will not happen again." Rafe's declaration was rife with mockery. He was thinking that he had never made more perfect love with another woman. Kacey had stirred his blood as no other had. And now he, Rafael Assante, was being dismissed. The thought caused his jaw to clench, but he could not stop the stirring in his loins as her hands came to rest on his waist when he urged the stallion forward.

"We are of the same mind, then. We should get along magnificently." Kacey felt more than heard Rafe's reply of a grunt. She was not feeling the conviction in her voice. Every nerve in her body was at attention at the mere nearness of him. She would have to stay away from him in the days to come. She would find plenty to do at the site and become absorbed in her work.

That seemed to be the only salvation from the situation. Rafe was not the marrying kind. He had just told her. And she knew she would never feel the same about another man. She cursed herself a million times. And the thought occured to her—what if she became pregnant from their encounter?

Why hadn't she thought of that when she had melted in his arms and given herself up to him? She cursed herself and she cursed Rafe, but she could not bring herself to deny the ecstasy she had known while he made love to her. Nor could she bring herself to accuse him, even as she tried. She was as much to blame as he was. She dropped her gaze to her belly, which might now very well hold the aftermath of their passion, and her nerve endings tingled at the thought of carrying Rafe's child.

They both had lapsed into a deafening silence and rode toward Pueblo Mesita in the wake of the waning sun. Twilight was setting in when the pair rode into camp. Colin came toward them as they dismounted.

"My dear, I've been concerned about you." Relief was evident in his voice.

Rafe spoke for Kacey.

"I'm sorry, Professor. It took a little longer because the mare developed a limp."

"Yes, yes, but I'm glad you're back. It seems that we had a hostile visitor to camp today. Made some threats to John, but he says the Indian has always tried to cause trouble and never followed through. He doesn't think it's anything to worry about."

"That's good, Professor." Rafe seemed distracted even as he spoke.

"Come along, you two." Colin motioned for the pair to follow him. "John and Clate prepared bacon, beans, and coffee, and we are just about to sit down to eat."

"I will be there as soon as I see to the horses, Professor." Rafe's hooded gaze darted to Kacey. Never before had he wished time could roll back as he did now. Regret at his words to Kacey after her declaration shadowed another stronger emotion that occupied his heart. In a single, sad glance he tried to capture her gaze but she refused to look his way.

Kacey was relieved that the question-and-answer period had lapsed. She gratefully moved toward the campfire and filled a plate before turning to sit on a nearby log.

Victoria, leading Isis on a leash, came to sit beside her. The small, fluffy terrier sat at their feet while Victoria fed her scraps from her own plate.

"Kacey, dear, did you make any discoveries while at the other pueblo?"

Kacey momentarily lapsed into recollection of all the discoveries she had made at the ruins. Quickly her mind flashed with memories of a naked Rafe poised above her, then moving with a frenzied rhythm that matched her own. She was thankful for the near-darkness that spread beyond the campfire. She could feel her face flush hot from the memory of their lovemaking.

"N-no, we weren't there very long. Just long enough to look over the site, then leave." The lie tasted of gall to her tongue. What was it her mother had always said? The words forced their way to her mind. "Oh, what a tangled web we weave when first we practice to deceive." She looked at Victoria and smiled, hoping to assuage the deceit she felt, but feeling as she had when stealing Sarah's cookies as a child.

"Was the pueblo as large as this one?"

Realizing she was taking a long time to answer Victoria's question, she offered, "N-no, it was somewhat smaller. A-and after seeing it I will be content to work this site . . . for the time being, anyway."

"After today I can see why you are an archaeologist. The possibilities for discovery are absolutely endless. Making a find must be very exciting." Victoria paused. "Kacey, are you all right? You seem . . . distracted."

"Oh, I'm fine. Just a little tired, that's all." Kacey was quick to reply, and she shot Victoria a forced smile. Her lips were on the verge of trembling, but she fought against that as her gaze moved momentarily to where Rafe had seated himself near the fire. She shivered as the night seemed to steal around her and sap the leftover warmth of the afternoon sun.

"I'm going to have another cup of coffee. Shall I warm yours, too?" Victoria stood and waited for Kacey's reply.

"Yes, thank you." Kacey gave her cup to Victoria, who moved away, leaving the small dog at her feet. Kacey ate a few bites of the food, which might as well have been sawdust, before setting her plate aside and reaching for the nbtiny animal. She cuddled its softness in the fold of her arms. The chill still wrapped itself around her, but she refused to move in closer to the fire where Rafe sat, and she did not feel better after having eaten. Right now she felt an unexplained sadness that reached her bones, and she was sure no amount of nourishment could cure that. As if sensing her need, Isis reached to lick her cheek. Kacey snuggled the dog closer.

She looked toward the campfire once more to see Victoria talking to Rafe. The man was absolutely unshakable. He seemed to be talking as if nothing out of the ordinary had happened to him. His easy manner with Victoria nettled Kacey. She continued her perusal until Victoria turned and came toward her with the promised coffee.

"My dear, Rafe says you had a practically horrible afternoon. I'm sorry your horse went lame."

Kacey shifted her weight and took the proffered cup. "Yes, well, so am I." Victoria would never know just how sorry.

Victoria's gaze went to the furry ball in Kacey's embrace. "So, you and Isis have become friends. You know, she doesn't take to everybody. She's very particular." Victoria talked as if she were a proud parent and Isis her child.

"She's very sweet and lovable. I don't believe she intends to move from this spot." Kacey began to feel better from the comforting attention of Isis, and she laughed at the small dog's insistence on staying ensconced in her arms.

"Isis is very intelligent, *n'est-ce pas,* mademoiselle? She knows a comfortable spot when she sees it."

Kacey's pulse leaped at the low, taunting voice beside her.

"Yes," she managed to elicit between quaking lips. "She does seem to possess more intelligence than some among us." Kacey looked up at Rafe, who stood just inches away. His eyes seemed to smolder as she looked into them. She was beginning to feel some of the same emotions that she had felt earlier, too. But she would never let on to Rafael Assante that his mere presence caused her skin to tingle with delight. He would never know, she vowed.

She refused to be a Pygmalion's Galatea.

Fourteen

Weeks had passed since Kacey and Rafe had ridden out alone to the other pueblo. She had avoided him and thrown herself into her work. She wanted to put the affair behind her. Her encounters with Rafe were cordial but cool, and he reciprocated.

At the moment, Kacey was kneeling in the dirt, brushing a complete piece of pottery. She worked in an area where the roof was still intact over the pueblo, affording the artifacts a dry, limestone-based soil. She lowered her brush and marveled at the delicate painted lines. She wondered about the artist who had created such lovely work. She closed her eyes in an effort to imagine the artist, and she instinctively felt that the person was a woman. What kind of life had she known? Had she loved a man? Had she been a mother? Had she been happy? Kacey knew she would never know all the answers, but she hoped to learn as much as possible about these ancient, mysterious people.

Kacey brushed the final bits of dirt from the pot and set it aside momentarily to continue the slow process of digging. She was alone in the chamber and in the tomblike quietness she heard a footstep, and turned.

"*Chérie,* I must speak with you." Rafe stood in the doorway, his frame nearly filling the opening, while his hat sat low on his forehead.

"Rafe, I . . . don't have anything to say to you." Kacey met his gaze head-on and dared him to say otherwise.

Rafe stepped farther into the room. "Please just listen, then, to what I have to say." He paused briefly, then continued. "I'm sorry, *chérie,* for the things I said at the pueblo. I'm not apologizing for what happened between us, only for the words afterward. Please believe me—I care for you very deeply, but seeing how you feel, I won't come to you again." Without waiting for a reply, Rafe disappeared through the door.

Kacey's heart drummed a frenzied meter. Could she believe what Rafe declared? Did he care for her deeply? Maledictions to the man! She refused to think about the implication of what he had said. She shoved the trowel into the hard dry soil. Concentration on her work became more and more difficult. Rafe's words refused to leave her mind. *I won't come to you again. I won't come to you again.*

Kacey started when Rainey spoke to her from the door. "Your father wants to know if you can come to the supply wagon, Kacey."

"Yes, I'll be right there. Is something wrong?" Even as she spoke, Kacey stood and walked toward the young woman.

"I'm not sure. John and your father were looking at the wagon."

Kacey and Rainey walked the short distance to the campsite, where she spotted her father and John.

"Kacey, dear, John has been telling me that our supplies are running low, and he doesn't believe that we have used them all."

"You mean you think someone is stealing supplies, John?" Kacey's tone was incredulous. "Who would do that out here?"

"Well, it could be anyone, and I don't want to accuse anybody falsely. The bottom line is that we need more supplies, so I'm sending Clate to Mancos."

"All right. John, tell him to put it on our account there," Colin said.

"Thank thee, Professor. I feel really bad about this."

"It's not your fault, John. We'll take care of it." When the rancher had gone, Kacey turned to her father. "Now who do you suppose could be responsible for this?"

"Probably just a drifter, my dear," Colin offered.

"I don't think so, Father. A drifter would have been welcome to eat with us."

"Yes, dear, but by not showing his face, he could take some with him."

"Maybe you're right, Father. I hope so." Kacey felt uneasy about the whole business, and instantly she pictured the stone-faced Navajo she had seen more than a few times. She would have to ask John about him.

After the evening meal the women retired to their tent. Rainey and Beth had settled into their beds on the opposite wall and were already sound asleep. Kacey sat on her cot, braiding her long hair, readying herself for sleep. Victoria, in her nightgown, made her way from the makeshift table in the middle of the tent toward Kacey.

"Kacey, dear, I've finally put together the chart that I promised to do for you. Would you like to go over it now?"

Kacey smiled at the older woman, who in the soft light wore an almost girlish expression on her face. "Why, yes, Victoria, I'd like to know what the stars have to say. This would be a perfect time." Kacey did not want to hurt the woman's feelings by telling her that she did not believe in astrology. Besides, she thought it might be interesting to see her chart just for fun. After finding out earlier in the day that someone had rifled some of the camp's supplies, Kacey felt she needed some lighthearted recreation.

Victoria sat beside her and spread the charting sheets between them. She pointed to the one that looked like a wheel with twelve sections and various signs and numbers in each segment.

"You will see here, dear, that you were born when the sun was in Pisces and the moon in Libra. Whatever you are drawn to, it appears that you have an almost spiritual and devotional feeling for it."

Victoria eyed the quiet Kacey before moving her index finger to another chart. "And here we see that at the time of your birth the sun was in conjunction with Mars, and Mercury was in conjunction with Saturn. Children with these aspects are generally known as difficult, but not always. Usually in later years they show audacity and don't know the meaning of fear." Victoria laughed softly. "I'll bet you were the child who wouldn't give in no matter how hard your pigtails were pulled."

Kacey echoed the muted laugh, remembering a certain brat who sat behind her in school and used to pull her braids. "You're right about that. Benjamin McCleod. I haven't thought of him in years. I got even, though. I kicked him in the shins."

"Good for you, dear. All bullies should be kicked. That brings us back to one other aspect of your reading—Mars square Uranus. That means temper. I've not seen that aspect in your personality, but it might be something you want to bridle if the need arises. On the whole, you are very broadminded and uncritical of others. You accept people for what they are. Those born under the Piscean sign are generous, good-natured, and unusually perceptive." She paused a moment to take a breath. "Your rising sign is Leo, and that reinforces your generosity and ability to lead others." Victoria's voice lowered somewhat as she continued. "But I see also that . . . soon the moon moves into Cancer, and for the Piscean that can lead to feelings of uncertainty."

Kacey could tell that the woman took this interpretation

quite seriously. She tried not to make light of the reading for fear she would hurt Victoria's feelings. Actually some of the things that she had said might be true. According to Rafe, her devotion to her father went beyond what was necessary or what he wanted. With that thought she turned to the older woman. "Thank you, Victoria, for your reading and insights. And . . . may I ask you another question?"

"Of course, dear, you can ask me anything."

"Are you attracted to my father?"

Victoria's face flushed slightly, then she replied candidly, "Yes, Kacey, I am. I consider your father an extremely intelligent and handsome man. Does that bother you?"

"I had never thought about it before. Where women have been concerned, Father has always seemed so uninterested. Ever since my mother passed away, it's just been the two of us. I've never actually considered that he could be romantically interested in a woman."

Victoria carefully considered her next words. "Kacey, I like Colin very much and I think he feels the same. But I would never want to cause friction between you and your father."

"It's all right, Victoria. I just never understood how it can be between a man and a woman, that's all." Kacey smiled, then momentarily pictured Rafe gently lowering her to the ground of the ruins and taking her completely. *Until now,* the voice in her head declared.

Rafe paced the outer perimeter of the campfire and inhaled the smoke from his cheroot. With Clate gone, there was one less man in the camp. A niggling in the back of Rafe's mind kept him from feeling at ease over the incident of the missing supplies. It was not something that a drifter would do in the Southwest, according to John. Rafe tried to figure what the person's game might be, but came up with nothing. There was nothing of great value in the camp. The bits of pottery that had been found were valuable only to a museum or anyone studying the history of the Anasazi. He failed to come to a conclusion.

"Well, Rafe, I'm turning in. I think the professor had the right idea. I'll see you in the morning." John removed his hat and rubbed at his head.

"Oui, bonsoir." Rafe nodded before the rancher turned and walked to the darkened tent.

He noticed that a faint light still filtered through the light-colored canvas of the other tent. Silhouettes were visible on the material. He would recognize the tilt of that chin anywhere. Kacey. She seemed to be lost to him forever. He would give his soul if the past few weeks could be erased, and they could go back to at least being friends. Now she wanted no part of him. She wouldn't even look at him. He had tried to talk to her today, but she refused. *Mon Dieu*, but he had made a mess of things. He heatedly tossed the cheroot into the smoldering campfire.

An ache spread through his groin as he watched the familiar form against the backlit canvas. His lips thinned, and at that moment he made up his mind and headed toward the supply wagon. There he found the extra rifle and loaded it before going to his own shelter. In the darkness he groped to find his bedroll, and then went back out to sleep not far from the ladies' tent. Anyone coming into their camp would have to get past him. The rifle was in easy reach just under the edge of his bedding.

Rafe lay there a long while, listening to the noises of the night and thinking of Kacey. She had become his reason for being. She was part of him, and he felt as if her rejection of him would consume him like a plague.

The fire died out, and the only light came from overhead. Stars filled the sky as if someone had released a million fireflies into the night. A horse whinnied, and a bush rustled. Rafe became fully alert as he scanned the area. A rabbit scurried by, then all was quiet again.

•   •   •

In the stillness of the night Kacey lay wide-eyed and thoughtful. Her mind whirled with the happenings of the day, not the least of which were the words Rafe had declared. *I won't come to you again.* Even now her body cried out for his touch, for his lips crushed against her own. Sleep seemed to elude her this night. Soft breathing issued from the other three women, but she had tossed and turned on the small cot until she was completely tangled in her gown. She had to get up. In the darkness of the room, she pushed the blanket from her and stood. Her feet felt for the furry mules beside the cot. Her eyes had adjusted to the obscurity long moments earlier, and she could see well enough to make her way to the tent flap without disturbing anyone.

She moved outside, just beyond the entrance, her long white gown stark against the velvet black. The night wind brushed her cheek, beckoning her to revel in the beauty of the night. The campfire no longer glowed. It must have burned out hours ago. Feeling confident that the men were in their tent and sound asleep, Kacey felt free to go a short distance in her gown before she returned to her bed. A walk in the night air might help her to relax and induce sleep. She crossed her arms and pulled the long sleeves of the gown closer to her as the air grew chilly around her.

She walked softly and carefully, not wanting to disturb anyone. She knew the campsite to be uncluttered after their meal, so she felt confident that she wouldn't stumble over any debris.

At her next step and before she could see it, her foot came against a dark, solid mass, causing her to lose her balance and fall headlong across the heap. A low guttural sound erupted with the volcano of blanket and man.

Suddenly Kacey found herself wrapped in the arms of Rafael Assante and lying on his bedroll. She would know his scent and the feel of his arms anywhere. Her eyes widened in the moonlight, and she could sense more than see his eyes burn into hers.

"*Mon Dieu, chérie*, what do you think I am made of? You come to me out of my dreams dressed as an angel and fall into my bed. And I would wager that you expect me to let you go, *n'est-ce pas*?"

The husky quiver of his voice, along with the musky male scent of him, stunned her. She mentally reeled with memories of their lovemaking.

Her reply did not come quick enough.

Rafe's lips closed over hers in a heated wave of passion, bent on tasting the sweetness of her to her very soul. His lips plundered her mouth with all the pent-up longing inside him—longing that had not been sated since that day at the ruins. And that had not been enough. He would never have his fill of Kacey. She was like a never-ending feast to which he was not invited. And now he was inside the banquet hall.

With one touch of Rafe's kiss, Kacey's resolve had melted like hard candy in a flame. She reveled in his scent and the feel of his muscles pressed hard against her. Her arms came up to envelop him while she tried to inch closer into his maleness.

Incensed, Rafe moved his hand to cup a breast poorly concealed by her linen gown. He caressed the peak through the material, then began to undo the buttons at her neck. She was yielding and soft in the darkness. He did not have to see her to know her beauty. He had memorized every line of her face, every curve down to the creamy softness of her thighs. He continued to kiss her, drowning in the ecstasy of her response.

A twig broke somewhere nearby, shattering Rafe's encapsulated existence. He released Kacey from his hold and listened cautioning her with his glance. He gently put his fingers to her lips. They remained motionless for long moments as they listened intently to the sounds of the night.

When nothing stirred, Kacey gathered the folds of her gown and stood. The noise had hit her like a splash of cold water, bringing her back to her senses. Her skin still tingled from Rafe's touch, but she had to distance herself from him before she became caught up in the throes of passion again.

Rafe got to his feet in a fluid motion, but did not try to touch her as he kept his voice low. "Kacey—"

"I'm sorry, Rafe, but I just came out for a breath of fresh air. I didn't mean to fall—"

"I'm well aware of that, *chérie*." Sarcasm edged his voice.

"Why aren't you in the tent with the others?" Her breathless whisper was almost accusing.

"I thought I would keep an eye on the camp tonight to make sure we did not have anymore visitors." His gaze moved around the darkened area before returning to her. "I did not know that I would be rewarded for my efforts. I shall plan to sleep under the stars every night from now on."

Kacey had no reply to the husky declaration as it seemed to caress the very air around her. She made a sound in her throat that was almost a moan as she turned to flee to the safety of her tent, still feeling the effects of desire.

She slipped quietly inside the tent and went to her cot. Without Rafe's arms around her, she felt a void that precluded sleep. She felt hollow and incomplete as she once more began to toss and turn. In his arms she experienced a fullness that she could not explain.

Rafe lay awake on his bedroll, recalling the softness of Kacey in his arms. Sounds of the night drifted by while sleep escaped him now. The ache that had settled in his groin increased with each thought of her lips pressed against his own.

Without warning, a loud crashing sound came from the direction of the supply wagon. Instantly Rafe was on his feet with rifle in hand, and before he reached the buckboard, John stood beside him. The two advanced catlike toward the noise. Rafe motioned for John to stand opposite him at the back of the wagon. Together they cautiously leaned in to see who was inside. When their eyes adjusted, both men burst out laughing at the scene in front of them. A filmy whiteness covered the inside, and in the middle of the floor two ghostlike creatures sat licking dainty paws. A pair of raccoons had invaded the supply wagon, and a bag of flour had spilled open in front of them.

"Quite a night's catch, wouldn't you say, Rafe?" John said with good humor. "What do we do with the culprits now that we've caught them?"

"We're short on mascots, *n'est-ce pas*? I suppose we let them go and fasten the wagon better in the future."

Kacey's voice came over the two men's shoulders. "I'm in complete agreement, Rafe. Who could harm those two cuddly creatures?" She moved as if to go past them and into the wagon but was stopped short by John's words.

"Excuse me, Miss O'Reilly, but has thee ever tried to cuddle a wild raccoon?"

Kacey turned. "I wasn't going to cuddle them, John. I was merely going to pick up the sack of flour before they consumed the whole bag and we starved to death."

"I'm not too sure that thee will even get close to that flour sack, ma'am."

"Watch me."

Kacey turned and walked up the steps into the supply wagon. She cautiously approached the powdered animals, who seemed oblivious to anything but the delicacy they ate from the floor. When she came into the larger one's space, the animal instantly bristled and bared sharp teeth as a warning. Kacey suddenly remembered everything she had learned about animals. When cornered, they all become hostile. She also remembered the large tin of cookies that Miriam Dunning had sent along. The whiteness of the surroundings allowed enough light for her to see the container on a shelf nearby. Without moving further, she reached for the tin and took out two large sugar cookies before reclosing the lid. She stepped back and squatted low before making her peace offering.

Both raccoons smelled the sweets at the same time, and both came cautiously toward her. The one who had bared his teeth seemed docile now and seemed almost to plead for the cookie as she held it out to him. Both animals took the cookies from her hand and scampered away through the front opening of the canvas.

"I would never have believed this if I hadn't seen it with my own eyes." John's tone was incredulous. "Where did thee learn to do that?"

There was humor in Kacey's voice. "It wasn't anything unusual, John. Animals are all alike, human species or not. Give them something sweet, and they'll be your slave for life."

Rafe answered from behind John in the opening. "Mademoiselle seems to know much about animal psychology, John. I think we can take a lesson from her. Give an animal something sweet, and he'll be your slave for life."

Kacey did not miss the undertone as Rafe repeated her declaration, or the way he seemed to say the words for her ears only. Her skin tingled as she digested his insinuation, reaching for the sack of flour at her feet.

"Well, I'm ready to put this episode behind me and go back to my tent. John, can you close the supply wagon where they can't get back in?"

"I don't know." John scratched his head. "It may take another couple of cookies."

Kacey knew he was teasing her, and she smiled. "Whatever it takes, John." She put the sack of flour on a shelf and made her way out of the wagon past the two men.

She was caught up short at Rafe's words near her ear. "I will walk you back, *chérie*. You don't have any more cookies in your hand to ward off wild animals."

"Sometimes it takes more than cookies, Rafe."

"*Oui, chérie*, how right you are."

Once more Kacey's skin tingled, and she made a sound

in her throat. ''I was speaking of a weapon such as a big stick or a gun, monsieur.''

''Kacey, dear.''

The sound of Victoria's voice startled Kacey, and she saw the woman standing just outside their tent.

''Yes? Is something wrong?''

''Beth and Rainey both seem to be very sick . . . and I don't feel so well myself.''

At the woman's words Kacey covered the short distance to the tent with Rafe beside her. He stood outside while Kacey entered the dwelling.

Fifteen

As soon as Kacey saw the ghostlike whiteness of the sisters' faces, the gravity of the situation struck her. They were doubled up on their cots, groaning with pain. Kacey turned to Victoria to speak, and she caught the woman rubbing her stomach with a definite look of half-concealed agony.

"Victoria, you need to lie down, too. Tell me what I can get for you." Kacey put her arm around the woman's shoulder.

"I'm all right, Kacey, just a stomachache."

Kacey walked to the entrance and stepped just beyond the opening to see Rafe pacing nearby. He looked her way and quickly covered the distance between them.

"Rafe, will you check on the others? The women are sick with stomach cramps, and I was wondering if any of the others have the same symptoms." She turned, paused, then looked over her shoulder. "How do you feel, Rafe?"

"I feel as if a herd of wild boars were rooting through my midsection, but it has nothing to do with illness, *chérie.*"

At his low declaration Kacey's blood coursed like rapids

in a mountain stream. His dark, hooded gaze and husky
voice did strange things to her own equilibrium. She momentarily swayed toward him before summoning her reserve to walk into the tent.

Reaching the bowl of cool water on the makeshift stand,
Kacey grasped two cloths and soaked them before placing
one on Rainey's forehead and the other on Beth's. The
two girls elicited a feeble sound of gratitude, but Kacey
felt helpless. Her braid had come undone, and wisps of
hair worked around her cheeks and into her mouth to annoy her. She shoved the strands aside and saw Victoria a
few feet away, slumped on her cot.

"Victoria, you should lie down. I'll get you a cool
cloth."

Kacey hurriedly wet another washcloth and handed it to
the woman.

"Thank you, dear."

"I don't know what to make of this, Victoria. It must
be something we've eaten, and it's probably just a matter
of time before the rest of us come down with it."

"Maybe not, de—" Victoria winced and doubled over
in her pain.

Kacey hated seeing suffering around her and not being
able to do anything about it. The kit they carried had iodine
and bandages for wounds, but nothing for pain. Her fingers
curled into fists at the helplessness she felt.

"I have a small bottle of laudanum for emergencies in
my bag. If the girls get worse, you can use it for them.
I'll be all right." The contortion of Victoria's face belied
her words.

Kacey looked toward Beth and Rainey. She could tell
they were trying to be brave, but there was no hiding their
anguished countenances.

"Kacey, I need to speak with you." The low French
accent filtered through the tent flap. She did not miss the
urgency of his words, or the way his tongue caressed her
name as it flowed from his lips.

She gathered her robe around her and spoke to Victoria. "I'll be just a minute." She stepped to the entrance and went outside.

"What is it, Rafe? Are the others ill?" Even as she spoke she felt pain shoot through her abdomen, and her hand involuntarily sought to ease the discomfort.

Even in the dull light of the moon, Rafe did not miss the movement. "John is fine, but the professor seems to be having stomach distress, also. How are the ladies?"

"Not very well. They're all sick, and I don't have anything to give them other than a small amount of laudanum that Victoria keeps for emergencies."

"Whatever you do, don't give it to them. It could make matters worse. John is scouting for fennel to steep an infusion . . . he seems to think the symptoms resemble poisoning from a type of ivy grown around here. He said very seldom does anyone die from ingesting it, but it makes them wish to die."

"Who would put ivy in our food, Rafe? That makes no sense, unless . . ." Kacey's words trailed off as she remembered the stone-faced Indian.

"It is only a theory that John has, but . . . there are some who do not want us here, *chérie*." Rafe was standing only inches from Kacey, and he reached to take her into the fold of his arms.

Momentarily she allowed her senses to feel the rapture of his embrace before she pulled away.

"I must go see about Father." She moved and started in the direction of the men's quarters, and Rafe followed, catching her wrist in a grip before relaxing his hold.

"I will tend to your father, *chérie*. Why don't you go lie down. I saw you trying to soothe your stomach back there."

"It's nothing." Kacey straightened her shoulders and stood at her full height. "I appreciate your concern, Rafe, but I want to see Father for myself. Now, if you'll excuse me." She eyed his hold on her wrist.

Rafe released her and nodded in resignation. "As you say, *ma chérie*." His brows lifted in sardonic amusement. "But may I make a suggestion?"

"I think you're going to whether you have my permission or not."

"As soon as you see to your father you need to try to get some rest yourself."

"You weren't so worried about my *rest* earlier." Kacey couldn't resist the gibe as she whispered, "As I recall, if it hadn't been for a certain nocturnal animal, to whom I owe my undying gratitude, we would have been in a very compromising situation."

"*Oui, chérie.*" Rafe continued in his low husky accent. "And is that why you feel you must bite my head off? Because you have feelings that you don't want to have? The untouchable professor's daughter at last has been touched, and she refuses to recognize what has happened to her."

Rafe caught her arm in midair and held it in a viselike grip before she could make contact with his jaw. Sparks flew from both eyes now, and tension was a tangible thing, like a hungry beast in the night, skirting and teasing its prey. His gaze burned into hers, and just as quickly he caught her in a crushing embrace, his ravenous lips seeking hers.

Kacey's insides became liquid heat—a volcanic lava that threatened to consume her sanity as Rafe's bruising kiss compelled the surrender of her lips. As she melded to him, he released her like hot coal and walked away, leaving her to stand alone in confusion.

Kacey brought her hand to touch her swollen lips before she moved toward the men's quarters. Inside, ignoring Rafe's presence, Kacey saw her father lying on a cot next to a dimmed lantern. His eyes were closed, and his face looked ashen. She went quickly to him and kneeled beside his bed.

"Father, is there anything I can do?"

Colin slowly opened his eyes. "No, dear. Just take care of yourself and the others. I understand the ladies are sick, too. How do you feel?"

"I'm all right, Father." Even then her stomach shot through with pains, but she continued, "Rafe says John thinks it is poisoning, but I don't understand why they're . . . we're not all sick."

"Well, John asked me several questions about what we had eaten or drunk since this morning, and I almost forgot about the tea that I drank with you ladies this afternoon. If you recall, the pot was left near the site, and we thought he must have made it. He says he didn't make the tea, and that after Clate left he was with Rafe all afternoon. That's the only thing we can think of that Rafe and John didn't eat, too. And if that's what it is, then you'll be sick also."

"Don't worry about me, Father, I'll be fine."

"I hope so, dear. I hope so." Colin's face contorted in pain.

"Oh, Father, I wish there were something I could do." Kacey's voice nearly broke in a sob.

"There is, dear. Go back to your tent and see to the others. Promise me you will do that."

Kacey protested, "I can't leave you here."

"I will be all right as soon as these blasted pains subside. Besides, Rafe will be here if I need anything."

Kacey did not argue with her father. She knew Rafe would take care of him and that the others needed her. "All right, Father, but I'll check on you later."

"Yes, dear, you do that."

Kacey stood, and without saying another word, she went through the opening in the tent. Even now her stomach ached intensely, but she managed to walk several steps before doubling over in agony.

Rafe had moved to the entrance and watched Kacey go into the night. He intended to see her safely back to the tent. When he saw her unmistakable motion, his whole body tensed as if shot through with darts. He quickly moved beside her and swept her into his arms. She did not quarrel with the maneuver, and he continued on toward her tent.

Inside, he laid her on the empty cot. She groaned in anguish, overwhelmed by the excruciating pain that consumed her consciousness. Hovering on the brink of lucid thought, she knew that someone had mercifully carried her to her bed. But what of her father, and Victoria, and poor Beth and Rainey? Her mind whirled at the thought of death. Would they all die from the poison? What was it her father had said? *It was the tea.* She'd had two cups. In the distance she heard muffled voices.

"Rafe, is Kacey sick, too?" Victoria asked from her bed.

"*Oui,* madame."

"There's laudanum in the satchel at the foot of my cot, Rafe. There's very little of it. I don't need any, but the girls and Kacey . . ."

"*Oui,* but I think that under the circumstances, madame, that would be the wrong thing to give them at the moment."

"Why, Rafe? What do you know?"

"Not much, madame. Only that the tea you and the others drank this afternoon was quite possibly poisoned."

The woman's face turned a paler shade of white, and Rafe rushed on.

"But John thinks it was only meant to make us ill. Please try not to worry. He is searching for something to ease the pain. In the meantime, is there anything I can do for you, madame?"

"I would appreciate a cool cloth, Rafe." Victoria's voice was raspy and weak.

"*Oui,* madame." He moved swiftly to remove the cloth from her brow and resoak it in the cool water before returning it to her.

"Thank you, Rafe. Now you must see to Kacey." Quickly she added, "And, Rafe, is Colin all right?"

"He has the same symptoms as you do, madame, but he is very strong. I'm sure he will be all right."

"Thank you."

He nodded and walked to stand beside Kacey. She had almost slipped into unconsciousness, except for her thrashing about. Her eyes were shut and her face screwed into deep lines.

Something inside him reeled, and he muttered a curse at the helplessness he felt. *Mon Dieu*, but would John never get back? Rafe raked his trembling fingers through his hair. He could not bear to see her suffer this way.

Slamming his fist into his palm, he strode to the water basin and dampened a cloth. He did the only thing he knew to do, which was to bathe her forehead in cool water, hoping to bring some relief. For a while he also kept the others' cloths cool before he went to check on the professor.

As he neared the other tent he saw John building a fire under a small kettle. He quickly covered the distance to him.

"John, *mon ami,* I'm glad to see you. They're all sick now, and Kacey seems to be the worst. I hope you found what you were looking for." Rafe squatted beside the man. "Can I help you?"

"As soon as the water comes to a boil, we'll need these seeds crushed." John held up a small pouch with one hand and continued to feed the fire with the other. "Thee can help me do that."

"*Oui,* I will be right back. I need to look in on the professor." Rafe lightly slapped John's back as he stood.

"This should be ready by the time thee gets back."

"*Merci beaucoup.* I will tell the professor," Rafe answered as he strode off.

Rafe found Colin still lying on the cot, his appearance no better. The older man stirred.

"Rafe, my lad, is Kacey all right?" The professor's voice was tenuous.

Rafe realized he didn't know how to answer. "*Oui,* Pro-

fessor, and John has come back with the herbs he was
looking for. I'm sure everyone will feel much better
shortly."

"I hope so, Rafe. I don't know when I've ever had such
pains."

After John had finished making the herbal tea, he and Rafe
distributed it to the others. Beth, Rainey, and Victoria accepted the drink, as did Colin. But Kacey did not respond
to Rafe's insistence that she drink the liquid, tossing her
head from side to side.

She drifted in and out of consciousness. Someone was
trying to make her swallow something, but she wanted
nothing to drink. Someone had already tried to poison
them all. Maybe this was the person come back to finish
the job. She opened her eyes slightly, unable to focus on
anything. Where was Rafe? She wanted him near. She tried
to say his name, but her lips seemed . . . Oh, God, no! They
had forced the liquid down her throat. And more followed.
The pain in her stomach was almost unbearable.

"Dieu merci, ma chérie, at last, against your will, you
have let me help you. Sleep now, *mon ange."* The husky
declaration was almost a benediction for Rafe.

He looked around at the others who seemed to have
found some ease, and he prayed it would be only a short
while before Kacey did the same. John had gone to sit
with the professor. Rafe did not intend to leave Kacey. He
settled himself on the ground beside her cot. It was well
into the early morning hours by now, only a short time
until daybreak. He would slip out at the first signs.

*Kacey drifted in a cloud of uncertainty. She was hesitant
to believe that the awful pains had eased, but they surely
had. Now she seemed to float in a mist of blue, her long
diaphanous gown flowing with her, moving toward a wonderful warm light. Her mother was there, near the light.
She looked the same as when Kacey had last seen her. She*

was still as beautiful as ever. But the others behind Kacey were calling her back from this journey. She had no recollection of how she had gotten here. The force of the light was strong, and she felt a great urge to continue on toward it, but the voices seemed so plaintive, pleading even, for her return. Momentarily she turned from the brilliance and saw their faces. Her father was there, and Victoria, and Rafe, all pleading for her to come back, not to go. She glanced back to her mother, who spoke to her. "Not yet, dear daughter, you have so much to live for, so much yet to give. Go back for now, child. Will you? For me?"

Kacey's soft voice answered, "Yes, Mother. For you."

She opened heavy eyelids from her dream state, and in the dimly lit interior she saw the other women lying on their cots. They appeared to be sleeping. Had she dreamed the whole thing? Maybe none of them had been poisoned at all. Then, as if to remind her differently, a slight pain shot through her middle, but nothing like the ones she had battled earlier. She sat up in bed, and that was when she saw him. Actually she saw his boots first. Then her gaze traveled the length of him beside her cot. Her first instinct was to pull the cover higher. What was Rafe doing beside her cot? She faintly remembered that it must have been him who brought her here from her father's tent. Another pain stabbed her insides. This one felt more intense than the last, and she could not hold the muffled groan that escaped her lips.

Rafe stirred. His hat had fallen low over his eyes, and Kacey could not see if she had awakened him. Then he came to a sitting position beside her.

His whisper caused her skin to prickle.

"*Ma chérie,* it's good you are better."

"Rafe, I . . . I just had a dream about my mother. She was so beautiful, Rafe. I wanted to stay with her, but she was telling me to come back here."

"I am so glad you listened to her, *chérie.* You have been very sick." Rafe's lips curled into a smile while he reached to take her hand in his. "Such a delicate, beautiful hand, *mon ange.*"

He slowly brought her palm to his lips, and Kacey trembled from the sensuous caress of his kiss as flecks of flame darted up her arm, eventually reaching her breast. She was powerless to take her hand from him and was thankful when he released it.

"I will go now, *chérie.* You seem to be much better."

"Yes. And Rafe, thank you . . . for being here." She sounded breathless as her pulse raced to catch her heart.

Rafe stood in a fluid movement. "I will always be here for you, *chérie,* believe it." He bent to brush her forehead lightly with his lips before he left the tent.

Kacey watched him go, and through the open flap she could see the first light of daybreak. Her stomach still ached somewhat, but not at all like it had before. *Rafe.* Thoughts of him circled her mind like a great fog moving in to shut out all else. She could not now deny that his very nearness caused a breathlessness in her, an aching need that might never be filled. Since their lovemaking at the pueblo, that need had grown to great proportions, despite her attempts at denial.

Rafe watched the sun move over the horizon like a ball of gold. The sight was glorious, and Kacey was going to be all right.

John emerged from the other tent and walked toward him.

"How are the patients, Rafe?"

"I think they will be *très bien,* thanks to you, John. But I have to tell you that I was worried for a while." Rafe kicked the dirt with his boot and continued in a quiet manner. "You know who did this, don't you, John?" The words were more a statement than a question.

"No. I just have my suspicions. I'll try to keep a better watch in the future. The Indians around here . . . Well, if thee knows who Geronimo is . . . he is their hero and he was captured last year and sent to a prison in Florida. They don't trust the government—can't say as I blame them. But it doesn't take much these days to upset them, and they seem to be taking great offense to our digging in their ancestral grounds."

"That does not give them the right to poison us all."

"No, but that's not the way some of the renegades see it."

"John, if you think it is dangerous here . . . I won't have Kacey or the others face any more danger. I—" Rafe's voice almost cracked.

"I understand. I feel the same way, but I think this is an isolated case. And I believe we can keep better watch from now on. When Clate gets back, that'll be one more in our favor. And I would like Professor O'Reilly to be able to stay the length of time he needs."

"As you say, *mon ami.*"

"Good morning, John, Rafe." The two men whirled at Colin's greeting. "How are the ladies? I would have checked on them myself, but I didn't want to disturb them."

"They are much better, Professor, and how are you this morning?" Rafe asked.

"I have felt better, but then I have felt worse." Colin chuckled as he spoke. "I'll be all right." He paused, then continued, "What's that you were saying about the Indians, John?"

"Well, Professor O'Reilly, as thee may already know, the Navajo and the Apache are cousins. The capture of Geronimo last year brought about much added bitterness toward the white man. There are some renegades about who try to do what they can to get even."

"Do you think that's who poisoned us, John?"

John scratched his head. "I wouldn't be surprised, Professor. But the Utes around here are awed by this mesa, and they give the area much supernatural importance."

"In other words, John, none of them want us here."

"Something like that, Professor O'Reilly." The Quaker's eyes twinkled with a keen intelligence.

Colin whistled through his teeth before all three looked to see Clate riding into camp. He dismounted and in his cowboy gait joined them.

"Where can a parched man get a cup of coffee around these parts?" Clate's lips curled in an easy smile.

John moved to fill the coffeepot from a covered tub of water. He looked at Rafe then took a sip of the water. Silently testifying to its safety with a nod toward the Frenchman, he continued, "Coming right up, Clate, dear brother of mine. How was your trip?"

"What's with this 'dear brother of mine' business?"

"Does thee love me anymore, brother?"

"I'm not sure. What does thee want this time, big brother?"

Continuing with his efforts to make coffee, John placed the pot on the fire Rafe had started, then declared with a look of wounded innocence, "Thee sorely wounds me with that statement, Clate." Then on a more serious note, he added, "We've had visitors in camp."

"Again!"

John nodded. "After thee left yesterday. Someone brewed up a pot of potent tea for us. Everyone drank some except Rafe and me." John eyed his brother in a fashion that revealed more than the words alone.

"Are Beth and the others all right?" Clate looked from his brother to Rafe and Colin. "Where are they?"

Rafe answered first. "They will be all right, Clate. But I suspect that they might be a little late in rising this morning. We all had a long night."

Clate looked toward the ladies' tent as if he wanted to verify the words.

John announced, "I'll have some breakfast cooked right away, Clate, and thee can see if they want anything to eat. But I have my doubts." John's voice trailed off as he looked past his brother. The others followed his gaze to see Acowitz moving toward them.

John stepped toward the aged, wrinkled Ute. "Good morning, my friend. It is good to see thee."

"And I, you, Quaker friend. It is good to know the spirits have not yet had their vengeance."

"Oh, there's been vengeance here. But not from the spirits, friend. Someone left us a poisoned tea yesterday. Definitely manmade."

The old man appeared saddened by the news. "Sometimes the spirits make use of human hands. Beware, my friend. I wish you and your scientists to leave this place, but if you will not, beware of forces beyond my control."

Colin stepped forward to speak. "Sir, I wish you could understand the importance of the preservation of these dwellings to future generations."

"My people already know their importance. That is why we wish them left alone." At the words the old Ute turned, and with his royal bearing left the site.

Sixteen

Kacey reached to move the lantern closer in the dimness of the cellar room. She gently brushed at the soil again and again. At last the object was perfectly clear. She focused on the mummified toe section of a foot that had been covered in the arid, limestone-based soil. Her mouth went bone dry as the tide of realization washed over her. She instantly stood and quickly went to the entrance of the pueblo.

"Father! You must come and look at this!" Kacey's voice shook with excitement.

Colin heard his daughter shouting from the section of the pueblo that still had its roof intact. "Kacey's found something, Victoria." He dropped his tools, and they quickly covered the distance.

Rafe, too, had heard her and came up behind Colin.

"What is it, *chérie*?" Rafe fought to steady his voice. Ever since the incident with the tea a few days before, he felt as though he were stretched on a tenter.

Her beaming eyes shifted to each one standing nearby. "I've found something that I know you will want to see. Come inside the pueblo." Kacey motioned for them to follow her and went into the chamber. Barely concealing her emotions, she scrambled down the ladder to the cellar room.

She dropped to the spot where she had been working. Colin and Rafe followed suit while Victoria remained standing.

Rafe was the first to speak. "*Mon Dieu*, Professor!"

"Exactly, my lad." Colin did not take his eyes off the foot. "Rafe, get the others in here, and bring more trowels, screens, and brushes." For the first time he looked at his daughter. "My dear, I think you've really done it this time. We've got to get the rest of this fellow uncovered."

"This should make the museum stand up and take notice, Father. Surely they can't ignore what's right under their noses."

"My dear, the museum will come around in time. They just have other rows to hoe at present. Meanwhile, we'll bask in the knowledge that we were here first. And you know what that is worth to an archaeologist." Colin winked conspiratorially at his daughter.

"Yes, but Father, I just hope you get the recognition when they finally do come around."

"You've got it all wrong, my dear. This is *your* discovery."

Victoria stepped closer. "Kacey, Colin's right. It's time women scientists received recognition well deserved. Accept it. You have made the discovery. Now, tell me what I can do to help. The poor fellow must have many tales to tell us if we can just get him uncovered."

Kacey looked at her father who nodded at her.

"All right, when Rafe gets back with the equipment, we'll start. I think that more than four would be a crowd." Kacey turned to see Rafe leading the way for the others, all carrying the tools Colin asked for. She stood from her kneeling position and stepped toward him.

"You've brought lots of help, Rafe." Kacey marveled at the effect his presence had on her. Her staccato heartbeat could not entirely be attributed to the recent discovery.

"Everyone wanted to see what you had found, *chérie*."

"The discovery is not quite complete yet." Kacey looked around Rafe. "John, I know you'll want to be part of this, too."

"Just tell me what to do."

"Is there anything Beth or I can do, Kacey? We'd like to help, if possible." Rainey's enthusiasm was mirrored in her sister's eyes.

"No, not yet. We may need a bucket brigade to dispose of the dirt. Once dirt is loosened, it seems to swell as if it were charged with yeast. And I don't want to dump it in here. It already looks as if this were a garbage heap."

"We'll go get buckets, then. Come on, Rainey." Both girls clambered up the ladder in a frenzy of excitement.

Morning flowed into afternoon with Kacey, John, Rafe, and Colin tediously troweling and brushing the shallow grave. Victoria and the sisters carried buckets of the screened soil to an area for dumping outside the pueblo.

Kacey worked in an area where she guessed the upper torso to be. And just when she was beginning to think the fellow didn't have an upper half, she reached something solid, and began painstakingly brushing with care. She continued with the gentle strokes until she saw the color.

"I've got something here—looks like turquoise. This must have been a fellow who was well off." She continued the brushing.

Colin leaned to look at his daughter's find. "Appears to be an exquisite turquoise necklace, my dear. And it looks as though it's still intact."

Kacey worked carefully at uncovering the necklace, which lay against the preserved bronze skin of a man's chest.

Rafe and John stopped their brushing to look toward Kacey.

"*Chérie,* this seems to be your lucky day, *n'est-ce*

pas?'' After he spoke, Rafe noticed the strained expression on Kacey's face.

"I don't know, Rafe. It's quite sad in a way. This poor gentleman reminds me of a passage from Ecclesiastes.'' Kacey lowered her voice, sounding pensive and mysterious as she quoted the verse from memory. " 'I returned and saw under the sun, that the race is not to the swift, nor the battle to the strong, neither yet bread to the wise, nor yet riches to men of understanding, nor yet favor to men of skill; but time and chance happeneth to them all.' "

Colin cut into the conversation. "Ecclesiastes is a very depressing book, dear. Just think of the joy this chap must have known in wearing this exquisite piece of jewelry during his lifetime. Besides, maybe he stole it from some unsuspecting soul and got what he deserved.''

"You've made my point, Father."

"Cheer up, dear. This fellow is going to help write your name in history. Now, let me help you finish uncovering that necklace. Better yet, why don't you go take a break? It's been a long day. As a matter of fact, why don't we all take a break?''

"You know I can't quit now, Father. I at least want to finish uncovering the necklace.''

"Dear, it will be waiting when you get back."

"You and the others go ahead, Father. I'll quit shortly.'' He was about to protest, but she added, "I promise."

John's face screwed into a look of distaste. "Does anyone besides me smell a strange odor?''

Colin and Kacey exchanged amused glances with Rafe. He turned his attention to John, resting his knuckles on his knees.

"*Mon ami*, did you think that a mummy buried for possibly hundreds of years would smell like fields of vanilla?''

"I've never smelled fields of vanilla, and I've never smelled anything like this.''

"The poor fellow just needs a bit of fresh air." Colin was caught up in the need for lightness. "Who wouldn't after being closed up in a cellar all this time?''

Victoria and the sisters descended the ladder from their task of dirt brigade. Beth moved toward the diggers and spoke to no one in particular, her gaze resting on Rafe.

''Clate says to tell everyone that he's prepared something to eat.''

''If Clate's prepared it, there might be some doubt about its edibility.'' John teased Beth and noted her slight frown at the insult to his brother's ability. ''But I'm willing to risk it for a break from this smell.'' He looked at the others. ''How about it? Anybody else ready to live dangerously and eat Clate's food?''

Kacey saw her father and Rafe look toward her. ''Please, go ahead. I'll be along shortly.''

''All right, dear. But make sure you follow soon.''

''I will. I just want to uncover more of the necklace.''

Accepting Kacey's agreement to follow soon, the others left the cellar chamber. With the back of her hand, Kacey pushed at the wisps of hair tickling her cheeks before starting the brushing once more. The tomblike stillness of the room magnified the whisking sound with each stroke. And each stroke brought more of the necklace to light. It was more magnificent than she had originally thought. Hundreds of tiny turquoise beads, exquisitely colored, blended toward a larger center stone that in its brilliance of hue seemed to wink at her.

A noise from the ladder caused her to look up. Rafe stood there, his expression unreadable beneath his low-slung hat. The silence stretched before them like an ocean of sand to cross. Rafe crossed it first.

''I came to get you myself, *chérie.* You need to take a break, *n'est-ce pas*?''

Ignoring the statement, Kacey shifted her gaze and her weight in the kneeling position. ''Rafe, look at this. It's more beautiful than I expected.''

He came to stand beside her and squatted, the stretched fabric of his pants brushing against her. Through the material of her split skirt, she could feel the hard, corded strength of his thigh, making no effort to remove itself from her touch. She fought to ignore the quick rush of blood that reached the core of her belly like a tidal wave.

Rafe looked at the turquoise. "It is *magnifique, chérie*. Such a vital quality of color. Centuries of burial have probably permitted the stones to mature to perfection." He turned his gaze toward Kacey. "It will be very beautiful on you."

Kacey watched, spellbound, as his lips slowly came down on her own. She didn't know what was more fascinating—the discovery she had just made, or the wonder of Rafe's lips pressed against hers. Every nerve in her body tingled from his touch.

The pressure of Rafe's lips increased, his arms moving to enfold Kacey in a cocoon of warmth. His fingertips massaged her compliant back through the material of her shirtwaist. The motion was an opiate to her senses, and she emitted a small noise, fighting the addiction to his touch. She pulled away from his kiss, but he did not release her.

"Rafe, please, not here, not now." Her breathing came in uneven rhythms, and she fought the magnetism that drew her to him like iron filings to a lodestone.

Rafe murmured near her ear, "*Ma chérie,* you are the most beautiful thing I have ever seen. I want to be close to you like your skin, your clothes. I want to be inside you, a part of you, and I will be jealous of that necklace pressed close to your breast. As exquisite as the turquoises are, they merely pale in comparison to your loveliness. Can you understand what I am saying, *ma chérie*?"

The heady male aroma of sweat and masculinity worked to confuse Kacey. She ran her tongue over lips swollen from his kiss, his taste lingering there.

"Rafe, not here, not now."

"When, then? If you think I will go away when we leave this place, *chérie,* you are wrong." His gaze traveled over her face and searched her eyes. "I will want you for the rest of my life."

Kacey could hardly lift her voice above a whisper. "How can I be sure of that, Rafe?"

"When you come to trust your feelings, *chérie,* you will know that what I tell you is true, will always be true." Rafe released his arms from around her and stood, staring down at her. "I will wait for you, *chérie.*"

"Rafe, please go on. I want to work here a while longer." Kacey's knees felt as though they were made of rubber. She needed to gather strength for her weakened limbs before she stood to leave the chamber. She doubted the food that awaited her would offer the sustenance to quell her shaking legs.

"I meant I will wait for you, *ma chérie,* for as long as it takes." There was determination in the smoldering depths of his eyes. Rafe strode to the ladder and did not look back.

Kacey turned to see Rafe's boot as it left the top rung of the ladder and disappeared from sight. For a long moment she felt as empty as the ladder rungs. Rafe's absence had a way of doing that to her. When he was around, she felt a wholeness that was unexplainable. When he was absent, the emptiness was almost frightening.

She looked back at the intricate stones lying against the leathery, bronze skin. She knew they would be cold to touch, yet she reached out to feel them. The last of the visible stones was almost uncovered. Taking her brush, she quickly worked to finish the job.

Short minutes later, Kacey gently lifted one section of the strand. The mummy's face and neck had not yet been uncovered. She would work on that after she had eaten. Alone in the chamber, Kacey lowered the turquoise gently once again to the mummified chest before she stood and left the room.

•   •   •

Clate's lunch turned out to be quite good, Kacey thought. The tinned corned beef, beans, and cheese quickly filled her. She had hardly eaten anything for several days because her stomach still cramped at times. She took the last bites of her food.

"Clate, the meal was absolutely delicious. Thank you," Kacey said to the young rancher.

"Thee is welcome, ma'am."

"John had us believing that your cooking might be hazardous."

"He ought to know. He's eaten plenty of it on the trail. But I never heard him complain." Clate's eyes beamed at the banter.

Kacey watched his gaze move to where Beth sat on a log nearby before coming back to rest on her. John and Rainey stood in the distance, deep in conversation. The others sat lazily around the campsite, momentarily enjoying the break. Colin cut into the conversation.

"My dear, I've been thinking about your mummy and that necklace. The quality of those stones looks to be enormous."

"It does, doesn't it, Father? I don't even know what the agreement is between you and John on what we find. I certainly can't keep the necklace. It belongs in a museum."

"My dear, we'll make those determinations later. I'm sure that we and John can come to an amicable agreement."

Rafe's dark eyes drank Kacey in, as though she were ambrosia. "*Oui, chérie*, I would like to see you keep the necklace. It is your find."

"Rafe's right, my dear. But we'll talk about it later. Right now I know we're all anxious to get back to work and get our ancient friend out of the cellar." Colin donned his worn fedora and stood, the others following suit.

Back inside the lower room, each one worked to uncover the mummy further. The professionals were sympathetic to the perpetual look of distaste on John's face.

"John, it might help if you used your bandanna to cover your nose," Kacey suggested. "The smell probably will not get any better."

"I'd already come to that conclusion. I guess it just goes with the occupation."

The silky sound of Kacey's laughter echoed in the chamber.

"But don't you think it's worth it, John?"

"Oh, yes, ma'am," John answered in his cowboy drawl. "I'd rather be right here than anywhere else in the world. I knew the first time I laid eyes on this place that it was an important find. I'm just glad I was able to convince someone." John glanced toward Colin.

"My lad, it's been a rewarding experience." Colin looked to where Victoria stood near the ladder, ready to hand up a bucket of dirt. "Very enlightening, indeed."

Rafe mused at the direction of the professor's thoughts. He glanced toward Kacey to gauge her reaction. Her attention was directed to the trowel in her hand.

Beth called through the opening above them, "Kacey, there's a man here to see you. Mr. Finn has brought him."

Kacey looked at Rafe, then at her father. "Who do you suppose—"

Her words were cut off by the masculine voice.

"Hello! I decided to take you up on your offer, Kacey."

She watched as the lean length of a man descended the ladder and removed a familiar Stetson.

"Logan!" Kacey stood and went toward the gambler. "It's good to see you. How was St. Louis?"

The gambler shifted his weight. "Fine. Just fine. I decided that I'd move on after the playoffs. I was kind of itching to see this pueblo you told me about." He flashed a spotless grin. "Besides, I was missing the sunshine of your smile. There's none like it in St. Louis."

Kacey could have sworn she heard Rafe make a noise that sounded like an angry bull.

"Logan, my lad, we're glad to see you." Colin had come to stand near the man and offered his hand. "We can always use another helper." His gaze moved to Rafe and John. "Isn't that so, lads?"

"Yes, sir." John stood and stepped forward.

"You know Rafe, of course, and this is John Dunning, Logan. If it weren't for him and his family, we wouldn't be here. We're grateful for his invitation."

"Thank thee, Professor, but I'm the one who is grateful for the opportunity to work with thee."

More from his upbringing than motivation, Rafe moved toward the gambler and offered his hand. "*Bonjour,* Monsieur Connor."

"Call me Logan." He accepted the gesture and nodded, his eyes locking momentarily with Rafe's.

Colin turned. "Victoria, my dear, Logan is a friend we met on the train coming out here."

"Good day, ma'am." The gambler inclined his head.

"It's nice to meet you, Logan." Victoria mirrored his smile.

"You're just in time, Logan. Come see our latest find." Kacey's gaze was momentarily drawn to Rafe's dark one as she led the way across the small room. Coming to stand beside her, Logan and the others looked down at the partially uncovered mummy, the exquisite turquoise necklace standing out like a rare flower against bronze.

Logan whistled through his teeth. "So this is what it's all about. That hapless fellow looks like he needs some air, and that necklace looks like it's worth a fortune." Logan's nose wrinkled. "What a peculiar odor."

"You smell it, too? It doesn't seem to bother anyone else." John's mouth quirked playfully as he gazed toward the professionals.

Rafe leveled unreadable eyes at Logan. "Perhaps monsieur would be more comfortable above ground, *n'est-ce pas?*"

Logan returned Rafe's gaze, keen understanding glistening in the depths. "Oh, I wouldn't miss this for the world, friend. That necklace is beyond anything I've ever seen." Logan squatted beside Kacey, who had dipped to her working position.

"It is very beautiful, isn't it? I'm hoping that after this, the museum will take an interest." Kacey began her brushing.

"My dear, I can almost guarantee when Putnam sees this necklace, his eyes will bulge like a bullfrog's." Colin grinned at the picture formed in his mind, of a cigar-smoking toad sitting at the intricately carved mahogany desk. "If the quality of that turquoise doesn't get them out here, then nothing will."

"They should be quite interested in this mummy, too. Don't you think, Father?"

"Yes, yes, dear. If they're not, they're absolute idiots. I think Putnam will be interested in everything we've found."

The brushing and troweling continued through the afternoon until a complete top view of the mummy was visible. Spiral buckskin leggings extended to his knees. More buckskin was bound around his waist, one end falling like an apron to the middle of his thighs; the other was thrown toga-fashion over his shoulder. Moccasins of the same material were found with soft insoles of cedar bark. Pressed against his side, a soft blanket of what appeared to be rabbitskin awaited his use. He must have wrapped endless narrow strips of fur around a loosely woven thin rope network.

"Hapless fellow is still gripping his *atlatl*," Colin offhandedly remarked.

"What is that, Professor?" Logan, looking at the stick about two feet long, with a notch at one end and two finger loops attached at the other, seemed truly interested in the workings of the dig.

Colin glanced at his daughter and Rafe to see if the implication of what they were seeing registered. The looks on their faces told him it did. "A spear thrower, or *atlatl,* is an old, old implement that preceded the bow. In principle it served as a mechanical extension of the arm. The user inserted his first two fingers into the loops, tipped his wrist so that the instrument extended backward, and inserted a long spear or dart into the notch at the farther end, balancing its length on the heel of his hand. With a mighty heave he cast the whole thing at his target, retaining the spear thrower by the finger loops."

"A true warrior would take it with him into the afterlife," Kacey interjected, meeting her father's eyes. "This burial is very, very old, isn't it, Father?" Her question was more a statement than an inquiry.

"Yes, my dear. I would say very old."

"This man died before the bow was ever invented, *n'est-ce pas*, Professor?"

John made a noise through his teeth.

"That's my calculation, Rafe." Colin doffed his fedora and took his handkerchief from his pocket, dabbing at his forehead.

Later, as everyone sat around the campfire, eating the evening meal of bacon and beans, Rafe glowered at Logan, who was seated near Kacey. She smiled and laughed at everything he said. The fellow took every opportunity to be near her, Rafe seethed. To make matters worse, she seemed to be exceptionally friendly to the man. The woman was a study in foolish trust, he mused. She didn't really know anything about the man, except what he had told them on the train. He was probably an international thief posing as a gambler. Even if that were not so, who could trust a gambler? *Ah la vache!* As if the previous days' events were not enough to worry about, now this . . . this *voleur,* thief, comes into camp. *Mon Dieu,* but the mademoiselle needed her head examined. Maybe he was just the one to do it.

Seventeen

The next day's work progressed rapidly, and by early afternoon the mummy was nearly completely uncovered. The area around his grave also was partially excavated.

"Father, have you noticed anything different about this lower level of the pueblo?"

"You see it, too, dear?"

"Yes, I see what's missing, what's different from our other excavations. There is no pottery here, only baskets." Kacey's eyes widened at the impact of her statement. "Father, I believe we're looking at a specimen much, much older than the former occupants of the pueblo." Kacey's gaze steadied to meet her father's before she looked toward Rafe, directly across from her. His eyes shone with an unreadable gleam that caught her off guard.

"What do *you* say, Rafe?" Kacey's voice held a challenge and something more as she looked into the dark magnetic eyes that seemed to hold some sort of new determination. Last night his behavior toward Logan had bordered on impudence. She was not going to mistreat someone just because Rafe acted like a cad. Logan was her friend, and Rafe had no hold on her.

Refusing to release her gaze, Rafe slowly brought the back of his hand to rub across the shadow of beard on his jaw. "I think it may be too early to say, *chérie.*"

The velvety murmur of the endearment skipped across her skin like angel wings, leaving prickles as it went and causing her dratted heart to skip a beat. "I believe it's a theory I'll stay with until proven otherwise," she replied. Breaking the eye contact, Kacey shifted in her kneeling position, hoping to rid herself of Rafe's effect. To prove she had, she directed her attention to Logan who knelt beside her.

"As you can see, Logan, even the experts disagree on archaeology. We're a very argumentative group."

"I see that." Logan dipped his head before giving Kacey a sidelong glance. "But I'm just wondering one thing here." He paused. "Who's going to be pallbearer for this fellow to the light of day?"

Kacey couldn't control her burst of laughter. She played along with the banter. "Are you skittish, Logan? This gentleman is not half as intimidating as his descendants. Take my word for it." She looked toward the rancher. "Isn't that so, John?"

"Well, I suppose Acowitz could be . . . disquieting to a stranger."

"Disquieting is an understatement, John. And that other one I saw—"

John's face sobered. "What other one, Kacey?"

"I meant to ask you about him, John, but I guess it slipped my mind. There was another Indian near camp. Judging from the expression on his face, he didn't appear too happy to have visitors in the area."

"I'd say that may be an understatement, too, considering that someone prepared a nice little tea for us all." John exchanged glances momentarily with Rafe. "If thee sees him again, tell me. I'd like to know who it was."

"He might not have been the one who left the tea, John," Kacey declared.

"He might not have been, that's true. On the other hand, he might know who did."

"Well, if I see him again I'll point him out to you."

"Sounds like toting this fellow out of here will be easy compared to what you've been through. What about a tea? Did I miss that, too?" Logan's question was aimed at no one in particular.

Rafe answered, his voice hardening. "Someone wanted us to have a tea party, and everyone except John and me drank some. As it turned out, the tea was poisoned."

"Let me get this straight. The natives don't want you here, and someone is poisoning the food supply?" Logan pulled at his earlobe.

"Do not be overly concerned, monsieur. If you die, we promise to give you a decent burial." Amusement flickered in Rafe's eyes as he looked at Kacey. *"N'est-ce pas, chérie?"*

"Logan, Rafe's humor seems to be lacking, as usual." Kacey cast stormy eyes toward the Frenchman, who returned her gaze in mock innocence, the dark shadow of beard adding to his rakish appearance.

Logan looked at Rafe and smiled, his eyes crinkling at the corners. "Oh, I don't know, Kacey. I think he's pretty funny."

Rafe, smiling too, met the gambler's gaze, and for a moment he almost liked him. "Monsieur, would you like the distinction of being pallbearer for our resting friend? I assumed from your inquiry that you wanted that honor, *n'est-ce pas?"*

Rafe's eyes never wavered as he waited for the man's reply.

Logan nodded, his gaze gleaming. "That is very kind of you to offer, Rafe. I accept the honor. Just one thing, though. How is a mummy carried? Is it potato-sack style or cradle style? I want to do this correctly."

"Monsieur, when the time comes, you will know." Rafe laughed inside. He reluctantly admitted to himself that the gambler was a sport—but one that would bear watching. He still didn't trust the man, especially where Kacey was concerned. Maybe he didn't trust him because he recognized himself in the depths of the man's eyes. He admitted he had made love to a few women and left them. He'd made no promises, and they hadn't been heartbroken. Now he wanted only one woman, and that was Kacey. She stirred him as no other could, and the wanting never ended.

Kacey came out from under the cloth behind the camera. Colin had seen to the lighting, and she had determined the shots to be taken. "Okay, I have all the photographs I want. Father, do you want any more?"

"No, dear, I believe you've covered it. I think we can get our man outside now." Colin looked toward Logan. "So, lad, have you been appointed pallbearer?"

"Yes, sir, I believe I have." All eyes watched as Logan moved to reach for the mummy, then brought him to rest over his shoulder. "Tell me if I'm doing this wrong, now." Slowly turning to look at the others, his mouth crooked into a grin. "I think he likes me. But I'm going to have to tell him about his breath."

Kacey and Victoria's gentle laughter echoed in the chamber.

"Lad, make sure you've got a tight hold on him before you start up the ladder," Colin explained, concern for the specimen apparent on his face.

"Professor, I'll be right behind him in case he needs any assistance," Rafe assured Colin.

John strode to the ladder. "I'll go up first and help from above."

Logan somehow managed to climb the ladder with the specimen in tow and the Frenchman on his heels.

Kacey could not help but smile at the initiation process that Rafe had set up for Logan. He took it all in stride, and she admired him for that.

She had removed the necklace from the mummy and

held it carefully in her hands. She knew the perfect place to keep the necklace. She planned to place it in the silver box Rafe had given her on his return to America. Her hold tightened on the necklace, and she went up the ladder behind Rafe.

When she reached the top rung, Rafe stood there offering his hand. She took it as if it were the most natural thing in the world, then stepped to solid ground. Rafe continued to hold her hand and moved closer to her. His gaze captured hers like a butterfly in a net. The dark, sensual maleness of him and the urgency in his mahogany eyes seemed to rob Kacey of her breath.

"*Chérie*, you are trembling."

The velvet of his voice was almost like an epiphany to Kacey. His lips were near her hair, and she thought she felt them briefly brush the strands. Reluctantly she removed her hand from his and willed her heartbeat to largo, but the stubborn thing continued its staccato rhythm.

"No, I'm not, Rafe. You just startled me, that's all." Kacey knew the excuse sounded weak.

"Would you like me to keep the necklace for you, *chérie*? With the happenings around here of late, I'm not sure you are safe with it in your possession."

"I plan to keep it in a secure place, Rafe."

He moved even closer to her. "You misunderstand, *chérie*. It is not the necklace that I am worried about."

Kacey stepped slightly away. "Thank you for your concern, Rafe, but I would like to keep the necklace, for now anyway."

Victoria came up the ladder followed by Colin, and Kacey separated herself further from Rafe, moving toward the doorway.

Colin called to his daughter while removing a clean white handkerchief from his shirt pocket. "Here, dear, wrap the necklace in this. It could suddenly break."

Kacey took the cloth and laid the necklace in its folds.

"What would archaeologists do without their handker-chiefs, Father?"

Colin chuckled. "Lose a lot of important finds, my dear. If they're not wrapped up they seem to have a way of slipping right through your fingers." Sensing for the first time the charged atmosphere, his gaze moved between Rafe and his daughter. He cleared his throat. "I'm going to talk to John about making a protective crate for the mummy." Colin nodded to the woman standing nearby. "Victoria, do you care to come along?"

"Why, yes, Colin. I want to learn every aspect of this field." Victoria gave Colin a look of understanding. He waited for her to move in front of him, and they went out the doorway.

Rafe made a fluid movement toward Kacey, much like a mountain lion, she thought—swift, graceful, with pur-pose. She was close enough to him to feel his breath warm against her cheek. She watched in fascination, his gaze trailing over every inch of her face before seeming to rest on the hollow of her neck. When his gaze did drift back to hers, he looked as if he had found the Holy Grail. That was Kacey's undoing.

Rafe brought his hands up to gently cup her face. "*Chérie,* I want to be alone with you, and there never seems to be an opportunity." His baritone voice was thick and unsteady.

Kacey drank in the comfort of his nearness, and his hands pressed against her face. She remembered the magic of those hands when they had explored the nether regions of her body. Like a fog seeping into her every pore, a deep longing swept over Kacey. She wanted Rafe to hold her as he had when they'd made love. Lucid thought was be-coming difficult, a feeling Kacey did not relish, but one her body welcomed with enthusiasm. Her brain cursed her traitorous senses as the hunger deepened, and her body swayed toward him.

Rafe moved like a hawk, enveloping her in the fold of

his arms and capturing her lips with his. The kiss was urgent and hot, and Kacey gave as she received. Her tongue sought the fiery depths of Rafe's mouth, as if she could gain entrance into his soul, abiding there forever. His hard, muscular body pressed into her softer one as if to meld them like clay dolls.

Rafe was the one to end the kiss. He rested his cheek against her hair, bringing one hand to cup the back of her head while his other brushed up and down the length of her back. His nostrils drank in the aroma of her lavender-scented hair as if starved for her scent.

"*Bien-aimée*, beloved, when I kiss you, everything else melts away. It is as if we are the only two people in the world."

The low caressing murmur of his voice did delicious things to Kacey's insides. She stepped back and looked into his deep mahogany eyes, as if searching for life itself. "You feel that, too, Rafe?"

He pulled her back into the cocoon of his arms, his gaze never leaving her face. "*Oui.*" The urgency in his voice equaled the urgency in the tightening of his embrace. "*Chérie*, meet me outside the camp tonight."

Kacey gasped, feeling his hard male staff press into her belly. Anticipation and reluctance played around her senses like taunting elves. She looked away. "Rafe, I don't know."

"*Chérie*, look at me."

At that moment a voice called from outside the doorway, and Kacey stepped out of Rafe's arms and the shadows of the room toward the entrance. Shaking his head and muttering a curse that dealt directly with the gambler, Rafe put his hands on his hips and followed her outside.

"Ah, there you are. What aspect of archaeology are you two debating now?" Logan's tone seemed playful.

"Monsieur, we are debating whether or not you would make a good mummy specimen. I thought you might." Rafe arched one eyebrow mischievously.

"Rafe!" Kacey looked at Logan and forced a smile.

"I'm glad Kacey disagrees." The gambler removed his Stetson and brushed it against his thigh before flashing a brilliant smile at Kacey. "And speaking of mummies, our friend is resting in the men's tent until a crate can be made. The other young ladies did not find his presence so . . . welcome."

"Oh, dear. I guess Beth and Rainey just haven't gotten used to what archaeology entails. They weren't prepared for this."

"You'll have to admit, Kacey, the poor fellow is quite unsettling."

Kacey's gentle laugh floated through the air. "Yes, I suppose one could say that." Against the sun, low in the western sky, her eyes sought Rafe's. His questioning gaze pressed her for an answer. She knew she would have to come to a decision. Later he wanted her to go to him in the velvet night after everyone else had gone to bed. And there he would do all the things to her that her body ached for, craved for, even cried out for. And then what? He did not love her. He had never said so. Surely she could not be so foolish, her brain taunted. Rafe was a womanizer, and she knew it. Yet . . . now he seemed so vulnerable.

The campfire blazed like a beacon in the darkness. Supper was over, and everyone sat listening to Logan play his harmonica. Victoria, holding Isis in the fold of her arm, had requested "Shenandoah," and the lovely, haunting melody rode the evening breeze.

Kacey refused to look at Rafe. She felt his eyes pulling her to him like a magnet to iron. The urge to look his way was strong, but she knew if she did she would be compelled to do his bidding, and she was not sure if she wanted that. She kept her eyes on Logan and enjoyed the lovely melody he played, but her thoughts were of Rafe and the way his hypnotic touch turned her to jelly.

The music stopped, and Logan leaned forward, gently

slapping the harmonica against his thigh. "I think that's all for tonight. I don't want to bore you."

"Why, Mr. Connor, your music is anything but boring. Please play us one more." Victoria looked at the others. "What shall it be?"

Rainey spoke up, directing her attention to Logan. "Do you know the Stephen Foster song 'Beautiful Dreamer'? That's one of my favorites. If you'll play it, I'll sing."

"Deal, Miss Billings. You start it off, and I'll follow." Logan once again placed the harmonica to his lips. Rainey began the song:

> *Beautiful dreamer, wake unto me,*
> *Starlight and dewdrops are waiting for thee;*
> *Sounds of the rude world heard in the day,*
> *Lull'd by the moonlight have all pass'd a way.*

The listeners were spellbound by Rainey's lovely soprano voice. She continued and came to the last verse.

> *Beautiful dreamer, beam on my heart,*
> *E'en as the morn on the streamlet and sea;*
> *Then will all clouds of sorrow depart,*
> *Beautiful dreamer, awake unto me.*

Victoria was the first to speak. "What a lovely song to finish with." She looked at Rainey. "You have a breathtaking voice, my dear. Have you thought of going on the stage?"

Rainey's gaze darted to her sister, and she let out a near laugh. "Yes, I have thought of it, but Father and Mother nearly go into apoplexy if I mention the stage." Then her gaze moved quickly to John and back to Victoria. "It doesn't seem to be so important anymore. I just sing for my own enjoyment."

"Victoria's right, Rainey, your voice is lovely. Thank

you for singing for us.'' Kacey stood and said, ''Thank you, Logan, for playing.''

He started to speak, but Rafe, now standing near Kacey, cut in. ''The music was *extraordinaire,* mademoiselle and monsieur.'' Rafe's gaze moved quickly and captured Kacey's. She had avoided his eyes all evening, but now she had looked at him, and he refused to let her go. The question was in his eyes. Would she meet him outside camp?

Kacey's gaze darted away, seeking protection for her traitorous body. Then she made her resolve. She would meet him and talk to him, but that would be as far as it would go. Just talk.

Soon the campfire died down, and everyone retired to their respective tents. Rainey, Victoria, and Beth readied for bed, and Kacey sat near the lamp and pretended to read.

''Will the light bother you if I read for a while? I don't seem to be very sleepy tonight.'' She directed her question mainly toward Victoria.

''Of course not, dear. We're very adaptable, aren't we, girls?'' Victoria looked toward the sisters and smiled.

Beth dropped to her bed, her eyes sparkling. ''Certainly. As long as we don't have to keep company with our mummy friend. I mean, that bald head with the locks of loose hair and those receding gums makes one quite opinionated toward the poor fellow.''

''You girls are too hard on our friend. Why, I bet in his day he was quite handsome. Don't you agree, Kacey?''

''Oh, I'm sure he was, Victoria. Probably a prince or something similar.''

''Well, just the same, I'll take the walking, talking kind of prince,'' Beth declared.

Kacey laughed. ''You mean you don't like our mummy?''

''Let's just say I've seen all of him I want to see.'' Beth snuggled back into her bed, then sat up. ''Ugh. I just had a horrible thought. What if he shows up in my dreams tonight?''

"Well, sister dear, you'd better treat him nice. You know, the curse and all." Rainey winked at Kacey.

"What curse?" By now Beth's eyes were like silver dollars.

"Didn't you hear Acowitz's predictions?"

"Why, yes, but you don't believe all that, do you?" Beth seemed to plead for denial.

"Bill Finn does. I haven't made up my mind yet." Rainey looked at Kacey. "What do you think, Kacey? You've been around ancient sites and mummies before. Do they leave curses in their wake?"

"There've been tales of such. But I've never seen any firsthand."

"I'm thankful for that, dear. Now maybe we can all settle down. This talk of curses is giving me the jitters." Victoria took the pins from her hair, and its length cascaded down her back.

"Victoria, I can't picture you as ever having the jitters," Kacey declared. "You always seem so—so together."

"Well, thank you, dear, but looks can be deceiving sometimes." Victoria cast an enigmatic glance toward Kacey. "I can assure you that as a young lady when the War between the States broke out I had plenty of jitters. Since then, I guess it does take a lot to shake me."

"Those must have been very hard times," Kacey said.

Victoria drew the fine-toothed comb through her long tresses. "Yes. Very hard. My father was killed in that war. Mother died soon after, and . . . I stayed in Lexington for a while. But it was never the same, and I felt I had to get away. I did some traveling, and that's when I met Martin, my husband, on a steamer to Scotland." Victoria cast her gaze to Kacey. "Have I told you, dear, that Rafe reminds me so of Martin?"

At the mention of the Frenchman's name, Kacey felt her heart lurch. Instantly she visualized his dark eyes filled with an emotion that she could not name. "No, I don't believe you have."

"Oh, yes. It's not so much that they look alike as their manner of bearing, so gentlemanly." Victoria smiled. "Well, it's getting late. I'll see you all in the morning. Good-night." She moved to her cot.

"Good-night." The word came simultaneously from the other three.

Kacey put her book on the makeshift table. "It's a little stuffy in here. I'm going to take a short walk in the night air before I dress for bed."

"Watch out for the snakes," Rainey cautioned. "John says they can be bad news."

"I will. Thanks for reminding me." Kacey stood and moved toward the tent opening. Snakes were the furthest thing from her mind.

Outside a full moon beamed overhead, and Kacey momentarily thought of the biblical description of the moon: "The lesser light to rule the night." Had God created the night and the moon for lovers? She walked slowly in the moonlight, watching strange shapes and shadows appear and disappear. Where was Rafe?

Her mind had no sooner asked the question than she heard a soft voice.

"Chérie." Rafe covered the short distance to Kacey. "I'm glad you came." His hand reached out to touch her hair.

Before Kacey could reply, he swept her into his arms, and pressed his lips against hers like a man starved for life itself. Kacey felt herself quickly falling into a realm of desire—a realm so strong that all forces seemed to be working toward the same end. Where was her reserve slipping to? Why did his touch do such wondrous things to her insides? She melted into the kiss with him, reason abandoning her like a mutinous sailor.

She struggled for rational thought, but his kiss deepened. His tongue sought the deep moistness of her mouth, in imitation of his real need. His hands were trailing lower and lower down her back.

He moved his lips from hers and nipped at her earlobe before he huskily whispered in her ear, "*Bien-aimée*, I want you. I need you."

With Rafe's lips at a safe distance now, rational thought was coming back to Kacey. Her body ached for his touch, but her mind was still sane. "Rafe, I only came to talk."

"Are you sure, *chérie*?" His mouth was very close to hers once more. His unshaven jaw brushed her cheek, sending shivers of delight to her toes.

With all her strength that somehow lacked conviction, she replied, "Yes. I'm sure."

Eighteen

"Ah, *oui*. I see, *chérie*." Rafe was nodding as if he had been enlightened, and his voice became lower and hard. "And does Logan have anything to do with this decision?"

Kacey's gaze snapped up to meet his, and she responded sharply, "Why, what on earth do you mean? Logan is my friend. That's all. You're a cad, Rafe, to imply otherwise." Kacey paused. "I came out here to talk, but if all you're going to do is insult me, then I'll leave." She turned on her heel to do just that.

Rafe's arm snaked out to grab her wrist. "Wait a minute, *chérie*. If you will stay, we can talk." In the moonlight Rafe saw the skittish look in her eyes. "I promise." He still held on to her wrist as if it were his lifeline.

Most of her anger evaporated at his promise.

"All right, Rafe. I'll stay."

"We can walk awhile if you like." He swapped her wrist for her hand, holding it gently but firmly.

"Yes, that would be nice." The two fell into step and walked slowly side by side. "When you were a child, Rafe, I'll bet you always got your way." Kacey gave him a mischievous sideways glance.

"I did not, *chérie. Au contraire, mon père* took me firmly in hand at an early age, *Dieu merci.*"

Kacey was struck by the boyish charm in Rafe's voice.

"*Ma mère* was much more lenient than Father. He saw this and kindly but flatly took the upper hand. He saw to it that I knew the running of the estate at a young age." Rafe chuckled. "I think he was surprised when I announced that I wanted to study archaeology. I believe he thought that I would come back from Oxford and be ready to help with the estate. His illness came as a shock to everyone. He was always so healthy." Rafe turned to look at Kacey. "Even when I went back to France after New York, *maman* needed me more than he did. He came out of it fine."

"I'm glad, Rafe."

"*Merci beaucoup.* Papa is a strong man." Rafe stopped walking and turned to Kacey. "I know my family would like very much to meet you, *chérie.* Perhaps someday you and your father can travel to France, *n'est-ce pas?*"

"I'd like that, Rafe." Kacey drank in the comfort of his nearness.

Rafe was fast losing his resolve to merely talk. It was all he could do to keep from taking Kacey in his arms once again. The thought of her at his family's home was doing strange things to his senses. Never before had he wanted to take a woman home with him. To keep. For all time. He pictured in his mind what wondrous things he could do to her body. Her body that curved in all the right places. Her body that seemed to make all others pale. Rafe mentally shook himself.

"I think we should start back now, *chérie.*" His voice lowered to a husky murmur. "I am finding it more and more difficult to keep my hands off you, *bien-aimée.* And I do not want to break my promise."

"Rafe, I—"

He silenced her with a kiss that deepened until they both swirled in a vortex of emotion. His arms cocooned her soft body against his. Rafe fought for control and won a bitter victory. With deep regret he released Kacey, soft and pliant in his embrace.

His voice was husky with need as he murmured close to Kacey's ear, "We'd better get back. It's getting late." Rafe shut his eyes, his nostrils drinking in the heady scent of her hair, his body trembling at her nearness and refusing to do his mind's bidding. *Mon Dieu,* but she was intoxicating, Rafe mused through his muddled senses. He would have a difficult time getting through this night. His masculine stem ached as if in reply.

Kacey felt as if she had been given a potent drug. Nothing seemed to matter, except Rafe's lips and Rafe's body as it had pressed into hers. Her head reeled from his kiss, and her midsection churned deep and low—lower and lower into her secret woman part, giving birth to a need so powerful, so strong she trembled with desire. Her voice was strained as she fought for coherent speech.

"Yes. It's very late."

Rafe stepped aside, placing his palm in the small of Kacey's back, his gaze penetrating the moonlight to capture hers. "Thank you for walking with me, *chérie.* I would not have missed it."

His hand seemed to sear through the material of Kacey's dress like a branding iron, and she looked into dark eyes that promised more than words ever would. Mentally shaking herself, she broke the spell that threatened her composure, and glanced away before starting the walk back to camp.

"It is very lovely out here under the stars, isn't it, Rafe?" She was looking heavenward now, the lights filling the big, velvet sky while a whippoorwill sang nearby. "It looks as if a person could almost reach out and touch them, they seem that close."

"Yes, *chérie,* they do. When I am near you I believe anything is possible." Rafe stopped walking and faced Kacey. He stood so close he could feel the heat from her body. His desire urged him nearer, but sanity won out, and he did not take her in his arms as he ached to do. "Would you like a star, *chérie*?" His raspy voice dropped to a whisper. "I will try to get it for you."

Knowing full well he could no more get her a star than travel to the moon, Kacey stood still, feeling as though her heart and soul had been unlocked—and Rafe had disposed of the key. She sensed the barely controlled power that was coiled in his body and sought safer ground.

"Sounds wonderful, but I don't believe I'll take a star tonight, Rafe. Some other time." Kacey laughed softly and willed her feet forward.

Rafe's head jerked as something sounded behind them.

"Don't move," he whispered near her ear. "We seem to have picked up some company." He motioned Kacey to the nearest brush for cover. There they waited to see if anyone followed. No one did.

"What is it, Rafe?"

"I don't know, *chérie*, but someone was out there. And I don't think it was any of our people."

The campfire still launched swirling smoke skyward as Rafe saw Kacey safely to her tent. Clate was in his bedroll near the supply wagon, and Rafe moved to the men's quarters and peered inside. The professor, John, and Logan appeared to be sleeping. Rafe was glad he had taken up sleeping outside. It enabled him to keep watch at night. He moved to where he had placed his bedroll within sight of the ladies' tent. He had an uneasy feeling as he spread the covering on the ground. Someone had evidently been near the camp tonight. *Mon Dieu!* Maybe it had just been an animal. He was on edge for no real reason. Maybe he had just imagined the noise. He took a cheroot from his shirt pocket and reached for a match. He changed his mind and stuffed the cheroot back into his pocket. If someone was out there watching, he didn't want him to know where he was.

• • •

"Come to me, precious, come to me now."

Kacey watched in horror, speechless, as Isis slowly waddled toward Victoria, the ancient turquoise necklace dangling from her tiny canine teeth.

Victoria slowly reached to take the dog into her arms and finally convinced Isis to let go of her newfound treasure. "I'm so sorry, Kacey, dear. I don't know how she could have gotten hold of your necklace."

Kacey, sound asleep only moments ago, swallowed hard to gain her equilibrium before she spoke. She had opened her eyes to the sight before her. Thinking it was a horrible nightmare, she could only watch as the scene unfolded in front of her. Her precious necklace, which she had placed in the silver box, had become a tiny dog's plaything. She found her tongue.

"I-it's all right, Victoria. It doesn't appear to be harmed."

Still holding the terrier in the fold of her arms, Victoria walked to stand beside Kacey, offering the necklace to her. "Here, dear. Please look it over. I think it's survived, but please see for yourself."

Kacey reached trembling fingers to take the strands of turquoise beads. She could not let on to Victoria her absolute horror at seeing the necklace in the dog's mouth. "I'm sure it's fine." She clutched the beads close to her and shuddered.

She had placed the necklace in her silver box and put it under her bed. A mistake for certain. She would have to find a new hiding place. Perhaps she should let Rafe keep it. With her luck, if she buried it, Isis would dig it up.

"Dear, I'm glad that whoever made that necklace made it strong. I would have been devastated if Isis had broken it."

Kacey knew her sentiments exactly. "It wouldn't have been her fault. I shouldn't have left it where she could reach it. I hope you won't punish her."

"I never punish her. She does her best to be good, and that's all that anyone can ask."

Kacey agreed with Victoria and reached for the fluff of fur in Victoria's arms. She brought the animal to her cheek.

"I'll find you a new toy, darling Isis. Thanks for keeping my necklace safe."

The small dog uncurled its tongue and lapped repeatedly at Kacey's face. She let out a peal of laughter as the wet kisses covered her cheek. The commotion brought Beth and Rainey to a sitting position on their cots, rubbing sleep from their eyes.

"Time for me to get up, Isis. And thanks for pointing out to me that the necklace was not in a safe place." Kacey put the dog down and brought the necklace over her head. That was the safest place she knew of at the moment.

The women went about their morning ablutions and were soon dressed and ready to join the men around the campfire for breakfast. Clate turned salt pork that sizzled in a spider skillet, and John put another log on the fire. The inviting aroma of coffee wafted from a hanging pot.

Colin came to sit near Victoria, balancing his plate in one hand and his coffee in another.

"This has been one of the most exciting trips I've ever been on," she told him.

"Now, my dear, you're not exaggerating, are you?"

"I never exaggerate. Working alongside you and Kacey has been an experience I shall never forget. Kacey has the ability to be a leader for our gender." She paused and glanced at Colin. "It's in her stars, and I think she will go very far in the field of archaeology. She's very lucky to have you for a father."

"Why, thank you, Victoria, that's kind of you to say."

"Oh, I'm not being kind. Many men try to squelch their daughters, thinking they should be brought up to be wives and mothers only. Don't get me wrong. There's nothing wrong with that if that is what a young woman wants. But

Kacey seems to be special, and I think it is because you have given her her lead. It takes a special man to do that."

"Kacey was a precocious child. She had an inquiring mind that never stopped. Her mother died when she was very young, and she has been with me ever since. I've tried to teach her what I know about archaeology, and she has been a quick study."

Victoria nodded, then looked to where Kacey stood. She watched as Logan and Rafe hovered nearby. "She seems to have many admirers. But, of course, someone as lovely as Kacey would have many." Victoria smiled and looked back at Colin.

He chuckled. "For someone who doesn't want an attachment, she seems to keep them dangling."

"Smart girl." Victoria paused, then coyly said, "We women can't give away all our secrets, Colin. Maybe she has more up her sleeve than you know."

"You think so, do you?"

Victoria looked toward Rafe, his expression brooding. "I'm sure of it." She took a bite of the crisp meat, then expertly changed the subject. "It's amazing, isn't it, Colin, how food cooked outside and eaten outside always tastes so wonderful."

"You're a fascinating woman, Victoria. You love the outdoors as much as I do."

Victoria merely nodded, and the two lapsed into silence, finishing off their food.

Rafe watched in disgust as Logan draped his coat across the fallen log for Kacey to sit on before tipping his Stetson to her.

"Good mornin', ma'am. Did you have a good night?" Logan asked.

Kacey could not keep her gaze from flying to meet Rafe's magnetic one before she replied, "Yes, I slept very well, thank you." She shut her eyes and took a deep breath of the cool mesa air. Memories of the previous evening flooded into her thoughts. Rafe's kiss lingered against her lips, and his touch seemed to envelop her once again as she recalled his arms wrapped around her.

Rafe cut into the conversation. "And how did *you* sleep, monsieur?" His smile was sardonic, and his tone indicated that he could not have cared less how the gambler had fared through the night.

"I slept like a newborn baby when I slept." Logan paused. "But you know, something kept bothering me. I kept hearing this moaning sound. Or maybe it was more of a wailing sound."

"A wailing sound?" Rafe asked.

"Yeah, I never did figure out what it was."

"Well, monsieur, did it sound animal or human?"

Kacey's gaze bounced back and forth between the two men like a tennis ball. Rafe's impatience with the man was obvious.

"Well, you see, I'm not sure. Can you tell the difference?"

"*Oui,* monsieur. I think I could tell the difference."

"Perhaps it was a banshee from my father's homeland." Logan winked at Kacey and grinned. "But I don't know if they could make it all the way to America. Perhaps it was the Indian version. What do you think, Kacey?"

"I think you're full of it, Logan Connor, and I'm going to fix my plate." Kacey watched Logan's smile widen at her accusation. She stood and moved to where John was piling a platter held by Rainey with flapjacks and crisp salt pork.

"That looks and smells delicious, John. Have you ever thought of opening a restaurant?" Kacey teased.

John glanced briefly at his brother Clate and continued the badinage. "No, ma'am, I'm afraid the help would go on a sit-down strike. I think I'll stick to ranching."

Kacey laughed. "That's probably just as well, John."

Rainey set the platter down on the makeshift table, and Kacey helped herself to the fare before filling a cup with coffee. She moved back to where she had been seated near Rafe and Logan. By now the two men were helping themselves to the delicious food also. She took a bite of her food then sipped at the coffee, glancing toward her father and Victoria. They seemed deep in conversation. Kacey mused at how her father was smitten with Victoria. She didn't blame him. Victoria was a prize, and she hoped he could see that.

"*Chérie*, you seem to be enjoying your breakfast. I hope it is as delicious as it looks on your lips. But then, anything on your lips would be delicious." Rafe's gaze seemed glued to Kacey's mouth as she licked syrup from the corners of her lips.

Kacey felt the blood rush to her cheeks, and there wasn't a thing she could do about it. Her gaze riveted to dark, silky hairs on the back of Rafe's hands—the same hands that had made love to her. Her cheeks blossomed even more at the thought.

Rafe, holding his plate and drink, seated himself beside Kacey, some distance from the others. "You are *ravissante* when you blush, *chérie*. You should do it more often, *n'est-ce pas*?" His voice was low and husky, meant for her ears only.

Kacey was determined to change the subject. His low, sensuous voice sent prickles of delight along her veins and warning signals to her brain. She smiled and seemed to ignore his remarks.

"You know, Rafe, we've made a very profitable find. I know that after Harvard gets news of the mummy, they should certainly be interested in financing a dig here. I hope they'll ask Father to head it up."

"I think the professor would like to see them ask you."

"I doubt that would ever happen, and even if it did, I would refuse. Father is the person for the job."

"You're very loyal, aren't you, *chérie*?"

"Loyalty has nothing to do with this, but yes, when it

comes to those I love, I suppose I am.'' She met his gaze head-on.

"Then, *chérie*, one would be very lucky to be loved by you.'' His voice was a velvet murmur.

He was doing it again, and Kacey sought release as she saw Logan headed in their direction. She was struck by the contrast between the two men. Logan was light where Rafe was dark. Logan liked to tease, and she saw it for what it was. But Rafe made her heart leap and made her ache with desire. He had never mentioned love, and she would be foolish to think he would offer it, but that did not stop the longing that would not let go. Logan broke her pensive mood.

"Kacey, how about a short horseback ride before we start digging?''

"Sounds like a great idea.'' Kacey stood and looked at the Frenchman. "Would you like to come, too, Rafe?''

His dark countenance relayed his stormy thoughts. "*Non*, I don't believe so. I have some things to attend to.'' He stood and walked away.

"Let me put these dishes with the others, and I'll meet you by the horses.'' Kacey gathered her cup from the log and set out toward the small makeshift table near the fire. She watched Rafe's broad shoulders as he moved toward the pueblo.

Kacey presently met Logan where the horses were tethered. They each saddled their horse and soon where riding side by side.

"I'll race you to that far rock,'' Logan challenged.

"Okay, but don't get too much dust between your teeth.'' As soon as the words were out of Kacey's mouth, she urged the mare forward at a fast pace. The wind whipped at her cheeks and hair, and she reveled in the freedom of just being. It had been days since she had ridden, and she enjoyed the pure pleasure of it.

Logan's horse was bigger and faster, soon overtaking Kacey's smaller mare. He passed her at a brisk pace, then slowed as he neared the rock they had aimed for. Kacey quickly came up beside him, meeting his smile with one of her own.

"Well, you've won this time, Logan. But there'll be others."

"Ma'am, it surely troubles me to beat one as lovely as you."

Kacey laughed, her gaze taking in the gray eyes so different from Rafe's. "Yes, I can see how it troubles you, Logan. You're grinning from ear to ear."

"You wound me, Kacey. Would I lie to you?"

"Maybe not exactly lie, but you sure know how to stretch the truth."

Logan smiled a smile that could charm the socks off a snake. Kacey was not immune.

"Now, you know I wouldn't do that." Logan paused and seemed to search for words. "Kacey, I want to ask you something. It's pretty obvious how Rafe feels about you. I just wanted to know if you feel the same."

Kacey stared at him for a long moment. "Just how do you think Rafe feels about me, Logan?"

"The man is besotted with you. Didn't you know? He fairly growls everytime I come near you."

"You may be right, but that doesn't mean he's in love with me or anything."

"That is just what I think. Do you love him?"

"Why should I answer that, Logan?"

"You're a very beautiful woman, Kacey. And I don't want to make any advances that would not be welcome."

"Logan, you are a good friend, and that's the way I would like to keep it. You're like the brother I never had."

"Brother, is it? Well, I guess that answers my question." His gray eyes crinkled at the corners. "I suppose I could stand another sister."

Kacey smiled, and the two rode in silence at walking speed for some distance before she announced, "We'd better get back, Logan." Kacey nudged her mare, and she

quickened to a trot. Logan also increased his pace, and the
two headed toward camp.

Without warning Logan's horse reared, throwing him to
the ground. Kacey came to a stop nearby, jumped from
her mare, and ran to where Logan lay on the ground.

She stooped beside him. "Logan, are you all right?"
she asked breathlessly.

He stirred and raised his head, shaking it side to side.
His vision cleared, and he saw the snake before he heard
the rattle.

"Be still, Kacey." He slowly reached inside his coat
pocket and pulled out the double-barreled derringer he carried there, took careful aim, and the snake's head disappeared.

Kacey gasped. "Where did you learn to shoot like that,
Logan? I didn't even know you carried a pistol."

He rolled to his back and squinted into the sun. "Oh,
I've learned a few things along the way. Never underes-
timate a gambler, Kacey."

Relieved to see that he was all right, she said, "Well, I
hope you've got another horse up your sleeve, because
yours just ran off." She nodded in the direction of a cloud
of dust.

Logan followed her gaze. "Well, at least yours is still
here. You'll let me ride with you, won't you, sis?"

The twinkling stars at night didn't have a thing on the
twinkle in Logan's eyes, Kacey mused. He got to his feet
and brushed the dust from his clothes, then looked around
for his hat and found it nearby.

"It's a good thing one of us knows how to ride," she
teased, "or else we'd both be without a horse." She strode
to the mare and mounted. "Come on, before I change my
mind."

Logan mounted behind her, and they rode toward camp.
Logan's nearness did not have the same effect as Rafe's.
Logan did not stir her blood as Rafe did. Her heart did not
race as his arms came around her to hold the reins.

Soon they reached the camp. Rafe stood near the men's quarters and saw them ride in. The others were with Colin at the dig site. Rafe's jaw clenched when he saw that Logan sat behind Kacey and had his arms draped around her. Unfamiliar emotions ravaged his mind. A fierce need to knock the man's arms away overcame him. He scowled and muttered a curse before he sauntered toward them.

"What a cozy sight. I take it you lost your horse, monsieur?"

"You take it right. Kacey was kind enough to give me a ride."

"Logan was thrown when his horse saw a rattlesnake," Kacey interjected, feeling much like a recalcitrant child under Rafe's dark scrutiny.

"I see." Rafe's pouting gaze perused Kacey from head to toe.

Logan coughed, seemingly to fill the silence that followed, then dismounted the mare. Kacey followed suit, bristling at Rafe's attitude; he acted as if she and Logan were disobedient children.

"I can see you're more than glad to see us, Rafe. Your enthusiasm for the fact that we came back unscathed is heartening." Kacey turned on her heel and went toward the ruins, leaving Logan and Rafe standing beside the horse.

Logan whistled through his teeth. "I think you've just had a dressing down, partner." He paused. "A damn good one."

Rafe arched his brows, still staring after Kacey. "It would seem so, monsieur. It would seem so."

Logan started to lead the horse away, then turned. "You know, this mare is a fine animal. Now, that other horse that ran away, he didn't have sense that God gave a goose."

Nineteen

Kacey was fuming. She wanted to be alone at the moment, so she started off on a path into the scrub. She walked at a brisk speed that indicated her mood, her shoes kicking up dust as she went. The mid-morning sun was warm on her face that already burned with anger. Rafe was absolutely incorrigible at times, she seethed. And this was one of them.

She continued the fast pace for some while. Soon she discovered that she was quite a way from the ruins. She stopped and looked at her surroundings. A short distance ahead, a canyon spread out before her. The panorama was breathtaking, and she stood there taking in the majesty of the colors of the rainbow—mauves, greens, and reds painting a magnificent canvas.

Without warning, a hand clamped across her mouth from behind. She tasted dirt and sweat before an arm snaked around her waist like a steel cord. Kacey fought for breath as the hand threatened to shut off her air supply. She tried to scream, but the strength behind the palm that closed off her mouth was superior to hers. Only a muffled cry that was lost on the breeze escaped.

Her attacker mumbled a savage oath, a language she did not understand, and she was being dragged further from camp. Her feet scrambled to keep pace with the blackguard as he pulled her backward. She tried to call for help, but no sound would come through.

"Rafe, lad, have you seen Kacey? I want to show her another basket I've found near where the mummy was buried." Colin stood in the entrance to the ruins. He held his hat in his hand and dabbed at his brow with his handkerchief.

"Not for some time now, Professor. I thought she was with you." Rafe recalled seeing Logan ride into camp with his arms wrapped around Kacey. His mouth dipped into an even deeper frown. The emotion that he could not name once more galloped forward.

"Did she get back from her ride with Logan?" A deep crease lined Colin's brow.

"*Oui*, some time ago."

"Well, if you see her, will you tell her I'd like to talk with her?"

"*Oui*, Professor. I will tell her." Rafe frowned again as Colin turned to walk away. It was not like Kacey to just disappear. He had thought she was with her father in the cellar room. He had seen Logan only moments ago, and she was not with him.

Rafe searched each chamber of the ruins. Kacey was nowhere to be found. He searched the camp and the tents. Still no Kacey. A cold hand seemed to squeeze at Rafe's heart. If anything had happened to her, he would never forgive himself. She could have gone for a walk and been bitten by a snake; endless possibilities ran through Rafe's mind. He tried to shake his worry and decided that she had probably gone for a walk and was fine. Still, it wasn't like Kacey not to be at the dig site. He turned on his heel to look for John.

He found him near the supply wagon talking with Clate.

"John, I am getting worried about Kacey. She has not been seen for some time now. Do you have any idea where she might be?"

"No, I haven't seen her since breakfast. Logan was looking for her, too, a little bit ago."

Rafe rubbed the back of his hand across his jawline, then came to a decision. "I'm going to look for her."

"Clate and I will come, too. I think we'd better take the horses."

"*Oui*. Let's get saddled up." Rafe's pulse hammered as the three headed toward their mounts. He looked up to see Logan coming their way.

"You gentlemen look like you're on a mission," Logan said as he came face-to-face with the others.

"*Oui*, monsieur." Rafe eyed the gambler with uncertainty. "Kacey is missing, and we're going to look for her. Do you know where she is?"

"I was just about to ask if any of you had seen her." Logan paused, then added, "I'll come, too. Do we need to tell her father?"

"Not just yet. I don't want to worry the professor needlessly if she's all right," Rafe said, then mumbled under his breath, "And I pray to *le bon Dieu* that she is."

The men saddled and mounted their horses and spread out as John suggested. He and Clate were more familiar with the region, and they combed the outer perimeter of the area. It had been about three hours now since anyone had seen Kacey.

The longer Rafe searched, the stronger the sinking feeling he had in the pit of his stomach. His eyes scanned the rocky soil for some sign of Kacey, but there was nothing. Then he noticed an area where the dust still showed signs of a struggle. Leading away from that were markings that appeared as if something had been dragged across it. Rafe followed these indications for some time before they ended on rocks leading into the canyon.

• • • •

Kacey was bound and gagged and hefted belly down over the horse's back. The coarse blanket under her rubbed at her cheek while the gag cut into her mouth. Her hands were tied behind her back, and every jolt of the animal pushed more breath from her. A grunt rumbled from her kidnapper. Kacey felt that if she could just get her hands to his throat she could strangle him barehanded.

"Woman with red hair not so feisty in this position. I think I keep you this way."

Incoherent noises came from behind the gag as Kacey tried to rear her head while she kicked her feet.

"I bet they pay plenty money to get you back." The man laughed, and the sound was almost maniacal as it echoed in the canyon.

Kacey wanted to shut off the Indian's gravelly voice. He obviously thought something was very funny. She didn't know how she was going to break it to him that nobody she knew had any money, and nobody was going to pay him to get her back. She mused to herself how he had taken the wrong woman. Probably the Misses Billings' father had money. The joke was on the Indian, but she didn't feel like laughing. The only thing of value she could put her hands on was the ancient necklace lying next to her skin under her clothing.

"We almost to cave now. Nobody find you there. I leave you, but I come back. This my secret cave."

Kacey tried to talk once again through the nasty cloth pulled tight across her mouth. "Mmm-mmm." The garbled sounds were useless.

"No talk now." The Indian reined in his horse and got off.

None too carefully he pulled Kacey from the animal. She landed on her feet, and he pushed her toward a huge boulder. He shoved her again to divert her around the giant rock and behind it, where a cave entrance loomed like the mouth of a hungry beast waiting to swallow her.

Inside, Kacey's eyes widened at the overwhelming darkness. Surely the man was not going to leave her here at the mercy of wild animals. The thought did little to cheer her. He shoved her into a recess toward the back of the cave and used the rope in his hand to tie her to a boulder.

Noises issued once again from Kacey's throat, but she could not speak through the cloth. The savage was going to leave her here without water, she realized. Even if she had water, she couldn't drink it with her mouth gagged.

Kacey almost panicked when she heard the Indian walk away. But then she reminded herself that she was still alive and unharmed. Someone would find her, she told herself over and over. She could not give in to her fear. Her eyes began to adjust to the cave interior as light filtered in from the entrance.

Rafe slipped his watch from his shirt pocket. The men had agreed to meet back in camp in two hours if they found no sign of Kacey. The track that was possibly hers had come to a dead end at the rocks. Where would he go from here? He would report back to the others, and together they could follow up on the trail. John would be better at tracking in this territory than he would. He had grown up here and would know the canyon. Rafe turned his horse toward camp and urged the animal to a faster pace.

When he arrived at camp, the others seemed to be waiting for his return, and for some word of Kacey. Anxious faces watched as Rafe reined in his horse and dismounted. Colin came toward him, and with him came the aroma of freshly brewed coffee.

"Rafe, lad, any sign of Kacey?" Colin's voice nearly shook with concern.

Rafe glanced at John before he answered. "I'm not sure, Professor. I saw some tracks that might have been Kacey's. They ended at the top of a canyon."

John moved toward the two men. "Which way, Rafe?"

"Just west of here."

"Then we'd better not lose any time. The rest of us

came up with nothing. If you've got a lead, that's more than we found. Let's get going."

Colin put his hand on Rafe's shoulder. "I'm coming, too, lad. If anything should happen to Kacey, I would never forgive myself."

"Professor, I think it would be better if you stayed close to camp. If some word should come, then you would be here to receive it, *n'est-ce pas*?"

"Perhaps you're right, Rafe. She could just have gotten lost and find her way back."

"That's right, Professor." Rafe was not feeling the conviction of his words. A cold hand seemed to squeeze at his heart as a feeling of unease seeped into his every pore. He suspected foul play, but he could not express the thought.

Logan's voice came from nearby. "We'll find her, Professor. You can count on it."

"Send word as soon as you find out something, won't you?"

"Certainly, Professor," Rafe said.

Victoria came forward with a bundle wrapped in cloth. "The young ladies and I prepared some food for you to take with you. You're all going to need your strength."

Rafe took the package and nodded. "*Merci beaucoup,* madame. That was very kind of you and the mademoiselles."

"It's the very least we could do." Victoria looked into Rafe's eyes and in a hushed whisper said, "I know you'll find her, Rafe. You must believe that."

"*Oui*, madame."

"Rafe, are thee ready to show us the tracks?" John's quiet voice was filled with leashed tension.

Rafe merely nodded, and the four men walked to their respective horses. Soon they rode toward the canyon head where Rafe had seen the tracks. In no time they reached the spot and dismounted.

The four stood looking at the ground. "What do you think, John?" Rafe asked.

"If it's what it looks like, then we'd better not lose any time finding her. Whoever took her probably forced her down these rocks and into the canyon."

"Who would do this, John?" Logan said in a choked voice.

"Could have been anyone, I suppose." John paused. "I'm just sorry Kacey got caught up in the middle of all this."

Rafe's eyes were keen like those of a hawk. "All of what, John?"

"Well, thee knows what the Indian situation around here is. There are some renegades who intend to get revenge for Geronimo's capture."

"You think she was kidnapped by an Indian?" Logan asked.

"I'm not sure. But the Navajo around here know these canyons like the backs of their hands."

"Then let's stop standing around and go find her." Logan gave an impatient shrug.

"Monsieur, that is one thing we agree upon." Rafe inclined his dark head, his mouth twisting in a half-smile.

John looked toward his brother. "Clate, I want thee to find Acowitz and bring him here. Pronto. We'll find out if he knows anything. Even if he doesn't, he knows every cave and crevice in this country."

"All right, John. Can do." Clate reached for his horse's reins, put one booted foot into the stirrup, and jumped on the animal's back, digging his boot heel into muscled flanks.

When Clate took off, John mounted his horse and looked at the other two. "Let's go."

Rafe and Logan followed him to the canyon below, all eyes searching for a sign of Kacey as they went. But the rocky ledges and stone walls revealed nothing, standing as they had for centuries as sentinels against the outside world.

Kacey noted that the light filtering into the cave entrance was not as bright as it had been. She had lost all concept of time, but she knew it must be late afternoon. Her mouth was as dry as cotton. Her tongue felt swollen against the gag, and any sound at all was increasingly difficult to make. Was she to die here in this dark cave? The thought made her legs weak as the shadow of fear swept across her like a cloud.

The rough hemp burned into her raw wrists as she continued to attempt escape from the rope. Suddenly she heard someone coming. Her heart seemed to stop, and she prayed it would be a rescuer instead of her attacker. She tried to cry out, but only an inaudible sound escaped.

Kacey saw the hulking form against the dimming light behind. A cold hand seemed to clamp tightly around her heart as the Indian came toward her, carrying a bundle under his arm. Dropping his load nearby, he came to her and unbound the gag.

Feeling a renewed bravado, Kacey cried out, regardless of her swollen tongue. "Why are you doing this? I could have died here."

"You no die. I bring food and water." He turned to his bundle and untied it, lifting out a thin, flat, round cake.

"I can't eat if you don't untie my hands," Kacey declared, her anger overtaking her fear and making her bold.

The man chuckled, then moved toward Kacey, taking a long knife from its sheath belted to his waist. She held his gaze as he moved slowly around her. Then she felt the wrist bindings loosen and give way. Her shoulders were stiff and sore as she brought her arms forward to rub at her wrists.

Without a word the Indian held the round cake for Kacey to take, then walked to the bundle and brought out a bladderlike bag. He untied its top and offered the bag to Kacey.

At first, revulsion welled up inside Kacey at the thought of putting her mouth where his had probably been. But her extreme thirst overcame her pride, and she reached for the bag of water, taking it to her lips and drinking. When she had quenched her thirst, she continued to clutch the bag as if in fear the man would take it away.

"We stay here tonight. Tomorrow I contact your camp to make deal."

Kacey's eyes widened as recognition dawned, and she said accusingly, "You're the Indian I saw near the ruins."

The man remained silent.

"You won't get away with this, you know. They'll find you, and you'll go to jail."

"With money they pay me, I go long way from here. They no find me." He laughed and reached to take a strand of her hair in his thick, broad palm. "Maybe they no find you, too."

Kacey knew the meaning of skin crawling. Hers did while the imaginary hand tightened around her heart. Panic as she'd never known it before welled in her throat, but she forced a bold front. "My father won't pay you *any* money if I am harmed in any way."

The Indian slowly released her hair and shrugged, turning his back to her and moving away. A silent sigh of relief escaped as Kacey once more sucked air into her lungs.

Rafe watched as the sun sank below the horizon. A chill settled into his heart with the knowledge that Kacey was still out there somewhere at the mercy of some unknown kidnapper. *Mon Dieu!* If he hurt her in any way, he swore he would kill him with his bare hands. Kacey had become his life, and he wouldn't think about a future without her. *He loved her.* The realization hit him like a cannonball. He had wanted her body, even now could feel her soft curves as they had pressed into him in the shelter of the ruins. He wanted to feel himself inside her again, to be a part of her forever. *Oui*, he loved her, and when he found her he was going to make sure she understood his feelings. He would make her love him, too.

"It's going to be dark soon, and we won't be able to see anything. I think we should head back to camp to see if there's been any word." John removed his hat and wiped at his brow with his sleeve.

Rafe knew the truth of John's words. But his heart balked at giving up the search for Kacey. "You two go on back. I will continue to search for a while."

John looked at Logan, then back to Rafe. "Look, partner, I know how thee feels, but thee's not going to be able to see in the dark. Thee'll do more good to start out fresh in the morning."

"I cannot . . . will not leave her out here alone." Rafe was unmoving.

Logan turned in the saddle and looked at John. "You go on back to camp and see if anything's turned up there. I'll stay and help Rafe search the canyon."

The expression in John's eyes said that he knew further protest would be hopeless. The two were grown men and would do as they pleased. "All right, good luck." John nodded, then steered his horse around and rode toward camp.

"Why did you stay, monsieur?"

"Let's just say that I don't think one fool out here is enough." Logan slowly shook his head from side to side.

"When I find her I'm going to ask her to be my wife." Rafe had a possessive desperation in his voice.

"Good. I don't think she thinks of *you* as a brother." Logan's mouth twitched with humor.

"*Pardon*, monsieur?"

"To use her own words, she thinks of me as 'the brother she never had.' "

"I see." Rafe's smile was without malice, almost apologetic as he caught the gambler's gaze. He nudged his horse forward without another word.

Darkness soon covered the land and sky. The two men rode in silence, listening and searching for anything, a scrape, a voice, a cry.

Once more bound and gagged, Kacey leaned against the boulder to which she was tied. Mere feet away, the Indian slept, his horse standing nearby. If there were just some way that she could get her hands on his knife! But that seemed impossible under the circumstances. Kacey's mind whirled at the events that had followed and those yet to come. Would anyone find her? Would the Indian follow through with his threat and take her with him? She had to find a way to escape. The others would never find her here.

The Indian moved, and Kacey's heart lurched, as if he had heard her thoughts. Her eyes widened, and she stopped breathing, waiting for the Indian to once more appear to be sleeping. Momentarily she heard voices filtering through the cave entrance. Her mind must be playing tricks on her! She heard Rafe speaking. She was sure of it.

"I'm beginning to see Kacey's face in every shadow on the canyon wall. She's near here. I feel it! But where? *Mon Dieu*, I feel like a blind man."

Rafe's voice sounded like a voice from heaven.

"Yeah, kinda like looking for a needle in the proverbial haystack, wouldn't you say?"

That was Logan. Dear, dear Logan! Why didn't they know she was here? She closed her eyes tightly and tried to send a mental message.

"I know the intelligent thing would be to give it up tonight. John is probably right." Rafe sounded almost resigned. "But, *Mon Dieu*, I will not quit now. You understand, *n'est-ce pas*?"

I'm here! I'm here! she tried to scream. But only muffled sounds escaped the cloth stuffed in her mouth. She closed her eyes tightly as tears welled, spilling onto her cheeks as she realized they could not hear her and were leaving her here with her attacker.

The menacing chuckle that reached her ears sounded surreal, and the darkness seemed to swallow her up. Her body tensed as she realized the Indian was now awake.

"I tell you no one find you here." The Indian's whisper held renewed belief in his words. "Now you believe me."

Kacey tried to lash out at the man. But all that came through was garbled, muffled sounds. *This can't be happening,* she cried inside. She was spending the night in a cave with a lunatic. And no one else on the face of the earth knew where she was. No one.

Twenty

At dawn Rafe and Logan rode into camp with jaws squared, revealing a purpose that would not brook defeat. The blond man was contrasted sharply with the other's raven hair and stubble of beard that matched the dark clouds hovering above.

John and Acowitz stood near the campfire. Each man held a cup of steaming liquid.

Logan dismounted, and, holding his horse's reins, he walked toward the fire. "Have you got any of that coffee left? Anything hot would suffice."

John poured a cup of the brew and handed it to Logan. "I take it that thee's found no sign of Kacey."

"You take it right. The clouds covered what little light there was. You can't see much in pitch black." Logan took a sip from his cup. "What about you? Have you come up with any leads?"

"Not yet, but Acowitz knows every crevice in this area. He's agreed to help us look for Kacey. We're about ready to start. Clate is bringing the horses around."

Rafe had dismounted by now and came to stand beside the others.

"I know it's been a tough night for thee, friend." John's voice almost cracked. "But we'll find her." He reached to pour another cup of coffee and handed it to Rafe.

"*Merci, mon ami.*" There was nothing else for the Frenchman to say. Kacey had not been found, and until she was, Rafe felt as though a part of him were missing, too. He sipped at the coffee in silence.

"As I was telling Logan, we're getting ready to ride, and Acowitz is coming with us."

"I am coming, also," Rafe said.

The question in John's eyes never reached his lips. Instead he said, "Thee'd better finish thy coffee and get a fresh mount."

"*Oui.*"

"You're not going anywhere without me." Logan downed the last of his coffee while the meaningful sound of thunder rumbled overhead.

Kacey stirred at the bolt of lightning. Realizing her nightmare to be real and not some elusive dream, she gently rubbed at the flesh on her wrists where the rope dug into raw, sensitive skin. Her mouth, still gagged, was dry. But one thing was different. The Indian was no longer inside the cave. For this she was thankful, even though she felt as though her bladder would burst from the need to relieve herself.

The blessing was short-lived.

"We move to higher ground before rains come," the Indian said, moving toward her with light-footed ease. He unbound her hands but left her gagged.

She reached to remove the cloth from her mouth, slinging it aside. "I need a few minutes of privacy." Kacey felt like smashing something, namely the man's head. No one should feel the humiliation she experienced here.

"You need piss?"

"Your sense of delicacy and understanding is overwhelming." Her voice was heavy with sarcasm.

The man grinned, his misshapen teeth prominent now. "Go here, inside cave. We leave soon."

"I can't *go* with you watching me. You'll have to wait outside."

"Woman too bossy. Padilla decide to stay or not."

"Okay, Padilla, is it? You decide and you'd better make it quick. I just hope your nose is as strong as your breath."

The man seemed to come to a decision. "I wait outside. You hurry." He paused, then added, "No tricks."

"Of course not." Kacey watched as he gathered the rope and cloth and left the cave.

When she had relieved herself she quickly picked up a flat, jagged piece of stone that she thought might come in handy later. She put the rock in her side skirt pocket and left the cave.

Padilla caught her by the arm and started once more to fasten the gag in her mouth.

"Please don't do that. I promise not to call out."

"You think I am stupid? That is joke to trust woman."

"Even if I were to call out"—she eyed him quickly— "which I won't, who is around to hear? The thunder would drown out my words."

The Indian's gaze did not waver. "I not take chance."

"Please, I can't breathe with that on."

He almost seemed to give in, but something in his eyes told her he would not. Once more he fastened the gag, then led her to mount the horse nearby before binding her hands in front. He came up behind her on the blanket and nudged the animal forward just as a deafening thunder-crack struck nearby. Without warning, and before Padilla had a firm hold on the reins, the horse reared. Kacey's sudden weight slammed into him. The pressure was just enough to loosen his tenuous hold on the reins, throwing him and Kacey to the ground.

Stunned, Kacey groggily saw an opportunity to run. Padilla seemed dazed, too, and she took the chance. With bound hands she groveled to stand and started to run.

She didn't get far. Strong, thick hands lunged for her waist and brought both bodies down. He landed on top of her, and she fought for wind to breathe. His eyes were blazing now, and she knew he would show no mercy. She didn't plead for it as he dragged her to her feet.

He spat at the ground amid a flurry of curses, then shoved her toward the mount. Rain started to pound the earth and Kacey's face. She could not distinguish the rain from her tears.

Victoria heard the rock slam against the ground before she saw it. A dirty piece of paper that clung to its surface was wrapped around it like a blanket. She stopped stirring the stew that she had started under a makeshift tent. The rain poured as it had the first day they arrived at Pueblo Mesita, making outside activity nasty.

Victoria instinctively looked around to see where the stone had come from. She saw no one. Quickly she pulled an oilcloth over her head and went to retrieve the paper before it disintegrated into the mud.

Back under the lean-to, she unwrapped the mud-splashed paper from the rock and read the scraggly, uneven print written on the opposite side: *U TAKE 5000 DOLLA TO RUIN EST OF HEER IF U WANT WOMAN BACK.*

Victoria's gaze quickly scanned the perimeter of the camp. Then, with alarm threaded through her voice, she yelled, "Colin! Colin! You must come quick!"

He ran through the rain from his tent, shaving cream still clinging to his chin.

"What is it, Victoria?" Stopping in front of her, he clasped her upper arms. "Have you seen Kacey?"

Victoria held the note out, and he took it. Their gazes locked, hers offering hope, his accepting.

He read the note aloud, then dropped his arms to his sides.

"I must get word to the others."

"I'm sure someone will be checking in soon. They'll

know soon enough. You just can't go out in this storm, Colin. It won't do anyone any good.''

"I won't wait long. Someone has my daughter, and I can't sit here and do nothing. Somehow I have to get that money. I'll go to hell and back if I have to.''

"I know how you must feel, Colin, but John and Acowitz know the territory, and they've got Rafe and Logan with them. They *will* find her.'' Victoria's composed assurance helped to calm Colin.

Beth and Rainey splashed into the cooking area.

"What is it, Victoria?'' Rainey asked. "We heard you call.''

"There's been a note about Kacey. Whoever sent it is asking for five thousand dollars.''

The two girls gasped. Beth cried out, "Oh, Victoria! This means she *has* been kidnapped!''

"Yes, I'm afraid so.''

Rainey turned to Colin. "Professor, if there is anything we can do, just let us know. You may not know it, but our father is a banker in Denver. We can wire him if we need to.''

"Thank you, my dears. You are very kind.''

Beth turned plaintive eyes toward Victoria. "I wish there were something we could do.''

"I know how you feel, dear. We all do.'' Victoria paused. "And there is something we can do. We can pray and believe that Kacey will be returned to us soon.''

Kacey and Padilla had ridden for what seemed like hours. Her wrists were almost bleeding now, and her arms and back ached from the need to stretch. She was soaked through, her hair falling onto her face in dripping strands. The man's stamina was beyond belief. Since she tried to run away earlier, she had seen his eyes harden, and she knew he would show no mercy whatsoever at her discomfort.

Through her rain-drenched eyes she saw the dwelling

come into focus in the distance. The same dwelling where
Rafe had made love to her. She would remember it always.
She squeezed her lids tightly shut, the memory of that
moment flooding her like a tidal wave.

Pulling firmly on the reins, Padilla's words violated her
precious memories, moments relived in Rafe's arms.

"We stay here, in kiva." He got down from the horse
and once again roughly pulled Kacey from the animal,
showing no attempt at kindness.

She knew by now the futility of speech through the cloth
stuffed into her mouth. Silently and briefly she looked up
into Padilla's eyes, which spoke of years of white man's
injustice. He sought revenge. She shivered at the depth of
hatred expressed in that one look before he motioned for
her to turn.

Padilla held her by the arm and none too gently led her
to an inner room of the pueblo, where he uncovered a trap
door to a chamber below. He forced her down the ladder
in front of him. Dim light filtered in from the room above.

"This is kiva," he announced proudly, standing in the
middle of the round underground room, before reaching to
remove the gag from her mouth. "Many spirits in this
place. They all that hear you now." He laughed menac-
ingly, moving to unbind her wrists before turning to light
the charred logs resting in a central firepit. Soon dancing
flames cast eerie shadows on the walls and on the low
stone benches extending around the room.

Kacey wished she could rub the raw, bleeding areas
above her hands, but she refused to let the man see her
discomfort. All she could say for the amenities in the place
was that it was dry.

She made an attempt at lightness. "Lovely place. You
come here often, do you? I'll bet you bring all your friends
here."

"Woman has sharp tongue. Maybe I cut it out, make
you my squaw."

Kacey thought his lips curled back like a snarling wolf daring its prey to move.

"You wouldn't dare. Then you'd never get your money." She put up a brave front, but almost panicked, believing the man was capable of anything.

"Maybe woman worth more than money." He moved toward her.

Her brain refused to work, and her feet seemed to do her thinking for her, moving to back away.

"No!" She raised her arms in front of her and spread both hands. "I'm not. Believe me. Just think of what the money can buy."

The Indian stopped in his tracks. "Maybe I keep both." He grinned, his yellow, prominent teeth belying the rapture that he obviously believed himself capable of bestowing upon a woman.

"They won't pay you the money if they don't get me back unharmed. I can assure you that." Kacey was not feeling the bravado she tried to exude.

Padilla grunted, then turned away, saying, "Maybe we see when the time comes." With that, he climbed the ladder, closing the trap door behind him.

Kacey felt truly frightened for the first time, her hands flying to her chest, where the necklace lay beneath her clothing. Now she knew she had to plan her own escape and not rely on being found. The others could search for days and never find her in this tomblike chamber. Panic rose in her throat and stayed there like a bite too big to swallow. She knew it would be futile to try the closure, but she climbed the rungs anyway. The door refused to move, even a little.

Kacey had been missing one day and one night, and already it seemed like a lifetime to Rafe. The rain came in torrents, hindering the party's search efforts, and leaving in its wake the heady scent of mud, leather, and horse flesh. They combed every cave that Acowitz led them to.

Nothing. No sign of Kacey. Rafe had never felt so helpless in all his life.

Acowitz held out his hand to stop the others behind him.

"What is it?" Rafe asked, his nerves strung like a violin.

John immediately saw what the Indian saw. "Tracks! There in the mud!"

Logan moved his horse forward and shouted above the rain, "One horse, unshod. Moving east, and not long ago or these tracks would have disappeared in the downpour."

Rafe looked at Logan, uncertainty once again entering his mind. "For a gambler, you seem to know a great deal about tracking, monsieur."

Logan looked across the mesa, then back to Rafe. "I did some tracking for a spell. Learned everything I know from a Cherokee brave before I took up gambling."

"How interesting." Rafe hesitated, measuring the gambler for a moment. "How many other occupations do you have up your sleeve?"

"Can't rightly say. You probably wouldn't believe me if I told you."

"*Oui, mon ami,* I probably would not." Rafe briefly eyed the gambler with friendly skepticism, then the two urged their horses forward behind John and Acowitz.

As the men rode and the rain abated somewhat, Rafe felt a sense of familiarity with the surroundings. A sweet emotion filled him, and he remembered the feel of Kacey in his arms, rocking with the motion of the horse the day they had gone to the pueblo alone. The pueblo. The tracks had all but disappeared in the rain, but Rafe would wager the tracks led there. Whoever rode in that direction had probably sought shelter there. Kacey. Even now he could taste the sweetness of her lips, could hear her murmurings in his ear, could see the determined lines of her lovely face.

Rafe's musings were interrupted by John.

"Acowitz says we're not far from Pueblo Beshba. He

says he feels very strongly that her presence is near, my friend.''

Logan was within earshot, and he said in a low voice, ''Do you think the old man has inside information, or is he truly a spiritualist?''

''Partner, these Indians are downright spooky in their predictions. Who's to say? Maybe they do speak to the spirits. Honestly, I don't care how he knows, I just hope he does know,'' John said.

''Well, do we have a plan, or do we just go riding into the kidnapper's camp big as you please?'' Logan asked somewhat sardonically.

''Monsieur, what do you suggest?'' Rafe asked, matching his sarcasm and leaning forward to cross his arms on the saddlehorn.

''I say we ease in from all four directions. You and I could circle around to the other side and come in from the east and south. Acowitz and John could come in from this side, north and west.''

Rafe looked at John. ''Do you have a better plan, *mon ami*?''

''No. It sounds like a good idea to me. We could mosey in and take a look around without all of us being seen.'' John turned his gaze to the Indian. ''What does thee say, Acowitz?''

''I say Logan has right idea. Whether there is one or more, kidnappers will be on lookout.''

''Well then, what are we waiting for?'' Logan's words were more a statement than a question, and he urged his mount forward.

He and Rafe skirted the outside perimeter of the area to get to their respective locations on the other side of the ruins, while Acowitz and John continued to head toward the east.

Kacey watched the fire quickly burn away, leaving only a few small coals to give a feeble light. She heard the door

move overhead and looked up to see moccasins step to the
top ladder rung. Just for an instant she had hoped it might
be a rescuer, but reality set in, and she knew she was her
only salvation. She could not rely on someone finding her
here in this tomb. Her mind whirled while her hand slowly
moved to touch the large, jagged rock through the twill
folds of her skirt.

Padilla reached the stone floor, and in his right hand he
grasped a limp rabbit by the tail. He thrust it toward Kacey,
his gaze bold and raw. "Clean and cook this for eating."

Kacey knew the man expected her to flinch at the helpless, bloody creature in his grasp. She would not give him
the pleasure. She met his gaze decisively. "I can't cook
in here with no air. You'll have to leave the door open."

"I leave door open enough for smoke escape. You clean
rabbit now while I get firewood." Once again the Indian
thrust the animal toward Kacey, his expression brooking
any refusal on her part.

Her eyes met his in mute effrontery as she reached for
the rabbit, its soft body still warm. "I'll need a knife."
Her stomach growled, reminding her of her hunger, and
she despised her weakness, knowing she would eat the
meat if given the opportunity.

Without preamble Padilla handed her a smaller blade
that was also sheathed at his side, then turned and left the
chamber.

Kacey followed his exit before returning to the small
animal she held. The thought of skinning and cutting the
rabbit that had been alive only moments earlier sickened
her, but she had no choice. The Indian would be back
shortly, and she knew from his black, vengeful eyes that
she had better have the rabbit prepared for cooking. She
began the bloody task.

Her mind whirled to devise an escape plan. The small
knife, even if she could throw a blow to the man, would
probably not be sufficient to do him any real harm, she

decided. But the large rock in her pocket might do if she could strike at his weakest part . . . his head. The plan came to life in her thoughts. She had to find a moment soon, before it was too late.

Twenty-one

The meat roasted over the fire in the center of the room while Kacey sat on the stone bench, fingering the jagged rock in her pocket. Its edges were sharp, but she questioned if she had enough strength to knock the man out. She had to try . . . it was her best chance.

She cast a glance at Padilla sitting on the floor at the opposite side of the room. He was sharpening his knife on a whetstone, and the scraping sound magnified in the empty chamber, rubbing at her nerves like sand in an open wound.

She knew he was aware of her every move, but the time would come when she would catch him unaware. She had to be ready for that moment.

Anxiously Kacey stood and walked toward the fire.

"Sit down." The harsh words echoed in the room.

Kacey stared at the man. "Why? I was just going to check the meat."

"I did not tell woman to move. You want me to tie you again?"

"No. Of course not." Kacey spread her arms. "Where am I going to go in here?"

Ignoring her question, Padilla said, "See if meat is cooked." He watched her move toward the fire, then went back to his sharpening.

Kacey poked at the meat with a small spiked stick. Juices spilled from the succulent young rabbit, but she barely saw them because her mind was on her plan of escape.

Padilla looked toward her as if he read her mind.

"If meat is ready, bring it to me."

Kacey silently conceded to the man's wishes, taking him the back legs, the favored part. She handed the roasted rabbit to him and returned to the spit, taking a piece of the meat for herself. She stayed near the fire to eat and glanced sideways, watching Padilla. He ate ravenously, filling his mouth with each bite.

She slowly reached into her pocket and grasped the rock. Now was her chance. The man seemed almost drugged by the food, savoring each bite. Cautiously she pulled the rock from her skirt, inching closer and closer to him. When the moment was right, Kacey suddenly struck her blow to the side of the man's head.

Without pausing to see the damage, she ran for the ladder and the opening to freedom. She heard muffled, foreign curses, but continued to climb as if Lucifer himself were on her tail. She reached the top rung and hit the ground running as fast as she had ever run in her whole life, through another doorway and outside. She didn't pause for an instant, knowing that a heartbeat could mean success or failure. She could tell the man was coming fast behind her, but she dared not look back. She ran with all her strength, her long hair waving behind like a copper flag. The rain had stopped, but the mud slowed her down, sucking at her shoes like leeches.

Suddenly, to her horror, her hair was jerked from behind, and a sharp piercing pain surrounded her head as she was shoved to the wet earth below. She felt mud ooze into her pores, eyes, and mouth, and felt the weight of Padilla pressing into her back. She had gambled and lost. Once again she was in the clutches of her kidnapper.

When Rafe saw the woman run from the pueblo, he was stunned for an instant. From the distance he could see that her clothes were filthy and torn in places, but her tangled mass of copper hair was the dead giveaway. His heart pounded, feeling as though it would explode.

In the next instant, he saw the Indian, and the pressure in his chest increased while his heart seemed to lodge in his throat. Instinctively he gave his bootheels a quick jab to the horse's flanks and galloped hell-bent for leather toward the Indian and Kacey.

It seemed to take forever to reach the two. He did, though, just as the Indian caught up with her and shoved her to the ground. That was too much for Rafe to swallow. He swung from his mount before it came to a stop and rolled the man from Kacey. The Indian came up, wielding a large knife and shouting obscenities.

"Rafe!" Kacey screamed, scrambling to get to her feet in the mud. When she finally did get her footing she ran to the Indian's back, pounding at him with her fists.

Padilla continued to hold Rafe at bay with the knife, seeming to ignore the woman at his back.

"Move away, *chérie*, before you get hurt!" Rafe shouted.

Kacey returned, "Get the knife, Rafe!"

"I will if you will stand out of the way, *ma chérie*!"

Making her decision for her, Padilla swung around, knocking her to the ground. Once more seated in the mud, Kacey watched as the two men's gazes locked like rutting bucks' antlers. Padilla swiped at him with the knife, and Rafe jumped back, turning swiftly and bringing the heel of his boot up to knock the blade from the Indian's hand.

Rafe then swung his fist toward the man's jaw, giving a powerful blow that would have leveled most anyone. But

Padilla, though shaken, still stood, readying to strike his blow.

"Watch out, Rafe!" Kacey screamed again, trying to get to where the knife had landed before Padilla could retrieve it.

The Indian swung, but Rafe blocked the hit and gave another potent strike that this time landed Padilla on the ground. Without hesitating, Rafe jumped on him and hit him again. He finally subdued the man enough to force his hands behind him.

"*Chérie*, get some rope from my horse."

Kacey gladly did his bidding, and in no time the kidnapper lay bound.

"Don't forget to stuff his mouth full," Kacey declared. "He needs to know how it feels to have your mouth stuffed full of cotton cloth."

"*Chérie*, I am glad to see you are still your sweet, timid self." Rafe mocked her, but his eyes displayed another emotion that left no question as to his feelings for her. In one motion he swept her into his arms and held her tightly, nuzzling her neck before his lips trailed a line to capture hers.

Padilla grunted and said, "If this your woman, I feel sorry for you. She make no good squaw. She talk too much and she bossy."

Coming to stand nearby, Logan chuckled deep in his throat. "Maybe you can send her to the Indian reservation for lessons, Rafe."

Kacey broke the embrace, and before she had a chance to reply, Rafe declared while his eyes seemed to drink her up, "I like her just the way she is."

"That's very big of you, Rafe. You mean you won't send me away?" Sarcasm was thick on Kacey's tongue.

He made a noise in his throat and murmured into her ear, "*Au contraire, mon ange,* I will never let you go away."

Logan cleared his throat and brought Padilla to his feet.

"What do you want to do with this fellow, Rafe?"

"We need to hold him for the Indian agent," John said, he and Acowitz coming to stand near the others.

"I know the perfect place," Kacey said, lifting her chin and meeting Padilla's icy gaze. "Follow me. I think he'll be comfortable there. He seems to like it, and his dinner is waiting for him." She walked toward the kiva, the others following.

The trap door was still open, and John untied Padilla's hands, forcing him down the ladder to the chamber below before closing the door and securing it.

"I am sorry for trouble Padilla has caused you, Miss O'Reilly. My people will see that he is punished." Acowitz seemed truly saddened by the recent events. "But it would have been better if scientists not come here. These ruins are sacred ground. It is difficult for an old man to see them desecrated."

"I am sorry, too, that injustices have brought about the animosity between our peoples," Kacey said, "but I wish you could realize the importance of the finds we have made. It will change the way we view history. Your people have had a very important role in America. We only want to bring that forward, to show the importance that the Anasazi have had here."

Acowitz merely nodded. "We only want to be left alone." The old man turned and went outside to mount his horse. John and Logan followed, leaving Rafe and Kacey behind.

Rafe moved to pull Kacey into his embrace once again, his voice low and seductive as he said near her ear, "Kacey, *ma chérie*, I love you. You must marry me and put me out of my misery. Now I know I can never be without you. When you disappeared, I felt as though part of me was missing. I want you for always, *chérie*." Reclaiming her lips, he crushed her to him.

Rafe had unlocked her heart and soul. His kiss was like nothing she had ever known before, and she didn't want to give it up. Kacey's mind whirled. He had asked her to marry him. She had found paradise in Rafe's embrace and she knew she would always want to be near him, to be one with him.

She pulled away just enough to whisper, "Oh Rafe, I love you, too."

"I want us to be married right away. Is that possible, *ma belle, ma femme belle*, my beautiful wife?"

"I don't know, Rafe. Not before we get back to Cambridge. Sarah would never forgive me." She laughed gently, a warm, happy feeling belying the mud on her face.

Rafe stroked her neck, moving his fingers to caress her checks. "Who would have thought that I would be asking a muddy-faced angel to be my bride?"

"Oh, Rafe, I forgot I was covered in mud!"

"You look *ravissante* in anything, *chérie*. Even the mud cannot mask your beauty."

"Well, just the same I would like to get back to camp and wash."

"Your father and the others will be very glad to see you."

"And I will be very glad to see them. I was beginning to wonder if I would ever see any of you again," Kacey said.

"I would never have stopped looking for you, Kacey." Her name rolled from his French lips like a benediction. He took her hand and led the way outside to his horse. Mounting first, he took Kacey's palm to pull her up behind him.

Kacey leaned close to Rafe and wrapped her arms around his muscular torso. She would always want to hold him this way, she thought, love for him spilling over into her soul. Soon, she would be his wife, and he her husband. The thought filled her with much excitement.

Logan rode up beside them. "John and Acowitz have gone to see the Indian agent. Are we ready to ride back to camp? It's been a long two days. I could do with a good night's sleep and a full belly." He paused, taking in the couple. "Of course, I can see that both of those items are the last things on your minds."

"Shall we tell him, Rafe?"

"*Oui, chérie*, he needs to know that you are no longer available for his flirtations," Rafe teased.

"Rafe, stop it."

"I can't stand it any longer. One of you tell me." Amusement flickered in Logan's eyes.

"Rafe has asked me to marry him, and I have accepted."

"Well, I suppose the best man has won. I'm happy for you both." He paused. "I guess you don't need a chaperon on the trip back. See you when you get there." Logan dug his bootheels into his horse and galloped toward Pueblo Mesita.

Rafe also headed in that direction, but he did not gallop. He kept the horse at an easy gait, enjoying the feel of Kacey's body pressed into his back. His loins ached for her, but this was not the time. She would soon be his bride, and for the moment that thought was good enough.

Little more than an hour later, Rafe and Kacey rode into camp. Logan had given the others the good news that Kacey had been found and was on her way back.

Colin was the first to see her as she slid from the horse, Rafe dismounting after her. He ran toward his daughter and, with tears in his eyes, hugged her close.

"Kacey, dear, you can't know how good it is to see you."

"Oh, yes, I can, Father."

"We've all been so worried not knowing what happened, and then early this morning a note was thrown into camp requesting five thousand dollars." Colin hugged his daughter tighter before releasing her. "I don't know what I would do if anything happened to you."

"I'm all right, Father. It's over now." Kacey looked

toward her fiancé with dreamy eyes. "Thanks to Rafe and the others, Padilla was captured." She paused. "Father, I have something else to tell you."

"What is it, dear?"

"Rafe has asked me to marry him, and I . . . well, I have accepted."

"Kacey, that makes me very happy." Through misty eyes Colin winked at Rafe, who smiled very much like a cat he had seen once after it had eaten a sparrow.

"Kacey!" Victoria, Beth, and Rainey cried her name in unison, coming toward her with outstretched arms.

She moved toward them and hugged all three simultaneously. "Oh, you lovely, lovely people."

Beth replied, her eyes as big as silver dollars, "You have to tell us all about it, Kacey. Were you very frightened?"

Victoria laughed gently. "I'm sure Kacey wants to freshen up before she does anything. She'll be sorry she came back if we gang up on her."

"I'm sorry, Kacey. Do forgive me," Beth said.

"There's nothing to forgive, and I will tell you all about it later, but Victoria's right. I would like to get the mud off my face and clothes." Kacey's eyes widened as if she had forgotten something, then she reached to pull the turquoise necklace from inside the front of her tattered shirt-waist. "I had a fortune on me all the time, and the blackguard never knew it."

"Maybe if you had offered that to him, he would have let you go from the beginning," Rainey said.

Kacey looked at Logan as he came to stand nearby. "Not on your life, I wouldn't. It was my ace in the hole, to use your words, Logan."

"That's all very well, Kacey, but I forgot to tell you that sometimes you have to have an ace in the boot as well, and any other place you can stick one."

"Well, I had a rock in the pocket. That was just as good." Kacey smiled. "I'll see you all shortly. I'm going to change now.'' Her gaze moved to Rafe's, and a sensuous light passed between them before she moved toward her tent.

Rainey and Beth followed her while Logan followed Rafe to care for his horse. Victoria stayed beside Colin.

"Kacey and Rafe seem to have made up,'' Victoria said.

"My dear, not only that, but she has agreed to marry him.''

"Oh, Colin, I'm so happy for you. I know how you wanted them to be together.''

"That's true, Victoria. But now I know I'm going to miss her and . . .'' He moved closer to the woman. "When we leave here, I'll miss you, too. Victoria, you've made me feel like a new man.''

"What are you trying to say, Colin?''

"Victoria, hang it all, you know what I'm trying to say. I want you to be my wife.''

The full lashes that shadowed her cheeks flew up while Colin stepped forward and clasped her body tightly to his.

"Colin, this is all so sudden.''

"What was it you told me, Victoria, about one being willing to experience new things? You're not backing out now, are you? Please, dearest, say yes.'' The light in his eyes beckoned her.

She hesitated only a moment, then her lips curved into a smile. "Yes, my darling, yes!''

Later, around the campfire after Kacey had given her account of the kidnapping and both announcements had been made concerning marriage, Logan played "I Gave My Love a Cherry" on his harmonica. The melody rode the gentle breeze for a while before he stopped and gently tapped the instrument against his thigh.

"How much longer will you stay here now, Professor?'' Logan asked.

"Another day or two. We've pretty well found out what we wanted to know—whether it was worth a dig or not—

and I think we have our answer to that. I'm sure Putnam will be out here as soon as we show him our finds.''

"I'm sure he will." Logan paused, then continued. "I was thinking maybe I'd move along in a day or so myself. I have some pressing commitments that I'll have to attend to."

"Where will that take you?" Colin asked.

"I'm not quite sure yet. Somewhere in Mississippi."

"Well, stay in touch, lad. We'll be back in Cambridge probably within two weeks."

"Logan, we'll miss you," Kacey said.

A flash of humor crossed his face. "Now why do I doubt that? Rafe, I'm sure, will see to it that you don't miss me."

"You know what I mean, Logan."

"Yes, I do. It's been fun and very enlightening," Logan declared. "As a matter of fact, I won't forget any of you. You've all been great—even the mummy." He stood and yawned, pushing his hands into his pockets. "I don't know about the rest of you, but I haven't had any sleep in two days. I think I'll turn in." He started toward the men's tent, doffing his hat and calling behind him, "Good-night, ladies."

Everyone else bid their good-nights also and went to their respective quarters, except Rafe and Kacey.

He moved closer and drew her to him. "Are you cold, *chérie*?"

She settled against him, enjoying the feel of his arms wrapped around her. "Not now, Rafe, darling."

He nuzzled her ear, the embers from the fire barely glowing now. "*Mon ange*, I am the happiest man in the world. You are safe in my arms and will soon be my wife."

Kacey snuggled deeper into the fold of his embrace. "I could stay like this forever, Rafe. It feels so right in your arms. In the cave I wondered if I would ever see any of you again."

Rafe made a sound in his throat. "I could strangle that man for taking you, *chérie*. You have become my life, my love." His hand took her face and held it gently before his mouth covered hers hungrily.

His lips were warm and sweet on hers, their tongues teased and touched, filling her veins with ecstasy and need so strong she fought for breath, releasing herself from the kiss.

He whispered into her hair, his hands exploring the hollow of her back and gentle curve of derrière. "I need you *chérie*. I need all of you. I need your heart, your eyes, your lips. I need you now."

A wildfire seemed to spread through Kacey's blood. "I want you, too, Rafe." She paused. "But not here."

"We can go anywhere you say, *chérie*." He stood in a fluid motion, bringing her with him, his body trembling.

"Do you mean that, Rafe?"

His voice was husky and low, "*Oui*, anywhere."

Kacey paused, then said softly, "Cambridge."

Rafe stood motionless for what seemed like minutes. "Do you know what you're asking, *chérie*? Are you sure that is what you want?"

"Yes, I'm asking the man I love to wait for me. Is that too much?"

There was a gentleness in her voice that he could not resist. "*Non, chérie*, if the wait is not too long. I will count the minutes—no, the seconds." His lips curled in a smile.

Twenty-two

Cambridge, Massachusetts
July 23, 1887

"You both look lovely." Sarah's gaze moved like a pendulum between the two. "Mrs. McCracken, Professor O'Reilly is a lucky man. And, Kacey, darlin', I wish your mother could see you in this dress." Sarah seemed to beam with the pride of a grandmother, a trace of tears in her eyes.

Colin's bride-to-be placed her hand on Sarah's arm. "Please, Sarah, you're such a part of this family—if you don't call me Victoria, I'll feel like an outsider."

"Now, we can't be havin' you not feeling welcome. Victoria, it is."

Kacey moved to Sarah and hugged her. "Thank you, Sarah, for making it possible for me to wear Mother's wedding dress. The length is perfect now. What you've done is pure genius. The lace around the bottom looks as if it came from the same bolt as that on the sleeves and neckline. It means more to me than you know." She hugged the woman tighter. "I love you, Sarah."

The dam broke in the older woman's eyes, and a flood of tears rushed forward. "Kacey, me darlin', you're the light o' my life."

"You're pretty special to me, too, Sarah, and . . . oh, I can't wait any longer. I have to tell you."

"Tell me what, darlin'?"

"Sarah, after Rafe and I are settled in France, we want you to come visit us."

"Kacey, darlin', you know I don't have that kind of money."

"It was Rafe's idea. He wants to pay for your visit, Sarah."

"I knew I liked that young man as soon as I laid eyes on him. And I could tell he had his Frenchman's hat set for you. We'll talk about it later, darlin'. Right now you've a wedding to go to."

The sound of Wagner's "Bridal Chorus" drifted up the stairs, and Kacey and Victoria looked at each other, happiness mirroring each face.

"After you, Victoria." Kacey nodded her head toward the doorway.

"No, my dear, I wouldn't dream of going down those stairs ahead of you. This is your wedding day, one you will remember for the rest of your life. Rafe will be waiting at the bottom of those stairs for you, and I wouldn't dare keep him in suspense." Victoria gently laughed.

"Well, what about Father? He's waiting for you, too."

"My dear, when you get to be my age, minutes are mere seconds. Listen to your soon-to-be stepmother and lead the way."

Kacey pulled her veil over her face and held tightly to the orange-blossom bouquet Sarah placed in her hands. She looked around the room and realized she would no longer be living with her father in this cozy home. But he was embarking on a new life, too. She felt at ease because she knew that Victoria would make him very happy.

Kacey began the slow walk down the steps. When she

was halfway down, she looked to see Rafe, rakishly handsome in his navy suit, standing near her father. His dark mahogany eyes were brilliant with anticipation.

Rafe felt as though he would never tire of looking at Kacey. If she aged to one hundred, he knew she would still be beautiful. He did not take his gaze from her as she seemed to float down the steps, a vision of loveliness. He knew he would remember this day forever, the radiance of his bride dressed in yards of creamy satiny material and lace, her face mysterious and beautiful behind the veil.

It was a small affair. Just Reverend Parker, an organist, the two bridegrooms and their brides, and the fluttering, flitting Sarah.

When this was over, Rafe and Kacey would be on their way to Paris for their honeymoon, and then on to Nancy to see his parents. At last she would be his to have and to hold forever.

Rafe saw no one in the room but Kacey. Even the reverend's voice did not break the spell he seemed to be under.

"Dearly beloved, we are gathered here today in the sight of God . . ."

Rafe shut out all thought except of Kacey, but on cue he said, "I do." He knew "he did" whatever it was. He loved her more than life itself and he intended to prove it to her. And then he heard words filter to his consciousness again.

"You may place the ring on her hand."

Rafe grasped the emerald-and-diamond ring in his pocket. He had wired from Durango to have his grandmother's wedding ring sent to him in Cambridge. His *grand-mère* would have adored Kacey. He had never thought of their similarities before, but now he realized the beloved old lady had been just as strong-willed as Kacey. They would have liked each other very much.

He placed the exquisite ring on her finger. He heard her

intake of breath and was once more oblivious to the minister's words until short moments later the sound reached his ears again.

"Gentlemen, you may kiss your brides."

The double ceremony was over, and Rafe slowly raised the veil of the woman beside him, his wife. Misty violet eyes met his gaze and he recalled the first time he saw them on the paddle steamer. Those same eyes had held disdain and something more, he recalled now. Challenge. The call had been made, and now she was his. Rafe pulled Kacey to him and crushed his lips to hers. She clung to him like ivy on limestone.

Colin kissed his bride, too. He was gaining a son-in-law and a wife, all in the same afternoon. Life had never been better. Maybe he would see those grandchildren after all. He chuckled inwardly as Victoria returned the kiss.

"There are refreshments in the dining room," Sarah announced. But the only ones that seemed to be paying any attention to her were the minister and the organist. "Reverend Parker and Miss Galway, if you'll follow me, maybe the others will come to their senses in a minute and join us." Sarah smiled, looking over her shoulder at the happy couples.

Moonlight filtered through the porthole, spilling onto the plush red carpet and filling the stateroom with a strange, silvery glow. Rafe and Kacey lay *au naturel,* cupped like spoons on the feather mattress. He nuzzled at her ear.

"*Ma belle femme*, my beautiful wife, we will have so many wonderful moments together," Rafe whispered almost reverently, as if she were a goddess.

Half asleep and satiated from their recent lovemaking, Kacey turned and snuggled deep into the mat of thick, dark hair covering Rafe's chest, sighing contentment.

Rafe felt as though he would never cease to feel the excitement of her touch. Even now, so soon after their union, he hardened again as her nipples teased at his flesh.

He watched through the fringe of his lashes as Kacey raised drooping lids to meet his gaze. *Saint-Pere,* but she was beautiful. Her passion had thrilled him to the deepest ecstasy he had ever known.

"We will have beautiful children together, *chérie.* Even now you could be carrying my *bébé.* And that thought makes me ache for you even more, *ma femme.*"

Kacey smiled impishly. "Oh, I doubt it, Rafe. I've heard it can take quite a while sometimes to conceive."

"In that case we should practice some more. I plan to perfect the art of loving you, *chérie,* and I hope it will take me a lifetime." Rafe shifted his weight to cover Kacey with his muscular frame.

Feeling his need pressed against her, Kacey moaned softly. "Rafe, darling, it couldn't be any more perfect."

He began a tender kneading of her breast, gently squeezing the nipple between his fingers, then moving his hand ever so slowly down her silken belly to the secret part that she shared with him. His fingers explored the short tangles of hair and probed the moist recess hidden beneath.

She moaned again. "Rafe, will it always be like this?"

"*Oui, chérie,* I will love you always." Even as he said the words he sheathed himself within her and moaned into her ear. He began a slow, rhythmic movement, their bodies in perfect tempo.

Kacey, feeling as though her mind would explode into a million colored lights, gasped and cried out his name.

He moved faster with a purpose until his seed spilled once more into the woman he loved.

Long moments later, Kacey slept, using Rafe's chest as her pillow. Rafe, near the point of sleep himself, opened his eyes wide. A familiar shrill voice outside the open porthole grated down his spine. *Mon Dieu!* It couldn't be, he told himself. Not the widow from the ship! Then he heard the voice again. He hugged his wife tightly, as if for protection, while Mary Carlisle's coarse laughter echoed in the night.